D1121338

But Nobody Lives In Bloomsbury

About the author:

Gillian Freeman was a scriptwriter for Robert Altman; her many novels include *The Leather Boys*, *Nazi Lady* and *His Mistress's Voice* (Arcadia). She is married to the novelist Edward Thorpe.

Praise for *His Mistress's Voice*:

'Freeman's fascinating tale is first and foremost a portrait of Jewish life in late Victorian England' – Michael Arditti, *Independent*

Gillian Freeman

But Nobody Lives In Bloomsbury

ARCADIA BOOKS

Arcadia Books Ltd
15-16 Nassau Street
London W1W 7AB

www.arcadiabooks.co.uk

First published in the United Kingdom 2006
Copyright © Gillian Freeman 2006

Gillian Freeman has asserted her moral right to be identified as the author of this work in
accordance with the Copyright, Designs and Patents Act, 1988.

ISBN 1-905147-22-8

Typeset in Bembo by Basement Press, London
Printed in Finland by WS Bookwell

Arcadia Books distributors are as follows:

in the UK and elsewhere in Europe:
Turnaround Publishers Services
Unit 3, Olympia Trading Estate
Coburg Road
London N22 6TZ

in the USA and Canada:
Independet Publishers Group
814N. Franklin St.
Chicago, IL 60610

in Australia:
Tower Books
PO Box 213
Brookvale, NSW 2100

in New Zealand:
Addenda
Box 78224
Grey Lynn
Auckland

in South Africa:
Quartet Sales and Marketing
PO Box 1218
Northcliffe
Johannesburg 2115

Arcadia Books: *Sunday Times* Small Publisher of the Year 2002/03

For Alison Hawkes

Chapter 1
But Nobody Lives in Bloomsbury

It was raining. Two college porters, their heads protected, were unloading trunks from upright trolleys. The porters carried a trunk into one of the narrow, arched doorways. Concealed behind a stone pillar Lytton Strachey and Leonard Woolf observed a hurrying figure wearing a long undergraduate gown and mortarboard entering through the lodge gate. He was partly concealed by a large umbrella. He turned along a path edging the lawn and was almost lost from view in the shadows.

As he approached Lytton asked in a whisper, 'Is that him?'

'I believe it is. I'm not sure...'

The man passed the spying undergraduates and Lytton ducked to see the face underneath the umbrella. 'Born to blush unseen. I'm not sure he is beautiful enough...'

'It's the beauty of his *brain* that concerns us!'

The man stopped by the next doorway, put down his umbrella and shook the rain from it.

'Concerns you, Woolf,' Lytton replied. He paused. 'Was he really so brilliant at Eton?'

'Let's leave our investigation for a drier night,' Leonard said.

As the two men emerged cautiously, a lamp was lit in an upper room and a figure was seen in silhouette. He moved across the room and drew the curtains.

'Well, for heaven's sake pursue it with discretion. We've been asked to give an opinion on whether he is worthy of membership to a secret society, not to...' Leonard left the thought unspoken.

The porters approached with a trolley and a heavy strapped trunk. They heaved the trunk, hoisting it between them.

'Begging your pardon, sirs.'

The two undergraduates flattened themselves against the wall to let the porters pass. Lytton gave a high, triumphant laugh which he quickly stifled. He followed the porters into the doorway, looking over his shoulder for Leonard to follow.

In the darkened gloom of the stairway, the porters grunted and puffed. All four of them arrived on the first floor together. The porters lowered the trunk and Lytton knocked. A few seconds passed before the door opened and the full light illuminated all three young men.

'Good evening. Your trunk? I am Lytton Strachey and this is Leonard Woolf. Trinity College. Forgive us for calling unannounced.' A quick glance at Leonard. 'We are here on behalf of our friend, Mr Thoby Stephen, to invite you to tea with his sisters.'

Leonard looked horrified, but the third man regarded Lytton with composure, stretching out his hand. He stepped aside as the porters were entering with the trunk which they put down on the floor. 'John Maynard Keynes. Good evening, gentlemen. Delighted to accept.'

A dinner gong resounded through the house. Virginia Stephen, in her early twenties, beautiful, slender, intense, with a high forehead and green eyes, turned away from the mahogany looking glass. She was dressed for dinner.

The room was lit by an oil lamp, and the night table was piled with books, several of them with silk markers. There was a washstand with a flowered basin and jug, a brass bedstead with a curtain behind it and a flowered chamber pot just visible beneath. A small coal fire burned in the grate and the mantelpiece was cluttered with framed photographs, ornaments and papers. As Virginia turned from the glass, her elder sister Vanessa appeared in the reflection in the doorway of the room. She was equally beautiful, but with a more sensual appearance, an oval face, grey-green eyes and full, sensitive mouth. The eyes of the sisters met, and Vanessa adjusted Virginia's necklace before they faced the family gathering downstairs. A dinner gong was struck again and as the sound died away the two young women went downstairs. They were wide sweeping stairs with carved banisters, and on the newel-post stood a bronze Ceres.

Holding up her skirt full of corn and flowers, Vanessa walked a few steps ahead with apparent serenity, in comparison to Virginia's gawkiness.

They reached the foot of the stairs and their brother, Thoby, strong and handsome with a marked likeness to Vanessa, came forward to take them in to dinner. They exchanged conspiratorial glances, a mixture of sympathy and resignation at the ordeal.

The dining room, large and high-ceilinged, was lit by gas wall-brackets and candles. The wallpaper was dark and the gloomy pictures were heavily framed. The furniture was massive and highly polished and the table was laid with all the formality and pomp of the Victorian age. Dominating the room was a large portrait by Watts of Sir Leslie Stephen, and he was sitting beneath it, older and more gaunt. On the table was his ear-trumpet. Aunt Adeline, in widow's black, and Aunt Mary Fisher, a faded beauty, sharp and bitter, sat on either side of Sir Leslie. George Duckworth, aged thirty-six, handsome and suave, with a moustache and sensual dark eyes, sat beside Aunt Mary, and Herbert Fisher, well into his eighties, was seated on the other side of Aunt Mary.

'I trust a chaperone has been arranged,' asked Aunt Mary, sharply.

'You don't imagine I should allow my sisters to visit Cambridge unchaperoned,' replied George.

'I cannot understand why you are putting on that disagreeable face, Virginia. You complain constantly that you are not allowed to go to Cambridge, and now that Thoby has arranged it you sulk,' said Aunt Adeline.

'Because we are not going,' Virginia said. She looked intense and defensive.

'We have all just heard your brother inviting you to tea,' said Aunt Mary.

'That is not going to Cambridge, Aunt Mary. That is going *to tea*. Don't you understand it is like putting a whole banquet in front of a person with lockjaw.' Virginia sounded exasperated.

Thoby exchanged a glance with Vanessa. 'A few crumbs...' he said.

'That isn't amusing, Thoby. At all.' Virginia was defensive.

George was half affectionate, half disapproving. 'You haven't been denied an education...'

Virginia continued, 'George is not my brother, he is my half-brother. He is a Duckworth, not a Stephen. I think I am quite as clever as my brother Thoby...' (Thoby made a deferential bow of the head.) 'And regarding Adrian...'

Adrian, who was the youngest of the four Stephen children, said sardonically, 'You mean you consider yourself brilliant and I am merely clever.'

'Exactly. And tomorrow you both go up to Cambridge and the daughters of the house wither at home.' Virginia sighed.

Sophy, the family maid, entered, cleared the plates and served the pudding. She was concerned, listening to every word.

'What? What? What is all this?' Sir Leslie picked up his ear trumpet but didn't use it. He spoke loudly, as the deaf do.

'Oh, father, you know you heard every word!' Vanessa smiled as she spoke.

'I don't like jam pudding, Vanessa,' said Sir Leslie.

George turned to Virginia. 'How many young ladies have Greek lessons? You're both privileged. Vanessa goes to art school...'

'On a bicycle,' said Aunt Mary disapprovingly.

Aunt Adelaide smiled. 'Your father is generous...'

Sir Leslie put the ear trumpet down again, still unused. 'And enlightened, wouldn't you say?' He smiled,

'And boys have to be educated, whatever Virginia might feel,' Aunt Adeline put in.

'I think Virginia feels if *she* had been a boy...' Thoby ventured.

'She isn't a boy, and there is nothing to stop her reading any book in the house. There is no shortage of books here. And in due course, God willing, she'll find a husband,' said Aunt Mary conclusively.

Adrian laughed. Virginia gave him a chilling look.

'Think who you might meet when you go to heaven,' responded Virginia.

Herbert Fisher helped himself to the dish that Sophy offered him, and immediately began to eat. He didn't look up but mumbled through a mouthful, 'Don't blaspheme.'

'Somewhere else I shall never go,' said Virginia.

Adrian whispered, 'Girls not allowed?'

'Of course you will go to heaven,' said Aunt Adeline.

'Aunt Adeline, there isn't such a place. When you die, you die.'

Sir Leslie, an atheist, gave Virginia a slight smile of commendation, quickly surpressed as Aunt Mary fixed her eyes on him.

'And what about your mother? You disgraceful girl,' exclaimed Aunt Mary.

Virginia rose to her feet. She was on the point of tears. She flung down her napkin and rushed from the room. Sophy and Vanessa exchanged anxious glances.

'May I, father..?' Vanessa went after Virginia. Thoby looked upset, and George began to apologise. 'I'm afraid she still hasn't quite recovered... she's so highly strung...'

'You shouldn't have discussed Cambridge... and you shouldn't have mentioned mother...' said Adrian.

'Nonsense.' Aunt Mary turned to Sir Leslie, 'You should say something to her, Leslie!'

Sir Leslie picked up his ear-trumpet and lifted it in the direction of his ear. 'Couldn't hear what was going on,' he bellowed.

In the morning room Virginia was crying on the sofa. There was a high ceiling, carved cornice, wall gas mantles and a fire burning in the marble fireplace which had a black leaded surround. Among the random assortment of furniture was a crowded bookcase and a glossy new pianola. The room had a lived-in appearance. There were several framed photographs of the family, including one of Sir Leslie looking pompous in a dress suit. There was an easel with an unfinished water-colour and, pushed up in a corner, a lectern-writing-desk with ink, paper and pen.

Vanessa leaned over the arm of the sofa trying to calm Virginia. 'Darling Ginia, don't be so upset.'

'I can't bear it when term starts and they go. I even miss Adrian...' She smiled through her tears.

'You shouldn't answer back, it only makes it worse.'

'Week after week, these deadly dinners... and George will start that round of social events all over again. Dressing up, making ridiculous conversation, dangling us before one unsuitable man after another...'

Vanessa said, 'He's given you up.'

'But not the warm brotherly embraces.'

The door opened and Thoby came in. He spoke affectionately, gently. 'That is what I call stubborn silly goat behaviour. Why antagonise the Aunts?'

'I can't stand it much longer,' said Virginia. 'The smell of their old clothes, the smell of the food, the smell of this house without you. You cannot begin to know what this house is like without you.'

'I know it's dull...'

'Dull? It is like being made to live in the back of Aunt Mary's wardrobe and packed in with mothballs.'

Adrian came in and stood with his back to the door, observing without sympathy as Thoby took Virginia's hands in his.

'That's why you are going to visit me in Cambridge and meet the most brilliant men I know!' said Thoby, consolingly.

Vanessa had a pencil in her hand and was drawing Virginia.

'Of course the Aunts want father to punish me and not let me go,' Virginia said.

'Do stop moving. I wish you wouldn't talk.'

'Oh, I'm not really talking. I'm small-talking. Anyway, I hate you drawing me. I can't think why you bother when there is a perfectly willing model in the Life Room.'

The lectern-writing-desk had been pushed into the centre of the morning room where the sunlight from the large window illuminated Virginia, who stood behind it, pen in hand, in a pose. Vanessa was at her easel, the half-finished water-colour was on the floor beside her. The fire was not lit, and there was a vase of spring flowers on the mantelpiece.

'You know I can't go to the Academy on Wednesdays. Father likes to go through the accounts.'

'Then I hope you'll be able to justify the three-farthings overspent on beef suet.'

'Oh, do try to stand still.'

'Where is father now?'

'In the study.' In a slightly mocking tone of voice Vanessa added, 'Deep in his dictionary of national biography.'

'Let's have a cigarette.' Virginia took a couple of books out of the bookcase and removed a packet of cigarette papers and a tin of tobacco. 'One wouldn't think he could find enough sufficiently interesting people to fill twenty-six volumes, would you? Especially as most of them are men.'

She took the tin and papers to the sofa and carefully rolled two cigarettes. Vanessa locked the door. 'You aren't going to draw any more, are you?' Virginia asked.

'Only upon the vile weed!'

They both giggled. Virginia reverted to her previous mood. 'Is writing always going to be considered the male prerogative? Novels and "ladies" novels?'

She handed Vanessa a cigarette and Vanessa struck a Swan Vesta and held it up like the Statue of Liberty torch.

'I feel resentful and melancholy,' Virginia said.

Vanessa lit another match and they both inhaled. Virginia got up and, cigarette in hand, opened the pianola with the other. 'Let's listen to the new toy. I shall have something to suit my mood.'

She balanced the cigarette on the edge of the pianola, selected a metal music roll and put it in. The mechanism whirred as she pumped the pedals. The pianola began automatically playing 'The Last Rose of Summer'; the keys worked as if being pressed.

Virginia said, 'Look at those invisible fingers. A musical ghost… travelling from drawing room to drawing room. The ghosts of Bach and Chopin.'

Vanessa stubbed out her cigarette, put the butt into the unlit coals of the fireplace, and walked towards the door.

'The accounts! Think of me, Ginia!'

Virginia went over to the pianola and put on a Chopin Polonaise.

Sir Leslie sat behind his desk, which was piled high with reference books and papers. On the bookshelf behind him were the bound volumes of the *Cornhill Magazine* which he edited, and the twenty-five volumes of the *Dictionary of National Biography*, upon all of which his name was prominent in gold lettering.

Vanessa stood beside him, leaning over an open ledger.

'We'll have to move if this goes on. Too much extravagance! We'll have to move, Vanessa. We will have to move house to Wimbledon.'

'Because of five shillings for the meat?' She sounded weary. She picked up the ear trumpet and held it towards him. 'Because of five shillings for the meat, father?' she bellowed.

'The boys aren't here to eat it. Who indulges? Is it the maids? Is it you? Is it Virginia? I am a simple man. My demands are small. Do I smell cigarette smoke on your breath? This is not a public bar.'

'Father, I need your signature on a cheque.'

With a groan Sir Leslie dipped his pen into the ink well. 'Your mother was an angel of thrift. If only she had been spared.'

Virginia was sobbing, a fit of misery brought on by a memory. The day of her mother's funeral. Virginia was fifteen. There was no pianola in the morning room then and it was pouring with rain. She was wearing a black dress, a black veiled hat, and she had flung herself sobbing on the sofa.

The door opened and George Duckworth, in funeral clothes, sat down beside her and gently removed her hat. He began to stroke and kiss her. She stiffened and lay rigid, and George's hands slid up her legs, caressingly, and then moved to her buttocks.

'Poor little Billy Goat. Poor little Ginia. Mother is with Jesus. I'm going to take care of you.'

There was the sound of knocking at the door. It took Virginia some time to recover from the unsettling memory and the knocking continued. Without turning round Virginia called out, 'Come in.'

Sophy entered carrying a hod of coal. 'Are you all right, Miss Ginia? Didn't you hear me?'

'I didn't hear anything.' Virginia paused. 'I was thinking about mother and half-brother George.'

'You don't quite look yourself.'

'Is yourself itself at this moment, Sophy?'

Sophy set down the hod. 'I don't know what you're talking about, Miss Ginia, and neither do you.'

Virginia replied with a touch of malice, 'Do you think I'm going mad again?'

'I never thought you was mad. You were just upset over poor Mrs Stephen passing on. And quite natural, too.'

'That was not the opinion of Dr Seton.'

'Good gracious! You don't want to listen to doctors.'

Vanessa entered silently, and saw Sophy about to light the fire. 'Oh no, Sophy. Not in May, I can't start justifying coal…'

'I'm sure Sir Leslie won't mind, the air's taken quite a chill to it now the sun's going down.'

'Anyway, we won't be sitting in here this evening.' Vanessa's eyes met Virginia's. 'We need an early night. Tomorrow we're being released from the cage, Sophy. We're going to Cambridge,' Vanessa explained.

It was a warm late spring afternoon. Aunt Adeline, acting as chaperone, handed Vanessa and Virginia over to Thoby. He walked to the lodge gate beside her and arrangements, which Virginia and Vanessa could not hear, were being made. Thoby gave her a half bow and Aunt Adeline went out to sit in an hotel for lunch and tea.

The girls were wearing long white dresses, with lace collars and cuffs, shady hats and carrying parasols. They were walking one either side of Thoby, across the quadrangle.

'Well, go on. For goodness' sake, don't stop. Who else is going to be there?' Virginia said, impatiently.

'You'll see for yourself.'

'Oh Thoby, don't be so trying,' Vanessa said. 'We're dying to know. Apart from "alarmingly cultured" Mr Strachey, with his French paintings and his passion for the poetry of Alexander Pope...'

'There's Mr Bell. He's an astonishing fellow. A sort of mixture between Shelley and a sporting country squire. Keeps two or three hunters up here.'

'Does he have straw in his hair?' asked Virginia.

Thoby laughed. 'You can't see his hair for straw! And I wrote to you about Mr Woolf didn't I? Another astonishing fellow. Very violent. Very savage. What's more, a Jew. Trembles perpetually! All over!'

'Why? Why does he tremble?'

'Part of his nature. Despises the whole human race.'

As they approached the college they caught sight of Adrian leaning out of the ground floor window, waving. The sisters waved back.

'I left him to guard the tea,' said Thoby, 'They're a greedy bunch.'

They were almost at the court entrance. 'Who's that with him?' Virginia asked.

'That's Clive Bell. And there's Leonard Woolf behind him...'

They went into Trinity College and Thoby flung the door open, it was his room after all. The men all stood and there was a slight, general awkwardness. Adrian came over to kiss Vanessa and Virginia and Thoby said 'Mr Strachey, my sisters, Miss Vanessa Stephen, Miss Virginia Stephen.'

Vanessa and then Virginia held out their hands. Lytton bowed, smiled, took their hands in turn.

'Mr Clive Bell. Mr Leonard Woolf.' The hand-shaking formalities continued. Adrian murmured, 'I'll tell the servant to brew up.'

'Mr Forster... Mr Keynes... Mr Sydney-Turner who is absolutely the most brilliant talker here.'

There was mocking laughter from both Lytton and Clive. Morgan Forster bowed, polite, almost demure. Maynard Keynes was formal and unsmiling. Saxon Sydney-Turner was serious and earnest and the girls had the impression that he was an oddity.

Morgan said, 'Do please take a chair, Miss Stephen.' Vanessa sat, arranging her skirts. Virginia took the chair beside her, sitting bolt upright. Most of the men sat in silence and then Clive coughed, hesitated, then said, 'I trust you had a good journey.'

'One sees such extraordinary people on a train!' Virginia said.

Lytton leaned forward. 'In what way extraordinary…'

Adrian came back into the room, followed by an elderly manservant with the tea tray.

'Set it down here, will you. Are you going to pour for us, Vanessa?'

'If you'd like me to…'

'You always do.'

Vanessa got up nervously, but with her eyes sparkling, and went to the tea table where there were thin sandwiches, two cakes and napkins. She seated herself in front of the tea tray and took up the pot. A moment's hesitation, then Leonard took the vacant chair beside Virginia.

'You were about to tell us of the extraordinary people in the railway carriage, Miss Stephen.'

'I observed that the stern dowager's volume of Christian Thoughts concealed an extremely low-class novel.'

Lytton murmured, 'First-class carriages do not always transport first-class minds.'

Vanessa was as delighted by Lytton as he appeared to be by her. She laughed and everyone smiled. The ice had been broken.

Tea and formalities over, the whole group went for a stroll along the 'backs' under the willow trees. An occasional punt passed by. An undergraduate was lying on the grass reading. Vanessa, Clive, Adrian and Morgan Forster were walking together. Virginia followed with Thoby and Leonard. Lytton, his arm around Maynard's shoulder, was a little way behind, deep in conversation. Saxon Sydney-Turner was wandering apart from everyone, occasionally listening, smiling to himself or at one remark or another.

Virginia put a hand on Leonard's arm. 'Do you really despise the human race, Mr Woolf?'

'Your brother has been maligning me!'

Thoby laughed. 'Well, it's true, isn't it? I've heard you expound on civilisation until two in the morning...'

'The truth is, Miss Stephen, I feel a profound compassion for mankind.'

'I generally feel an immense irritation...'

Adrian overheard and turned round, putting an arm round Vanessa, '...while my elder sister always remains the pillar of patience.'

Vanessa smiled. 'I just manage to keep my irritation to myself.'

'Like mother,' Adrian said, softly. Just for a moment Vanessa's smile faded.

They were baulked by a couple of men approaching in the opposite direction and the conversation momentarily faded away.

'That's the man who will change the conscience of the world,' said Leonard, after the men had passed.

'Which one? The one with light brown hair and the thin, intense face, or the one with dark brown hair and trimmed moustache? The wild looking one?'

'No.' Leonard spoke dismissively. 'That's Mr Bertrand Russell. The other one is Mr George Moore.'

A yelp from a dog made them turn to see Mr Moore untangling himself from a dog's lead – to its lady owner's consternation – while still talking animatedly.

Clive was taking off his jacket and laying it on the ground for Vanessa. He made a mock bow, she gracefully accepted it and sat down. Maynard, acting faster than Leonard, did the same for Virginia, and she flung herself down, giggling. 'I suppose the grass is rather wet,' she said. 'Arise, Sir Walter Keynes.'

Lytton arrived, breathless. 'Doesn't anyone have a cloak for me? If I don't rest I'll collapse like a pile of dominoes. You all forget I am an invalid.' He propped himself against a willow tree and surveyed them. Except for Morgan Forster, the others sat on the ground.

'Who is he? How is he going to change the world?' Virginia asked.

'Ah... Mr George Moore! Who has damned forever the concept that man has fallen from a state of grace,' said Morgan.

Virginia answered rather gleefully. 'No original sin? So none of us may be redeemed. That won't do for the church!'

'Which is why it doesn't bother Mr Woolf!' said Clive, slyly.

'It wouldn't bother me if I were a Christian, Mr Bell,' replied Leonard, 'I repudiated *all* religious belief at the age of fourteen.'

'If you *were* a Christian it wouldn't bother you. Christians don't repudiate Christianity!' put in Maynard.

Lytton gave Maynard an approving glance and shared it with Leonard. Two undergraduates ran along the bank keeping pace with a rowing boat – five pairs of oarsmen and a cox calling out, 'Together – one, two.' One undergraduate called out, 'Come on, Jesus,' and Virginia burst out laughing. Leonard smiled.

'Divine intervention?' He paused. 'Mr Moore's philosophy is concerned with goodness, beauty and absolute truth.'

'My grandfather saw Halley's Comet when he was a boy,' said Sydney Saxon-Turner suddenly. 'If we survive our examinations and live another seven years we may see it ourselves in 1910. April 1910.'

No one paid any attention. Clive made a mock bow to Vanessa from his sitting position. 'Truth and goodness and beauty, Miss Stephen.' Lytton flashed him a contemptuous look.

'If you ask me,' Adrian said, 'Moore is a bit of a fraud.'

Morgan coughed. 'I disagree. In the simplest terms, what Mr Moore is saying is that the most valuable things in life are exactly what we are doing now. We are enjoying pleasant company, good conversation and beautiful surroundings. By honestly being oneself, regardless of contemporary attitudes, society benefits.'

'Private passion, public profit!' Lytton gave a short laugh. 'It all makes life so much more a-gree-able.'

Maynard spoke thoughtfully. 'So man isn't born evil! Ergo! No dogmatic moral code.' He paused. 'No god-given sanctions, we have to have others. Ergo! The end of violence. Possibly even war?'

The rowing boat returned, splashing Lytton as it passed. He took out his handkerchief. 'Someone is trying to soak me in sin! It is becoming increasingly dangerous to venture out of doors.'

Virginia, enjoying every moment, looked up at him as he dabbed the splashes on his suit. 'And how would Mr Moore interpret that?'

'Without doubt splashing is an act of violence.'

Clive, a little sourly, replied, 'Perhaps you should devote a meeting to it!' He turned to Vanessa and Virginia. 'You see, Mr Moore has *his* disciples. Or should I say, his *Apostles*.'

'That is the secret society everyone knows about!' said Adrian.

Morgan Foster gave a gentle smile. 'All you know about it, Mr Stephen, is that it is secret.'

Virginia looked from one to the other, avid for details. 'I want to know all about Mr Moore's apostles.'

'Not exactly Mr Moore's apostles. The current members are Apostles. Past ones – Angels!' Leonard smiled.

'Are you an Apostle, Mr Bell?' Vanessa asked.

'Not elite enough.'

'Are you, Mr Woolf?' Leonard smiled and did not answer. 'That clearly means yes.' Vanessa went on, 'Mr Strachey, I'm sure you're an Apostle.'

Lytton replied laconically, 'One can be sure of nothing, Miss Stephen.' As he spoke, a handsome student walked by. Lytton looked at him meaningfully – and Virginia didn't miss it. His eyes still on the student, Lytton went on, 'Except the pleasure of human intercourse and the enjoyment of beautiful objects. We want to make people happier.' He returned his attention to Virginia. He used a mocking tone to conceal his serious content. 'But don't tell a soul.' He lowered his voice to a stage whisper. 'The late Queen left us a murky heritage. We are three years into the twentieth century. It is up to us to blow away the fog of hypocrisy and superstition that poisons our lives.'

'Before lunch – or after?' Virginia's tone was equally mocking as she scrambled to her feet.

The railway seats were covered in plush, the panels finished in mahogany and framed sepia photographs of Cambridge and Ely Cathedral flanked the central mirror above both seats. On the window a Ladies Only sign; small lights with glass globes dimly lit the carriage. The curtains were partially drawn but one was held back by Virginia looking out at the summer night sky, smoke from the locomotive streaming past her. The window was open. Beside Virginia Aunt Adeline slept, with Vanessa on her other side. Vanessa was relaxed, dreamy, going over the day in her mind. Virginia was restless, agitated. Aunt Adeline opened her eyes.

'Pull up the window, please. There's a draught and the smuts are coming in.'

Virginia turned, looked at her, looked at Vanessa, then pulled the window up.

'Drop the curtain when we pass through a station. It wouldn't be respectable to be seen looking out.'

Vanessa smiled to herself. Virginia seemed about to answer back and then controlled herself. Aunt Adeline shut her eyes and in seconds was asleep, mouth dropping open and snoring softly.

Virginia moved cautiously to sit by Vanessa. It was a bit of a squash, and they whispered very quietly.

'It was so perfect it just makes me feel worse. I knew it would.'

Vanessa shook her head. 'Don't spoil it.'

'Nothing could spoil the day. It's now. It's tomorrow. It's our whole life.'

'Mr Bell paid a great deal of attention to me. Did you see?'

Virginia said, 'The least interesting mind of them all.'

'How can you say that, how can you make a judgement...'

'Oh, I'm teasing. Yes, I did observe his splendid blue eyes saw no one but you.'

Vanessa said, 'Thoby has promised to invite him... them, all home during the vacation.'

'That won't do us any good. No one is interested in us... no, not even Mr Bell, in *that* way. Our ideas don't count. We're never going to hear Mr Moore expound...' Virginia was growing angrier and angrier. 'We could be no more than Chinese, we...'

'The window is still open,' Aunt Adeline said reprovingly. She didn't even open her eyes.

Virginia went back to her seat. 'Too small a gap to escape through.' Aunt Adeline looked at Virginia as if she were demented. And Virginia got up and slammed the window up by its leather strap.

'Well now, Mr Keynes, you have uttered the Secret Curse! You have been born into our Society!' Lytton was seated close beside him in Moore's room in Trinity College.

Maynard did not respond to his slightly mocking tone. He was watching Moore engaged in deep conversation with two unidentified young men. As he paced backward and forward, the heads of the young men moved as if they were watching a tennis game. Moore talked with intensity and passion, his face occasionally lighted with a seraphic smile while he physically attempted to light his pipe, forgetting what he was doing, burning his fingers with match after match.

'George Moore. A myth,' said Maynard. 'And to have been elected and to watch him in the same room arguing with that wonderful intensity...'

'Literally if not philosophically burning his fingers!'

Maynard raised his hand slightly, smiling at Lytton's remark, in order to listen to Moore.

'...because one's main purpose in life – as a philosopher – is to help discover that which is good. I believe that every action, by every human being, must be judged by his asking himself, if I perform it, will it have good results?'

Sitting a little apart from Maynard and Lytton were Leonard Woolf and Bertrand Russell with his dark eyes, dark hair and a trimmed moustache. He was about ten years older than the rest – a graduate Apostle!

'What I wish to point out,' Moore went on, 'is that "right" does and can mean nothing but "cause of good" and is thus...'

Leonard whispered, 'How simple he makes it sound. After all the dogma.'

'I admire him almost beyond idolatry,' Russell whispered back.

'Genius! He makes right behaviour sound as easy as chopping the top off one's breakfast egg.'

Moore continued, 'What things are intrinsically good? Good in themselves? Some of you might say...' at this point Moore addressed everyone in the room... 'Books are good – but this answer is obviously false, for some books are very bad indeed.'

'My books,' Lytton whispered, 'will be indisputably good.'

'Concomitantly, it seems to me to be self-evident, not to be doubted by anyone who has ever asked himself the question, that the states of mind brought about by the affection for another person and the appreciation of what is beautiful in Art and Nature are good in themselves.'

Lytton and Maynard were in excited agreement. 'He's right. He is right. Oh, we've buried more than Queen Victoria,' said Lytton.

An elderly servant brought in a tray of coffee and buttered toast under a dome. Maynard took a piece of toast spread with anchovies as the servant made the rounds. 'Love of another person! Love of beauty! Love of knowledge! Those states of passionate feeling. Yes, that is what it is about,' he said, taking a bite of toast. The servant gave him a look as if to say he'd heard all this pretentious twaddle from young men before.

'Drivel! Utter nonsense!' Russell raised his voice. 'Not my friend Moore's philosophy, but your interpretation of it, Keynes.' He stood, towering over Maynard. 'By concentrating on the one aspect of his thought you choose to conceive the good as consisting only in the mutual admiration of a clique of the elite. In short, being selfish.' Russell took a piece of toast and bit into it before seating himself again.

Moore glanced across to see what the row was about. Leonard leaned across, a hint of anxiety in his voice. 'But one must do good in the world, Mr Russell. And Mr Moore has shown us…'

Maynard was sardonic, not going to be drawn by Russell. 'But doing good, I fear, is much less beguiling than being good… automatically as it were!… Those states of passionate feeling.'

'Hear, hear!' Lytton said.

Russell pulled himself to his feet, incensed. 'You're misinterpreting Moore for your own interest. Great God in boots! Do you expect to be congratulated on diminishing Moore's philosophy to a series of isolated passionate moments? You have managed to degrade his ethics, Mr Keynes, into stuffy, schoolgirl sentimentalising.'

Maynard refused to be drawn. 'Not at all, not at all, Mr Russell. One must take from life and learning the things which fit one's purpose at the time.'

'Oh, Mr Keynes, you will go far with that credo. But not, I fear, as a philosopher.'

Russell sat down and Lytton put a hand lightly on Maynard's shoulder. He smiled maliciously at Russell. 'But a welcome addition, wouldn't you say, to our schoolgirl meeting.'

'In my day, Mr Strachey, a friendship between men accorded the platonic ideal. A friendship of *mind*. Of *intellect*. Not of the body.'

Lytton stirred his coffee and met Forster's eyes. Maynard, a little uncomfortable moved away. 'In this room we dare to call it as is,' said Lytton, 'We call it sodomy. In fact, in this most elevated company we call it… the Higher Sodomy.' There was general laughter, although not from Russell. Moore smiled gently, his mind had been elsewhere. He took up his pipe again.

'And that,' Russell said, 'you believe, is the greatest social communion to which man may aspire?'

'Matter of predilection, wouldn't you say, Mr Forster,' Lytton said in his high voice. Morgan kept his eyes down.

Russell went on to the attack. 'Philosophical and social, but not *sexual* intercourse have been the aspiration of…'

Leonard was anxious to save the situation. 'Gentlemen, right now my aspiration is for anchovies on toast! When I am in Ceylon…'

'When do you take up your appointment?' Moore asked.

'Not before your book is published, I trust. I want to read it on the voyage.' Russell spoke with irony. 'You might use it to convert the natives. Not Mr Keyne's version, of course.' He smiled at Moore, the final dig, but more good humoured.

Moore put down his pipe. 'Shall you read your paper first tonight?' he asked.

'Mr Strachey may have the honours,' said Russell.

Lytton rose to his feet. 'My subject, gentlemen, is – Is Death Desirable?' Everyone groaned.

Sir Leslie Stephen groaned. The door of his bedroom was open. A nurse hurried along the landing with a covered tray. Virginia ran upstairs and Aunt Mary came hurrying out of the bedroom holding a handkerchief to her face. She accosted Virginia.

'I don't like it. I don't like it at all.'

'Father likes it even less, I imagine,'

Aunt Mary dabbed her eyes, deeply affronted. 'You always were a cold, unfeeling gel, Virginia.'

Virginia stood aside to let Aunt Mary pass, and then went into Sir Leslie's room. It was dark and cluttered. There were big pieces of mahogany furniture, and Sir Leslie lay in bed, emaciated, weak and dying. The nurse was leaning over, holding an invalid cup with a spout to his lips. He groaned, pushing it away, and the nurse met Virginia's eye and moved away. Virginia went over to him and took his hand. 'Your groaning! Your groaning upset Aunt Mary, Papa.' She had to put her head close to him to hear his whispered answer. 'Had to do it… to get rid of her… bores me to death.' Their eyes met and both managed to smile.

Virginia and Thoby sat, paced, moved the heavy curtains and looked out at the dark night and stared at one another in despair. The constant groaning of Sir Leslie rose and waned in the background.

'I feel as if I'm murdering him.' Virginia walked about the room as she spoke. 'The dreadful part is he likes us all so much better now. For the first time we really interest him because we *think*…'

17

Thoby said facetiously, 'I think I have always thought…'

'As adults.' She threw herself into a chair. 'It is the awful inevitability. And I've longed for it so often. Oh God, Thoby, I don't want him to die.'

'I think he wants to,' said Thoby gently.

'I could cope perfectly well if the Aunts didn't come and cry and hold my hand and pump my emotions out of me. It really is the end of our childhood, isn't it?'

'Thank God.' He put his arms round Virginia. 'Don't keep looking back.'

'What is going to happen to us? Where are we going to go? I can't live with the Aunts. I can't live with George and his nineteenth-century bride…'

Thoby smiled at the last words. 'Don't worry. The Stephen children will leave the gloomy Victorian pile, their ancestral home at Hyde Park Gate…,' he declaimed. Virginia managed to smile. '…and assume their rightful place in the twentieth century…'

Virginia struck a pose. 'Sustained by their brother Thoby they will move forward to artistic freed…'

'Your father is on his deathbed, Virginia.' They turned round to see George standing in the doorway. 'This is not the time to indulge in jokes.'

Virginia stood frozen, drained. Thoby said, 'We were trying to distract ourselves by thinking about the future.'

'You can leave the future to me. I'm very concerned about the future. Things have been far too lax. Vanessa has done her best but without Mother to give proper guidance and protection…'

'I intend to guide and protect them, George,' said Thoby.

'I'm talking about marriage. Moving in the right circles. Control. I've spoken to Aunt…'

Thoby answered angrily. 'There is no question of living with any of the Aunts. They would not be happy.'

'Young women don't know whether they are happy or not. But I certainly would not be happy if I left the girls with you, without a suitable companion…'

'We shall of course take Sophy.' Virginia turned to look at him, amazed. 'Sophy is a servant!'

'Who has been with us most of our lives,' Thoby retorted.

'I can see you're not in the mood for sensible discussion.' George tried a new approach. 'Once Margaret and I are back from our honeymoon, settled in, she will do her duty and take responsibility.'

'It won't be necessary. Wherever I live my sisters and brother will live with me. We are all over age, brother George,' Thoby said emphatically.

Virginia turned to Thoby, a look of gratitude on her face. Simultaneously the groans from Sir Leslie reached a pitch and stopped. George, Thoby and Virginia looked at one another waiting for it to start again. It didn't. Their eyes turned to the dominating portrait of Sir Leslie on the wall. Virginia sobbed.

The removal men in green baize aprons carried Sir Leslie's portrait sideways out of the door. It was raining outside and the room was sombre. Much of the furniture had gone or was covered by dustsheets. Aunt Mary, Aunt Adeline and Virginia wore black, even to their stockings. Virginia was standing, but the Aunts were perching on the remaining high-backed chairs, stiff with disapproval. The dining room was stacked with china and silver. Sophy came in with a heavy silver tray with coffee and biscuits. She moved aside a dustsheet on the sideboard to put it down.

'You haven't shown me all the condolence letters,' said Aunt Adeline.

Virginia said irritably, 'They're all the same, Aunt Adeline.'

'Coffee, madam?'

'Where is one supposed to put the cup?' asked Aunt Adeline.

'Virginia! If people are good enough to write…' Aunt Mary said reprovingly.

Sophy cleared a space on the table. At the same time the removal men returned, murmuring apologies, touching their foreheads, and carried out the sideboard. Sophy rushed to take the coffee tray and placed it on a chair. 'They're… all at sixes and sevens…' she said.

Virginia said, 'They write because they believe they have to!'

Sophy brought Aunt Adeline her coffee, offering sugar, milk and biscuits.

'No, Virginia. They write because they respected and admired your father,' Aunt Adeline said. She helped herself to sugar.

Sophy took coffee to Aunt Mary and she shook her head. 'No, thank you, Sophy.'

'I'll have it, Sophy, I could do with it,' Virginia said.

Vanessa came in, a handkerchief tied over her hair. 'Oh, good. Coffee.' She turned to her Aunts. 'Sorting out which of Father's books…'

'You are the only one who doesn't mourn him.' Aunt Mary fixed her eyes on Virginia sternly.

Vanessa looked quickly from Aunt Mary to Virginia. Virginia took a deep, quivering breath. Vanessa said warningly, 'She's feeling upset, Aunt Mary…'

Virginia began to talk slowly, building up to an increasingly nervous frenzy. 'Upset? Why should I be upset? They write with such anguish. Great loss, esteemed career, devoted husband, devoted father... Well, I went for a walk yesterday in Hyde Park. And I knew when I got home he'd be here...' She gave a wild giggle. Vanessa looked at the Aunts accusingly, and they looked meaningfully at one another.

'So sorry. Deepest sympathy. Heartfelt condolences. Safe with God. Done their duty, merry as grigs. I dream every night he's alive. And I can tell him I did value him, we all valued him...!'

Sophy had been hurriedly pouring and sugaring a cup of coffee, which she put into Virginia's hands. 'There, Miss Ginia...'

Virginia took it, looked at it as if she had never seen a cup before, and fell silent. The Aunts exchanged significant looks. Aunt Adeline eventually broke the silence. 'To where are you actually moving, Vanessa?'

Vanessa paused. 'Bloomsbury.'

Aunt Adeline put down her cup. 'Bloomsbury? *Bloomsbury!*' She rose to her feet, horrified, '*But nobody lives in Bloomsbury!*' The removal men returned and took away the chair she had been sitting on. The rain still beat against the window.

The removal man carried the same chair from a horse-drawn pantechnicon into the open door of the new house. Other removal men emerged wearing bowler hats and green baize aprons. Vanessa threw open the upstairs window and waved and Thoby and Virginia, full of vigour and youthful excitement, waved back as they approached the house, arms full of feather dusters, brooms, flowers and cake boxes. The removal men took in the sideboard and Virginia's lectern-desk as they approached, and once inside they went into the drawing room where Adrian towered on top of a ladder, painting the biscuit-coloured ceiling white. Furniture was piled under dustsheets in the centre of the room. The walls were heavily papered and Vanessa and Sophy were ripping down dark velvet curtains.

'Dear Mr Woolf,' wrote Virginia. 'We have moved from the house in Hyde Park Gate and now live in Bloomsbury, in Gordon Square. I believe you are going to Ceylon and we would love it if you could come to tea – or dinner – or breakfast – before you go.'

Virginia ran into the drawing room and collided with Sophy who had just arrived to talk to Vanessa. Vanessa, out of mourning too, but with a black band on her arm, stood on a chair arranging the folds of green and white chintz curtains. The room, repainted all white, was in total contrast to Hyde Park Gate, light and bright and airy, with sunlight pouring through the large windows at either end.

'Whoops! Sorry, Sophy…' Virginia indicated the curtains, 'They look like summer…'

Sophy looked at them disapprovingly. 'The butcher's here for his order, Miss Vanessa. I'll tell him you want beef for Sunday, shall I?'

'Let's be wild and have muttonchops,' Virginia said.

Sophy's tone and expression was similar to Aunt Adeline's '*Nobody* eats muttonchops on Sundays.'

Virginia and Vanessa burst out laughing. Vanessa tried to pacify her. 'Order a short wing rib, Sophy, and some kidneys for breakfast.'

'What about suet?'

'If we need it, order it. I don't have to account to anyone anymore.' She threw herself down on the sofa. 'I don't have to account for anything. To anyone. Any more.'

'But I have to account to you, Miss Vanessa. So it's no good saying do what I want.'

'But I trust you. Please ask the butcher for some suet.'

Sophy went out and Virginia said with a sigh, 'How shall we ever liberate the serving class!'

'I don't think they want to be liberated. They don't know how wonderful it is. Total, utter, amazing freedom.'

'Let's do without table napkins!'

'Let's always have coffee after dinner!'

Virginia sat on the sofa at the other end from Vanessa. 'Imagine if they'd married us off!'

'We'd be trapped,' Vanessa said. She paused. 'We're very lucky, you know. Being on the shelf. There aren't many like us. Enough to live on. In mixed company.'

'We don't need husbands,' said Virginia 'We've got brothers. Or at least, we've got Thoby!' Vanessa giggled and blushed a little. 'Oh, Nessa,' Virginia went on, 'think what you'd be giving up for marital bliss! I know! You can be someone's mistress!'

Vanessa replied seriously, 'Only married women can be mistresses. Accepted by society, I mean. And their lovers have to be very connected. The Archbishop of Canterbury once asked Mrs Keppel to a party when everyone knew about her and the King!'

'Would you…without being married?' asked Virginia.

Vanessa shook her head. 'No. Would you?'

'I just want us to go on living here, the way we are now. It's perfect.'

Virginia's sitting-room looked organised, the books were in rows, the walls re-painted, although the mantelshelf was cluttered. Virginia was at her lectern-writing-desk, dipping her pen into the inkwell, three quarters of the way down a page…

'My first published book review, Vanessa, and my name isn't on it. Still, if everyone thinks it's a poor work, I'll be relieved to stay anonymous.'

Vanessa was addressing envelopes at a table and she spoke without looking up. 'You won't be anonymous to your friends. You've told everyone you know.'

'And being paid for it! Imagine being paid for something I've been doing all my life.'

'Everyone will have eaten before they arrive, won't they?' Vanessa asked anxiously.

'They won't expect champagne and caviar in Bloomsbury!'

A hansom cab emerged from the gloom and pulled up outside the house where the light from the downstairs windows penetrated the fog. As the cabman climbed down from his box and opened the door, assisting George Duckworth and his wife, Lady Margaret, to alight, a de Dion open car with wooden spoked wheels and hard rubber tyres turned noisily into the square. A chauffeur sat at the wheel and Kitty Maxse, dressed against the weather, was lolling in the rear seat. The cab horse reared, frightened, as the car drew up beside the cab.

'Why, Kitty…' George said, paying the driver, as Margaret and Kitty walked towards the house.

'I'm not sure whether we should be flattered or offended at being asked!' George, in evening dress and silk hat, joined them.

'Oh, flattered!' Kitty said. 'I thought we had all been discarded.'

'My dear, we have been invited to observe how differently the "twentieth century" entertains!' He smiled sarcastically and rang the bell.

One wall of the drawing room was dominated by a large poster of La Goulou at the Moulin Rouge, displaying much leg. Below it sat Clive Bell being offered a plate of buns by Vanessa. She was dressed in a Bohemian manner, with a flowing skirt and a Spanish shawl, but Virginia looked gawky in a polka-dot dress. No one was talking. In silence, Saxon Sydney-Turner sat across the room by the fire, filling his pipe and continuously attempting to light it. On the table was another large plate of buns and a tray with cups and saucers and a jug of cocoa. The silence was broken by the ringing doorbell and Sophy could be heard walking across the hall to open it. 'When we had parties in my parents' home,' said Vanessa smiling nervously, 'everyone talked all the time... about nothing.'

'And here no one talks about anything!' Clive tried to make her feel at ease.

Virginia came over and took the plate of buns from Vanessa. 'You're hogging the buns.' She strode across the room and thrust the plate towards Saxon who smiled and declined. Silence again, and then the voices of George, Margaret and Kitty were heard in the hall. Sophy opened the door and announced them as they swept in, looking with horror at the vulgar poster on the wall.

'Lady Margaret and Mr George Duckworth and Mrs Maxse...'

Kitty was elegant, precise, blue-eyed, fashionably and expensively dressed, as was the more establishment Lady Margaret. 'Vanessa, my dear...' Kitty avoided her eyes. 'How charming it all is...' She gazed at the awkward gathering.

Thoby came to greet them, shook George's hand, kissed Margaret's hand and then kissed Kitty's. 'Let me offer you...'

The doorbell rang again and Sophy's footsteps punctuated the silence. In desperation Virginia proffered the buns. 'Thank you, my dear, but we have had dinner,' Lady Margaret said. Kitty, game for anything, took Thoby's arm and went with him to the table where he poured a cup of cocoa.

The door opened and Morgan sidled in anxiously. 'Mr Forster,' Sophy said.

George looked on disparagingly as Morgan was greeted by Vanessa and Clive. Kitty took the cup and helped herself to sugar and whispered mockingly to Thoby '...as long as my husband never hears I've been drinking cocoa...'

Outside the front door the chauffeur was asleep at the wheel. Maynard and Lytton emerged from the fog and caught sight of the de Dion parked at the kerb. 'Then we are *not* the first,' Lytton said.

'What a charming boy... although his eyes are hidden. Still, a lovely mouth.'

'I cannot be tempted. I have fallen in love.'

'Again?' said Maynard.

'Passing Cambridge fancies, my dear Maynard. This is utterly different. I'm in love with my cousin Duncan. Lived with us all these years, and suddenly, across our thousandth breakfast together, I was pierced by Cupid's dart.'

They climbed the front steps and Maynard looked back at the sleeping chauffeur while Lytton rang the bell.

Once inside Lytton advanced on Virginia, carrying a cup of cocoa. 'Well, Miss Stephen, I read your unsigned criticism of that rather dismal book.' He sat down by Virginia.

'Was my criticism dismal, too? It can't be as dismal as my teaching.'

'Fortunately, you did not find it necessary to speculate on the author's private life.'

Morgan slipped unobtrusively into the chair beside them. 'Sometimes an author's private life elucidates his work,' he said.

'Whether my own torrid personal life,' Lytton announced dramatically, 'will throw light upon the great works I shall undoubtedly write remains to be seen. I am prepared to be dismissed by the critics in my lifetime.'

Virginia stood up. 'Then you will live longer. Failure will keep us young.'

Lytton was delighted by the cynicism. 'Mr Forster also intends to be a writer. Well, Morgan, dear fellow, will you be a failure too?'

'Ha! I'm risking divine disapproval. My book is called *Where Angels Fear to Tread.*'

Virginia took a cup of cocoa to Morgan, Saxon Sydney-Turner lit his pipe again and surveyed the room, and George, Margaret and Kitty stood together as if for support.

Kitty spoke very softly. 'We seem to belong to another world!'

Margaret drew closer. 'I've no doubt their friends are all very nice – but they do look deplorable!'

'Do you remember how lovely Vanessa looked on your wedding day?' Kitty remembered nostalgically. They all looked towards Vanessa as she leant against the wall in deep conversation with the attentive Clive. Her skirt was orange and her embroidered shawl pink.

Margaret said sadly, 'In white satin and pearls... and now I'm afraid everyone is gossiping. Vanessa's involved with some artist's club, they take tea with men alone, and for some reason Virginia's decided to teach English to girls of the working class...'

Virginia, in hat and coat with books under her arm, was striding towards The Old Vic in Waterloo Road in working-class South London. Beside the door was a sign which read Morely College, and on the door itself was written Stage Door. Virginia pushed the door open and climbed the stairs, going against the tide of working women clattering down, assorted ages and types. She went into the classroom which was a dressing room, rearranged with several rows of chairs and a lectern facing them.

'Good evening,' Virginia said smiling, as she went and stood behind the lectern, leaning forward on her elbows, eager and intense. On the chairs in front of her sat four women in a line. One, in her thirties, was handsome and well dressed; there were two young gaudily dressed shop girls and a thin, intense, shabby and earnest girl with glasses. 'I'm sorry that only two of you managed to write something for me. If some of you need pencils let me know. I had hoped that by writing about your own lives...'

'I don't consider my life particularly interesting, Miss Stephen,' said the first woman.

'Of course it is,' Virginia said passionately. 'Every detail of every human life is interesting. Fascinating.' The fourth woman gave a sardonic little laugh.

'We come 'ere to learn from you. And with all due respect we haven't learned much.'

Virginia said emphatically, 'Can't you see that in writing about yourselves you *are* learning. To express yourselves freely. To use the English language. To understand your own feelings.'

'We thought we were going to learn *better English*.'

'But this is the way to do it.' Virginia was exasperated. 'If you could only get into the habit of writing down the ordinary things that happen to you during an ordinary working day...'

The shop girl burst out laughing. 'What? 'Ow I sliced the cheese and done the butter pats...'

25

'*Yes*. You don't need age and wisdom to write, either. Just remember that the poet Keats died when he was only twenty-five...'

'Can you say that name again, Miss Stephen.'

'What did he die of then?'

'John Keats. K.E.A.T.S. And it doesn't matter what he died of, all that matters is he left us wonderful poetry...' She recited with feeling.

'Four seasons fill the measure of the year

There are four seasons in the mind of man:

He has his lusty spring, when fancy clear

Takes in all beauty with an easy span

He has his summer, when luxuriously

Spring's honey cud of youthful thought he loves

To ruminate, and by such...' Virginia stopped. The first woman stood up and gathered her things together.

'That ain't goin' to help us get 'igher wages, Miss Stephen. Don't expect me to be 'ere next week.' As she went out she turned and spoke derisively, 'Spring's 'oney cud!'

Virginia looked after her in helpless frustration. The second shop girl tried to make things better. 'It isn't that we don't want to write down, but we on'y get 'alf an hour for our dinner and by the time we've had it there wouldn't be any time to do any writin'...'

Clive and Vanessa were surrounded by stacked paintings, several of which were already on the walls – but there was an undercurrent to their discussion. Clive held up Vanessa's portrait of Lady Robert Cecil. 'I'm going to hang Lady C,' said Clive.

'Oh, don't do that! The poor lady doesn't deserve it. She *paid* me!' Vanessa paused. 'Do you think I should stick to portraits?'

Clive hung the painting and came closer to Vanessa. 'I think you should go in all directions. You are very talented. But you have to learn to display your wares, Miss Stephen.' He stood behind her, stretched out both arms, imprisoning her as he adjusted the portrait. Vanessa turned her head to look at him.

There was a commotion, running footsteps up the stone stairs as the door was swung open by Virginia, still wearing her hat and coat and carrying her books. There was a notice on the door – Friday Club Members' Exhibition – and Virginia left it open as she stormed into the room.

'What is it? What's happened?' Vanessa cried out.

'It's the girls, it's my class. I can't get close to them...'

Vanessa moved away from Clive's outstretched arms, but not before Virginia had seen. 'Oh, I'm sorry, Mr Bell, good evening, good evening... Why must they insist on putting a chasm between us?'

'You mustn't let them upset you...'

'What did they say?' Clive said.

Virginia replied vehemently, 'They think they are not interesting. They think they are born not to put pen to paper. They think because they work in shops and cut cheese the English language is not to be used for pleasure. Every week I go there, bursting with ideas and images...'

'Your sister will tell you,' Clive looked adoringly at Vanessa, 'that I couldn't convince a more enlightened audience of Cézanne's genius.'

'You did better than that.' Vanessa looked into his eyes. 'You shocked them.'

'And I've never been able to convince my father he should invest his capital in art,' Clive said.

Virginia turned to leave. 'You should try and make him buy one of Vanessa's paintings,' and she went out without waiting for a reply.

'I must go, too. Thursday again?' Clive asked. Vanessa nodded. 'Of course,' Clive went on, 'Thursday evenings in Bloomsbury...landmarks in London's social calendar!' He picked up a painting and surveyed the wall space.

'Oh, Mr Bell, I think you exaggerate!'

'No exaggeration at all! Everybody who is going to be somebody goes to Gordon Square.'

Lytton Strachey, wearing a cloak and greenish-yellow gloves, sailed through the front door, held open by Sophy. As Sophy closed the door behind him there was a hubbub of voices from the drawing room. Lytton peeled off a glove. He had become increasingly mannered and was growing a beard. He turned his head towards the party sounds with affected anticipation. The Thursday social gathering was well underway and there was a pall of cigarette smoke in the room. Vanessa, wildly dressed in a romantic gypsy style with a rose in her hair, was seated on the floor and Clive Bell had his head in her lap. Sydney-Turner was sitting in his usual place by the fire and Thoby was pouring wine into the glass of a

Bohemian and beautiful girl. Virginia stood with the inevitable plate of buns which she was thrusting towards a nervous and conventional young woman, Miss Cole, who sat on the edge of an upright chair, holding a cup and saucer. Maynard Keynes and Morgan Forster sat either side of a handsome young man, fair-haired and stalwart and with a healthy complexion. A sheepdog, Gurth, wandered around and was petted and given bits of bun. Adrian stood on a chair, a watch and chain in his hand, ready to time a game.

'Thoby, you must start. Thirty seconds. Ready. The letter is O. Begin.'

'Orange, orangery, ostrich, ordinance…'

Lytton struck a pose. 'Orgasm!' he shrieked. His voice was particularly high and piercing and everyone turned to look at him.

There was silence, and then laughter from everyone except Miss Cole who froze with embarrassment. 'I must be going,' she said, 'I didn't know you were entertaining… I only came to bring the maps…'

Lytton sailed over to Maynard, Morgan and the young man. 'I don't believe we have met. What a wonderful complexion. Don't you envy him, Virginia?'

'You've spoilt the game, Lytton,' Virginia answered, 'and you've upset Miss Cole. Hasn't he, Miss Cole?' Miss Cole blushed and rose still clutching the cup. The young man smiled up at Lytton. 'We met at Cambridge.'

'Impossible. Unforgettable.'

'Wait!' said Sydney-Turner. Everyone turned to look at him. 'Orifice!'

'We're not playing!' Clive whispered close to Vanessa's ear. 'Only with one another!'

'I won't hear of you leaving,' Virginia said to Miss Cole. 'Have some whisky?'

'I'm contented with cocoa, Miss Stephen.'

'Contented with cocoa?' Virginia said, looking round for an audience. 'How do you define contentment, Miss Cole? Do you wake up in the morning and think, I'm contented today? I am discontented today?'

'I was using the word carelessly…'

'No, no, not at all. Some of us find our contentment in the simplest things. In cocoa, for example.'

Miss Cole began to move towards the door. She managed to put her cup down as she went.

'I would like everyone to be seated,' Lytton said, moving between Morgan and the young man and smiling at him. 'And I shall read aloud the letter I received today from Leonard Woolf – lord of a million in Hambantota, Ceylon.'

'Miss Cole...you must wait to hear the letter,' said Clive.

'I really must be going. I have intruded.' Clive shot a look of complicity towards Virginia, enjoying the social persecution. Clive said sadly, 'Must we be deprived of your company so soon?'

'I have a cab waiting.'

'Is it because you don't like me?' Clive pretended he was crestfallen.

'Miss Cole has a very strong character. If she decides to go because she doesn't like you, we must applaud her integrity. I do, Miss Cole.' Virginia spoke authoritatively.

All conversation had stopped, all eyes were on the hapless Miss Cole. Everyone was smiling, waiting for the next barb. Saxon Sydney-Turner made one of his rare remarks in a mild flat voice. 'I was at Thomas Cook's this afternoon. There are several ways to go to Germany,' he said. Everyone turned towards him, astonished.

Miss Cole addressed Vanessa, social etiquette dominating her feelings. 'Thank you so much for your hospitality, Miss Stephen.' Vanessa scrambled to her feet, suddenly guilty.

'It was very kind of you to call and offer us the Greek maps...' she said.

'We will find them tremendously useful on our journeys,' added Thoby. Miss Cole looked at him gratefully and he was all at once protective and charming as he went over to her. 'I'm afraid we are old friends and you were made to feel left out.'

Virginia said wickedly, 'We hold an 'At Home' every Thursday. I do hope you will come again...' Miss Cole gave her a look of horror.

'Let me see you to your cab,' said Thoby, and they went out.

Virginia felt rather ashamed. 'Was I very cruel?' she said.

'You always are,' Adrian replied.

'She will survive,' Lytton commented. 'She is convinced of her superiority. She was taught by her nursery governess. She will dine out on your cruelty.'

'She was an outsider,' Virginia said defensively.

Thoby came back into the room. 'A dram more whisky, and we'll learn what Mr Woolf has to tell us.' He took the bottle round and filled up glasses and Sydney-Turner re-lighted his pipe. Clive stroked Vanessa's hair and Lytton opened the letter with a flourish.

'And now you shall hear how Woolf came down on the fold like an Assyrian...'

Clive with his hat and silk scarf came out of the front door. Vanessa stood in the golden glow of the gaslight in the hall. Clive took her hand and Lytton's voice rose and fell in the drawing room.

'Will you walk tonight or take a cab?' Vanessa asked.

'Walk. And think about you, Miss Stephen.' He paused. 'Vanessa, I must ask you again. I will not accept your answer as final.'

'If marriage was just a question of being good friends and caring about the same things...'

Clive said 'It is!'

'I do like you better than any other man...'

'But not better than Thoby.'

'Without him I wouldn't have been able to see you again. George and the Aunts would have made me banish you.'

'But now you live in Bloomsbury and you have your own rules.'

'So I won't banish you entirely.' She took a rose from her hair and gave it to him, half-mockingly, half-flirtatiously. He took it and put his lips to it, then he turned and ran down the steps. Vanessa watched him as he walked away, the rose in his hand.

The rose was on the bedside table. Clive and his married mistress were naked in bed together. They had just made love.

Dawn light was beginning to illuminate the room where Vanessa was lying in bed and Virginia, in her nightdress, was curled up at the foot.

'Of course, he loves you,' Virginia said. 'But you don't love him.'

'I *agree* with him.'

'On what?'

'He has a high regard for Jane Austen and a low one for Christianity.'

Virginia spoke in a flat voice. 'He also comes from a *nouveau riche* family, I'm afraid. The fortune comes from coal!'

Vanessa burst out laughing. 'You're a snob! You're like George! Don't tell me you want me to marry the equivalent of Lady Margaret?'

'You know I don't want you to marry at all.'

'We're all bound to marry in the end.' Vanessa put her arms behind her head, a gesture that was both yielding to inevitability and yet reluctant.

'Who'd want to be stuck with Adrian!' Virginia said, laughing. Then she was serious. 'Oh, Ness, every day I dread that Thoby is going to tell us he's fallen in love.'

'Where could I find anyone with your combined qualities?' They turned round and Thoby, in his dressing gown, was standing in the doorway, an open book of maps in his hand.

'Well,' Virginia said, 'What about that creature of vibrant beauty you were flirting with tonight?'

'Only flirting. No, if I were drawn to anyone, it would be the ravishing, scintillating and utterly contemporary Miss Cole.' Virginia and Vanessa burst out laughing.

'But do you want to marry one day?'

'Yes,' Thoby said with a smile, 'I don't share Mr Strachey's tastes.'

'I almost wish you did…except of course I would like to be an Aunt.' Virginia paused. 'Don't fall in love with a Greek Goddess.'

Thoby came across and sat on the end of the bed, opening out the folded map in the already opened book. 'Miss Cole earned her cocoa. She has even pencilled in a suggested route.' They all leant over the map.

'Then I forgive her for being a bore,' Vanessa said.

'Here's Athens…' Thoby pointed at the map, 'We'll have a week doing all the tourist things…'

'And the wine!' Vanessa exclaimed, 'Virginia, don't you dare to be ill. Don't you dare go mad in Greece!'

'I'm never mad,' Virginia said fiercely, 'It is the rest of the world. Not me!'

Lytton sat in bed reading aloud in a hoarse voice from a letter from Virginia. He was wearing a nightshirt with a scarf tucked in at the neck and there were medicine bottles on the bedside table. A breakfast tray with a half-eaten boiled egg and uneaten toast had been pushed to the foot of the bed. The bedroom was high and gloomy. The huge cumbersome window did not open but had a little circular ventilator worked with cords and pulleys. Duncan Grant stood beside him, with a towel in one hand and a steam kettle in the other. He was immensely attractive, with brilliant eyes, unruly hair and saturnine features, and Lytton was in love with him. He was wearing only flannel trousers, and his manner was gentle and sweet.

'You will be interested to know,' Lytton read on, '…that we have seen Greece from an unusual point of view, a series of hotel bedrooms in Athens, Corinth, Epidaurus, Tirynus, Mycenae, and here we are back again in Athens while the brothers imbibe Greek art and I boil goat's milk for poor Vanessa who was stricken the moment we arrived. For me it has been an educational tour. You know I like to make up stories about people in hotels, but for Vanessa it is a dreadful disappointment, three weeks with no walking, no museums… I'm amazed that I am the one who is well!'

'No inhalations!' said Duncan, throwing the towel over Lytton's head, and inserting the steam kettle under it. 'If you don't lubricate your lungs you won't be able to read me the rest of the letter.'

Lytton, concealed by the towel, waved the letter for Duncan to take. Duncan put it down among the medicines.

'Darling Cousin Duncan,' said Lytton 'promise me not to be ill in Paris.'

Duncan sat down on the bed beside Lytton and took his hand. 'I promise.'

Lytton threw back the towel, draping his head Arab-style, his face pink and damp. He took off his steamed-up glasses and dried them on the sheet. 'You know these foreign doctors are all quacks.' He clasped Duncan's hands and wailed, 'Why must you go?'

'To paint!'

'You'll fall in love with some handsome Gallic phallic artist. I shall rot here, forgotten…'

Duncan laughed. 'Nonsense! You are unforgettable! My God, Lytton, you look like a gypsy fortuneteller. How could I forget you?'

Lytton laughed with Duncan – rather wheezily. 'Well, I forbid you to leave until the Stephens are back. You must meet them and help me to regale them with all the London gossip.' He snatched up Virginia's letter and his glasses and disappeared again under the towel.

It was a winter's day in Gordon Square and Dr Seton, wearing a top hat and carrying a black bag, hurried up the steps and pulled the bell knob. Sophy answered the door, solemn-faced. 'Good morning, Doctor.' He went in and saw the strapped trunks, an easel and strapped canvasses. George Duckworth came into the hall.

'Good morning, good morning… and how are my patients?' Dr Seton asked.

'I understand they both slept. Exhausted from the journey.'

'Travel may broaden the mind but it plays havoc with the human body. I advise my patients to stay in England.'

Virginia and Adrian were playing piquet in the drawing room. They were doing their best to pass the time, but there was a sense of tension and unease. 'It's no good. I can't concentrate. He's been upstairs for forty minutes.'

Adrian sighed. 'It's the way George has taken over. As if he were Father…'

There was a knock at the door. Adrian leapt to his feet, Virginia turned and whispered, 'Dr Seton…'

'Come in,' Adrian called.

The door was opened by Sophy and Clive Bell hurried in, taking Virginia's hands. 'I've just heard…'

'How good of you to come.'

'I consider Thoby my greatest friend…and your sister… I cannot bear to think of her ill.'

George and Dr Seton came into the room and Clive went towards the door. 'I will wait outside…'

'Please stay Mr Bell. What is the news?'

Dr Seton puffed out his chest. 'Over the worst.'

'Thank God,' Clive said. George looked at him as if he had no right to be there, let alone have an opinion. Adrian and Virginia sighed with relief.

'Your brother's sharp attack of something or other foreign appears to be subsiding. As I thought.'

'And my sister?'

'Overstrain,' said Dr Seton. 'I'm keeping on the nurses. I want them both in bed for another week at least. Rest. Rest. Nature's cure!'

In the low gaslight a uniformed nurse was taking Thoby's temperature and as she removed the thermometer from his mouth she looked very disturbed. She called in the other nurse and said 'He's got a very high temperature. He's in a fever. We'll call the doctor in the morning.'

In the hall Dr Seton and Dr Fowler and George were gathered together. Virginia came in through the front door, lowered her umbrella and shook

33

it out over the step. She had been buying books, but she looked afraid when she caught sight of the doctors.

'Dr Fowler has diagnosed malaria.'

The doctor was very brusque and unsympathetic. 'I have prescribed treatment. We should be seeing the downward arc of the fever within two days.'

'There's no question that my sister…?' Virginia left the question unfinished.

'No question at all. Nothing the matter with her except the female complaint of nerves.'

Dr Seton said, 'I suspected malaria from the outset but the symptoms were not straightforward.'

Virginia wasn't convinced and she made her way to the stairs past the group of men. 'I shall take these upstairs to my sister. Thank you for coming, Dr Fowler.' He bowed perfunctorily. 'Good morning, Dr Seton.'

'Nothing newfangled in your library, I hope,' said Dr Seton. 'We don't want Miss Stephen upset.'

Virginia was halfway upstairs. 'Hymns of Praise. At her request!' And she went on up.

'But malaria never really goes away, does it?' Vanessa said.

'But you don't *die* from it. It can be controlled.'

'I couldn't bear to think of Thoby having to "take care". Not being free to do what he wants.' Vanessa paused. 'Everything comes from Thoby.'

'Everything!' Virginia echoed. She paused going towards the door. 'Look at your books, Nessa. The astute Dr Seton prescribed mild literature.'

'Thank you for complying.' She gave a little giggle. 'Elinor Glyn! Very, very calming. Dante…positively soporific…'

Through the open door the nurse and Dr Seton could be seen bending over the bed where Thoby tossed and turned. Vanessa and Virginia, in their nightgowns, stood holding hands. Then, through the crack in Vanessa's door, they could see Sophy showing the doctor downstairs. She was wearing a woolly dressing gown and her hair was in a net.

'Nurse!' Vanessa called. She and Virginia came out of the room and onto the landing. 'What's the matter?'

The nurse joined them. 'Nothing you need to worry about. Doctor's told me what to do. Not that I needed telling.'

'But is he going to be all right?'

'It happens in cases like this.'

'In cases like *what*, nurse?' Virginia said.

'In cases like Mr Stephen's.' She turned to go.

'Is he in danger?'

'He's sleeping now. We're doing all we can.' She paused, then in a different tone, stealthy and knowing, she said 'But if you ask me – I never like November for my patients.'

Vanessa looked astonished. 'November?' Virginia and Vanessa looked at one another, amused but fearful. The nurse bustled out importantly.

'Oh, dear God…' Vanessa said, quietly.

It was daytime in Thoby's room. Vanessa was arranging flowers and she said, 'These are from Kitty Maxse. Everyone seems to know you're ill.' She paused. 'Oh, Mr Strachey dropped in a book of Latin verse.'

Thoby said in a voice so feeble that Vanessa could hardly hear him, 'Did he remember the primer?'

Virginia, Vanessa and Adrian were waiting for the doctors. Dr Seton wanted another opinion.

'I wish to God we'd never gone away,' Adrian said.

'And it seemed so wonderful…' Virginia added.

'Shh…'

There were footsteps on the stairs and Dr Seton entered and said pompously, 'My colleague is talking to the nurse.' The Stephens drew nearer together. 'I'm afraid your brother seems not to have malaria. I'm afraid it now appears he contracted typhoid fever.' Instinctively Virginia, Adrian and Vanessa grasped hands. 'We will do all we can. He still has a chance of life.'

Virginia was sitting by the bed, her eyes on Thoby's face. The nurse stood on the other side. Thoby's breath was very shallow and for a moment it seemed to stop altogether. Virginia froze. Then he took another breath and Virginia said, 'Thank God.'

The nurse whispered, 'He's very weak. I'd like to say a prayer. I've been looking at the books. Doesn't he have a Bible?'

Virginia reached out to the bedside table and picked up the book that was lying there. *Principia Ethica* by G.E. Moore. She handed it to the nurse who looked at it, bewildered.

'I don't think you understood, Miss Stephen.'

Virginia didn't hear her, her concentration was on Thoby. His breathing stopped. She said tremulously, 'Nurse!'

The shutters were closed and straw was being swept away from the roadway and pavement by a road-sweeper. Outside the house stood a black horse-drawn conveyance. Two tophatted undertakers rang the bell. Virginia, Vanessa and Adrian, all pale and in mourning, stood huddled together. Adrian had an arm round each of them but in effect it was as if the girls were supporting him. He seemed more *gauche* and ineffectual than ever.

Adrian said with a shudder, 'Measuring him.'

Vanessa was almost motherly. 'Adrian, we have to accept it.'

'I can't do it all. Not all on my own,' he said.

'We're not going to ask for help from George,' Virginia said.

'But Thoby could cope. I don't know what we're going to do.'

There was a sound of muffled voices in the hall and the sound of the front door opening and closing. Virginia peered through the almost closed shutters and saw the two undertakers walking with sombre steps along the pavement. As they reached the conveyance, one suddenly turned his head and she saw he was laughing. Virginia looked away from the window and Vanessa was stroking Adrian's hand – neither had seen the laughing undertaker. The doorbell rang and Adrian said in a choked voice, 'I can't face seeing anyone.'

Sophy's footsteps sounded in the hall and the front door opened and closed. Then Sophy opened the door of the drawing room. She was in black and her eyes were red. 'Mr Bell.'

Clive entered, his eyes were moist. He looked at his friends with compassion. No one spoke and then Vanessa broke away from Adrian and Virginia and opened her arms. He held her close and Vanessa began to sob. Clive stroked her hair. 'Don't...I know, I know...my darling girl...'

Virginia spoke very, very quietly. 'We've lost a brother. And I think we've lost a sister, too.' She turned away and her face was stricken by her sense of loneliness.

Chapter 2
Private Passions

It was a rundown street and a small group of onlookers watched as the Carnarvon family carriage, its arms emblazoned on the side and driven by a liveried coachman, pulled up behind a dilapidated dray. The coachman opened the door and Vanessa, Virginia, Adrian, George Duckworth and the sheepdog Gurth descended, all attired for a wedding. Gurth was wearing a Pierrot ruff.

The wedding party, with some hilarity on Virginia's part, approached the entrance to the registry office where the doorman refused to let Gurth inside. Vanessa returned the dog to the coachman who took the leash with haughty displeasure.

Clive and his brother Cory were waiting. The registrar was wearing thick-lensed glasses and when he took out his watch he held it close to his face. Clive was pacing. 'Can't think what's holding them up. George's wife lent them the Carnarvon family coach.'

'Um, er, Mr Bell, er…' the registrar said.

Through the door came the radiant Vanessa, giggling, with Virginia, Adrian and George. 'They wouldn't let Gurth in,' said Vanessa.

'Where on earth were you?'

Virginia smiled. 'The coachman isn't used to coming to such plebeian places as St. Pancras.'

The registrar peered at the papers. 'Er… Miss…er Stephen, we must get on, if you would stand here…'

Clive and Vanessa stood in front of the desk. 'You have two witnesses present…'

Clive said, 'I was beginning to think you were standing me up!'

George and Adrian indicated they were the witnesses. 'Please have the ring ready,' the registrar urged.

Cory took a jeweller's box from his pocket and opened it, and as he took it out, let it half-slip from his fingers. He retrieved it and handed it to Clive. He whispered, 'Nearly dropped the fucking thing!' Vanessa caught the whisper and gave a gasping giggle.

Virginia craned to watch and her merriment suddenly subsided as she recollected that she had lost Vanessa to Clive.

With one hand Vanessa was rummaging in a suitcase which she had propped on one of the seats. Gurth, still wearing his ruff, was beside her and Clive stood watching. Also in the railway station waiting room was a mother with a small boy who tried to play with Gurth who was continuously yanked back by Vanessa.

'What are you looking for?' Clive asked.

'I want to write to Virginia.'

'But we haven't even been married an hour!'

She found her writing case, and the mother said angrily, 'Edmond!' The little boy answered, 'I only want to stroke him.'

'Do you think we'll have to sleep in the train corridor?' Vanessa asked.

'Probably!'

'Oh, Gurth, stop pulling. I'll remove your finery.' She fiddled with the ruff which didn't come off easily. 'Will we do "married things" in the corridor, Clive? I hope you're going to like *la cuisine francaise*! Do you think he'll like snails?' Gurth escaped and Vanessa sat down.

The mother said, 'He'll bite you,' and hung onto the child's arm.

'You'd better hold him tight, darling, or he'll savage that little boy,' Clive said.

'I told you. You don't play with dogs. Ever,' the mother said, angrily.

Vanessa opened her writing case and smiled as she began to write.

Virginia was in her dressing gown reading Vanessa's letter; Adrian stood in front of the fire. ' "There was a spoilt child on the train who kept trying to play with Gurth." Look, she's drawn a picture of the horrid brat…' Adrian came to look over her shoulder. Virginia looked up at him. 'Oh, Adrian. How are we going to manage without her. How are we going to manage without her until we go to Paris? I already feel quite numb and dumb.'

'How are we going to manage with each other?'

'Keep a truce!' Virginia said.

A flying pat of butter hit the wall. Virginia bent over the silver butter dish on the tea tray with butter rolled into little pats. She held her knife upright and was in the act of sending another pat. 'I will get you. You're exasperating and lazy and boring.' She let the butter go and Adrian jumped aside and it landed on the floor.

He grabbed a pat and with his fingers flicked it at Virginia. It hit the wall and stayed there.

Sophy came in to take the tray. 'You're behaving like children. Look what you're doing to the walls.'

'I'm afraid my brother has always been fifteen years younger than the rest of us,' Virginia said.

'She adores me really, Sophy. She's always had a maternal streak.' Adrian half closed the door behind him as another pat of butter hit it.

'You never give 'im a chance, Miss Ginia. Even when you was little you was always after the older ones.'

'Because they were more interesting.'

'It was hard for 'im always being compared to Master Thoby.'

Virginia said savagely, 'Well, now he's on his own, isn't he? Oh don't look at me reproachfully. I'm not dismissing him entirely. He does have the Stephen blood.'

'Mrs Bell...'

'I haven't got used to it yet. I hope you haven't changed your mind about going away, she'd be ever so disappointed. She must be longing to see you.'

Vanessa, naked in bed, held out her arms to a half-dressed Clive who laughed, came over to her and started to kiss her. Gurth, who was on the end of the bed, jumped down in annoyance.

'Darling, we can't...there isn't time! We have to meet Virginia for lunch.'

'She'll understand.'

Clive said wryly, 'I rather think – in this uncerebral matter – she won't.'

Vanessa caressed him, full of newly discovered sensuality, between kisseṣ. 'And,' he went on, 'it isn't…only Virginia and Adrian, darling… Lytton's painter cousin Duncan…'

'I don't care about Lytton's painter cousin Duncan. I only care about…I only care…oh…'

Clive pulled off his clothes and got into bed.

Lytton sat in bed in a nightshirt and cap, the quilt covered with papers and books. On the bedside table were several bottles of medicine. Standing by the bed was Maynard Keynes who had just arrived, and one of Lytton's sisters, Pippa, who was about to leave. She was thin and wore spectacles, a family likeness. Opposite the bed was a huge gloomy window fitted with a ventilator, a vast plate of slightly corrugated glassy material – a 'reflector' – on chains had been installed in an attempt to bring more light into the room. It reflected the yellow bricks from the backs of nearby houses.

Maynard looked towards the reflector. 'Very ingenious.'

'It's supposed to give him more light to read by,' Pippa said.

Lytton picked up the open book in front of him. 'My dear, how *not* to write a biography!' he said.

Maynard sat down and Pippa went out closing the door behind her. 'It is my sister who exhausts me. She is liberating women. Beware. She will attempt to involve you.'

'I did admit on the stairs that my sympathies are with her cause…' Maynard took the book from Lytton. 'So your sympathies have not been engaged by this memoir of the life of Henry Sidgewick?'

'The poor fellow has been incapacitated by Victorianism like an ornament under a glass case. The Glass Case Age. And, one gathers, physically impotent. I suppose it's damned difficult to copulate through a glass case.' He lent over and took a measured spoonful of medicine. 'I feel quite done in, Maynard. Horrid palpitations. Will I ever be able to copulate again? My darling Duncan will be meeting God knows who in Paris.'

Maynard said, 'My God, Lytton. What is the trouble?'

'He thought he was in love. And I really thought he loved me. How could I expect such a beautiful, desirable creature to remain faithful to a bag of bones. You've no idea the anguish I'm suffering. Look at the drawing he sent me…' He pointed and Maynard went over to the dressing table and picked up a page covered with Michelangelo-like sketches of naked Greek athletes.

'Who was his model? And you ask me what's the trouble!' He groaned. 'Do you think we'll come together in our old age?'

Maynard had to drag his eyes from the page. He put it down and returned to Lytton. 'Long, long before that, I imagine. But actually I was referring to your medical trouble.'

'Oh, they're feeding me special meat juices. And threatening to enlarge my torso. Too narrow the latest doctor said, to contain my liver and lights. Pressing inconveniently on my heart. But the heart is superb.' Lytton lay back on the pillow. 'But cracked so often. The immortal Thoby dead.'

'In a curious way, he now seemed doomed to die young,' Maynard said reflectively.

'What do I have to live for? It's a shoddy, maudlin, shifting world of vanity and illusion. The human race grubs along like hedgehogs. I want to make my mark upon the age.'

'You will.'

Lytton said sorrowfully, 'I want Duncan to love me again.'

'Write, Lytton.'

'To Duncan? I do. I do.'

Maynard shook his head. 'Your book reviews.'

'Oh, I grunt and sweat over one weary article after another for the *Spectator*. Still… I suppose you're right. Writing may be misery, but not writing would be hell. Better to be a painter. I know he's a genius…'

Maynard tipped his chair back and stretched to reach Duncan's drawing and looked at it intently.

Lytton said, 'He has given me a glimpse of heaven! I want to go into the wilderness of the world and preach an infinitude of sermons on one text. *Embrace one another*.' Lytton sank back, exhausted by the conversation. 'I simply can't endure the pain of anyone else embracing Duncan.'

Maynard still held the page of drawings and sympathetically lent forward and patted Lytton's hand.

Duncan Grant was sitting at a pavement table in Paris and sketching on the back of a menu. He poured himself a glass of wine from a carafe and looking up, saw Virginia and Adrian approaching. Adrian towered over the surrounding French pedestrians and guided the gawky but mesmerising

Virginia – she was taking in everything around her and everyone smiled at the sight of her. Duncan got to his feet.

'Miss Virginia Stephen? Mr Stephen?'

Virginia nearly burst with pleasure. 'How clever of you...and *thank goodness!* We didn't know how we were going to recognise you if my sister hadn't arrived first.'

Adrian extended his hand. 'How do you do, Mr Grant.'

They shook hands and sat down, and Duncan pulled over a couple of glasses and poured them both some wine. 'We're far from English formalities. I'd rather be called Duncan.'

The meal was almost over. Gurth was under the table, and Vanessa, Clive, Virginia, Adrian and Duncan were well-fed and relaxed. Duncan lit a cigarette for Vanessa and their eyes met for a second. She leant against Clive and inhaled, and spoke with sensuous enjoyment. 'I love French tobacco.'

'You smell it the moment you step off the steamer,' Adrian said. 'Tobacco and garlic.'

'And see those handsome young men in their blue overalls,' Duncan sighed.

'The most satisfying shade of blue!' Vanessa said.

'Four cognacs, one crème de menthe.'

'So will you stay here and paint forever?' Clive asked.

Duncan smiled lazily. 'I never make decisions.'

'You must have made a decision to come here,' Virginia said.

'It wasn't a decision. I was given enough money on my twenty-first birthday to do it!'

'And now you're to paint like Picasso.'

'I'm learning to paint like Duncan Grant!'

A maid was warming the bed with a brass warming pan. Vanessa, in her silk dressing gown, was watching. Clive was brushing his teeth at the washstand and Gurth slept under the bed. The maid bobbed and said '*Bonne nuit, Madame...Monsieur*' and departed. Vanessa took off her dressing gown and got into bed, wriggling under the quilt. 'Ooh...very warm...'

'We don't need anyone to warm it.' He rinsed his mouth, making a lot of noise. Vanessa deliberated for a moment and then said, 'I rather like Duncan Grant!'

Lytton, in a dressing gown, was reading a letter to Maynard. 'Duncan liked them! I knew he would! I've widened the circle. When he comes home they'll include him in their Bloomsbury soirées!' He continued reading. 'What a quartet. Though I fear too much Clive Bell on Art would bore me.'

'Astute perception.'

'Amused by Virginia...of course, of course. Who isn't? We are all *diverted* by her. Speaks affectionately of Adrian. They went to the Louvre...My God!' Lytton rushed to the window and tugged frantically at the ventilator cords. 'He couldn't...he couldn't fall in love with Adrian, could he?'

Maynard laughed. 'At least a foot too tall. But be warned. Anyone could fall in love with Duncan.'

Maynard, about three steps up, rested on the marble stairs of Exeter Hall above which a large banner proclaiming SOCIETY FOR WOMENS' SUFFRAGE was prominent. Two women stood by the open door to the street and a distant hubbub of voices and a band approached. The women looked towards Maynard who walked down to the bottom step and, as he reached it, Pippa Strachey burst in, exhilarated, flushed, hat not quite straight and the bottom of her skirt muddy. 'The whole procession went without a hitch! The mounted policemen have been topping!'

'But where is Lytton?' The voices were now loud and close.

Pippa shouted over them, 'The coward fled to Cambridge...'

The first phalanx of marching women holding placards arrived and flooded in. Maynard stood guard over the stairs. 'To the right, ladies! Fill the front rows first...to the right, please. To the right, ladies...'

In the sitting room of Clive and Vanessa's rented house in Cornwall on a Friday afternoon Vanessa was breast-feeding her son. The spring sunlight gave her the look of a Madonna as she gazed down tenderly at the baby. The calm was broken only by Virginia's voice. 'I feel guilty that I didn't do anything to help.'

Vanessa lifted the baby to her breast. Without covering herself up she looked towards Virginia who was standing in the middle of the room. 'Pippa actually organised three thousand women to turn up and march from Hyde Park Corner,' Virginia said. 'And helped by Maynard! Imagine!'

'Well, I couldn't have marched. Because Julian needed his lunch...didn't um?'

Clive entered and overheard. 'Which is exactly the reason that freedom for women is always going to be a half-hearted movement.'

'But it has to be fought for, Clive.'

'Of course. And preferably in Pippa Strachey's way. Constitutionally. Not by lying down in the House of Commons like Mrs Pankhurst.'

'It must feel extraordinary,' said Virginia, 'to want something in that way. For other people. To behave in a new way. Break windows for a cause.'

'Much too uncivilised for you, my dear!'

Vanessa flushed. 'Well, I'd throw myself under a bus to save Julian!'

'But would you do it to be allowed to vote?'

Vanessa didn't seem to hear and was peering down at the baby. 'Why is his mouth still open,' she cried in sudden panic. 'You don't think he's got an obstruction in his nose?'

Clive stood beside Vanessa and kissed the top of her head, but his irritation was apparent. 'He hasn't got the strength to close it. He's bloated with contentment!' His eyes met Virginia's with shared feelings.

Clive and Virginia were walking along the beach. They were apart but there was a strong communication between them. 'Is it going to be about you?' Clive asked. 'First novels are generally supposed to be about their authors.'

'It is about a sheltered girl, expected to adorn conventional society, but who recognises – on a voyage – that she can never be a part of it.'

'And is it also about falling in love?' Virginia gave him a startled look. 'Perhaps you have never been in love, Virginia?'

'Not like Vanessa. No.'

'Or attracted...against your better judgement?'

Virginia didn't answer and they walked on.

It was evening, the sky was cloudy and it was much colder. Virginia shivered but nevertheless she and Clive continued sitting on the cliff top, Virginia with her arms round her knees and Clive lying back smoking his pipe.

'Shouldn't we go back?'

'Oh, let's escape from the infant-howling a little longer,' Clive said.

'She finds his howling interesting.'

'My dear Virginia, we discussed the amazing range of howling throughout our breakfast.'

'Are you jealous of him?'

'Of course,' Clive said. 'What father isn't? And I'm also a little bored.'

'Well... I don't want to talk about the contents of Julian's nappy either. I'd rather have a conversation about...anything else!' They both laughed and drew closer together. 'I do try to understand. We haven't given birth, Clive.'

'At this point in their respective development, I have to confess,' he leant across and took Virginia's hands, 'I am more interested in your baby. I suspect the labour pains are just as overwhelming. Am I going to be allowed to read it?'

She nodded and her hand remained in his.

In the glow of the oil lamps Virginia and Clive sat close, reading the pages of Virginia's manuscript. Vanessa sat apart, threading a scarlet ribbon through the neck of the baby's woollen jacket. Gurth lay at her feet.

'I told them at the draper's it was for a baby. They were deeply shocked.' She snipped the end of the ribbon. ' "Not very nice. We have a lovely shade of white if you don't want blue".' Virginia handed a page to Clive. 'You're not listening.'

Clive looked up. 'Yes, we are.'

'So I said, "White is a symbol of death in some parts of the world you know".'

'You should have told them red was for His Order of the Bath.'

Vanessa laughed. 'The draper's assistant isn't very quick on puns.'

Virginia had not been listening and she looked up. 'You don't really like the title of my book, do you Clive?'

'*Melymbosia*. I'm afraid idiots won't know how to pronounce it.'

'They won't know what it is,' Vanessa said.

'It's the name of a ship.' Virginia paused, 'We don't often think about ships, do we? We think they dissolve when they vanish on the skyline.'

The baby started to cry and Vanessa put down the jacket and got to her feet.

'That's an interesting idea. Write it down,' said Clive.

Vanessa sighed. 'What makes you think she won't. She has always written *everything* down. In spite of your long walks together, you don't know *everything* about her.' She went out and Clive stood and looked down at Virginia. 'Yet!' He prodded Gurth with his foot. 'Come on, old boy. We'll go for a walk on the beach.'

Vanessa came in with Julian and they almost collided with Clive. 'I'm going to absent myself from your felicity awhile!' He went out and in a few moments the front door slammed.

Vanessa sat down and unbuttoned her blouse and put Julian to her breast. 'He always flees at feeding time. He doesn't understand about babies, does he?'

'He'll manage better when they can discuss art.'

'Whose side are you on? I thought you rather despised him. Or has he made the leap from commerce to art?'

'Thoby was right,' Virginia said. 'Do you remember what he said at Cambridge. "Mr Bell is a mixture between Shelley and a sporting country squire".'

'And until now you chose to ignore the poet.'

'Now I find the poet dominates!' The sisters looked at one another, a moment of awareness and rivalry. Then Vanessa smiled and looked down at her baby. She had opted out.

'Come here, Ginia. You have to smell him. It's heavenly. Warm wool and talcum powder.' She giggled. 'And regurgitated milk…' Virginia was horrified and gingerly sniffed from a distance.

Lytton was up and in his dressing gown. Duncan Grant, in an open necked shirt and flannels, was lolling on the bed. Lytton was taut and he fixed Duncan with a penetrating stare. 'You're always the lovee, Duncan.'

'That's a sort of compliment,' and he held out his arms. 'Come, cousin, and give me a kiss.'

'You see, you're not serious.'

'But you didn't expect fidelity when I was in France.'

Lytton sighed. 'I would have infinitely preferred it.'

'The Bible decrees that cousins can't marry.' He held up his hand. 'Serious! I promise! But you know I don't have it in me to pour all that molten passion into a single crucible.'

'But you're not in love with anyone else?' Lytton said.

'No one more than you.'

'And are you in lust with anyone else?'

'Not this afternoon.' He spoke with sudden warmth and generosity. 'I haven't changed toward you. Don't be jealous of me.'

Clive and Virginia were paddling; their shoes, socks and stockings were just out of reach of the water. Clive had rolled up his trouser legs, Virginia held up her skirt, both of them were wearing hats.

Clive stooped and in his cupped hands caught a baby crab. Virginia came to look and as she did so Clive kissed her on the cheek near her mouth. Virginia jumped back, shook her head and lost hold of her skirt which dropped into the water and was soaked at the hem. She snatched it up again; half panicking, half delighted.

'Come on,' Clive said. 'Come back.'

'No…really…no.'

Clive let the crab back into the water. Virginia waded away from him with a little shriek, out to sea.

'What are you trying to do. Drown yourself?'

Still wading, Virginia called back to him, 'I'm not going to allow you to!'

Clive laughed, wading after her and grabbing her by the arm. She turned to face him. 'All this walking and talking, Virginia!' Clive said.

'What about my sister?'

'Your sister is in love with her baby.'

'And with you.'

'Not in the way she was in Paris.' Going to kiss her, Clive turned her face towards him. 'You're very beautiful. You know it, don't you? And much too clever. And much too…damned amusing.'

Virginia released herself, and began to wade towards the shore. Her eyes were sparkling, she liked being admired. Clive waded after her slowly. At the waters edge Virginia wrung out her skirt.

'Without…anything else, Clive. We have achieved the heights, haven't we? Walking and talking.'

Clive passed her, sat down, stretched out his legs and wiggled his toes to dry them in the sun. A long pause and then he laughed. 'There are other things to do with a man…'

Lytton, Maynard and Duncan were having lunch at Simpson's in the Strand. The waiter lifted the silver dome on the trolley and inquired, 'All having the beef, sir?'

'We all decided on the beef, didn't we?' asked Lytton.

'You were the indecisive one. You toyed with the idea of lamb,' Maynard said.

'Beef. I like it *blue*.' Duncan watched hungrily as the waiter started to carve.

'So French in your eating habits,' Lytton said. A look of disdain from the waiter as Duncan spoke, a quick sweep of the eyes over Duncan's shabby and unconventional clothes. Amused, Duncan spoke to the waiter, who pretended he was not being addressed.

'I'm a starving artist dependent on my relatives and friends to buy me lunch. Unlike civil servants on a salary!'

Maynard looked from Lytton to Duncan, a dramatic pause for a portentous announcement. 'I am resigning from the India Office!'

'My dear, you always found it tedious.'

'And the risk to India of free speech is nil.'

Duncan said, 'You've accepted the lectureship in economics!' Lytton looked at him sharply. 'Because you are too lazy to go into an office every day. Too lazy to do any real work.'

Lytton suddenly felt the outsider as Maynard and Duncan talked with an air of teasing intimacy. 'Are you implying an authority on the currency arrangements of India, Mr Grant?'

'Oh, I don't doubt you are *the* authority on such useful artistic knowledge, Mr Keynes.'

'Frankly, for a chap who doesn't even know his multiplication tables…'

Lytton broke in, trying to re-establish a three-way conversation. He spoke to Maynard. 'It explains the rumours about you that I heard in Cambridge.'

Duncan spoke to Maynard, too. 'It also explains why, when we were in Cambridge…'

'When *you* were in Cambridge…'

Maynard and Duncan looked at one another, and then away. There was a silence, then Duncan broke it to cover up the double-crossing of Lytton. 'If one of you catches the handsome waiter's eye, I'd like some horseradish sauce!'

Lytton, dumbfounded, put his knife and fork together in a state of agitation. Maynard clicked his fingers and called over to the waiter, 'We'd like some horseradish.'

Lytton moved his plate instinctively away from him, so disturbed he could not eat a thing.

Lytton could not sleep. In a restless turmoil in bed he sat up and wrote feverishly, uttering groans. 'Oh God, oh God, oh God...' He got up, dressed, and a muffled solitary figure he hurried through the streets to Maynard's flat in St James Court. Maynard, half asleep and tying the cord of his silk dressing gown, opened the front door. Lytton thrust his way in. 'Is he here?'

'For heaven's sake...no one is here.'

Lytton pushed past and opened the bedroom door, but all that faced him was a single, rumpled bed. Maynard followed him in. The curtains were drawn and on a clothes stand hung Maynard's suit for the next day. There was a pile of books by the bed, but it was an otherwise impersonal room with service-flat furniture.

'The whole room reeks of semen,' said Lytton.

'Do you know the time?'

'You took Duncan to Cambridge. *When I was there!*'

Maynard sat down on the edge of the bed. 'Stop being absurd. Anyone may go to Cambridge.'

Lytton asked, 'Does he love you?'

Maynard answered slowly. 'Since you ask – yes. We love one another.'

Lytton regarded him with desperation and derision. His voice rose. 'You know numbers. You know nothing about love.'

'Think what you like.'

'You have as much romance and passion and affection as a safety-bicycle. With genitals.'

'You're being infantile.'

'Because it's stupid and absurd and incomprehensible. And I'm in agony. I'm suffering too much.' Lytton began to cry.

Maynard went over and attempted to put his arm round him. 'Which is why I didn't want you to know.'

Lytton sobbed into his handkerchief, 'Which is what makes it so ghastly and cruel. You have to tell me how long you've been so horribly secret.'

'Five and a half weeks.'

'When I left London,' Lytton wailed.

'Directly after you left London, I'm afraid.' Lytton sank down, his head in his hands. 'You knew it was on the wane when you left,' Maynard went on.

'Not with me. Not with me.'

'Be honest with yourself. Since Paris? Come on, pull yourself together. You're forgetting what you told me.'

'I told you everything.'

'Because we are friends,' said Maynard.

Lytton muttered after a long pause, 'Friends!'

'We are civilised and we are friends.'

'I suppose one might look at the whole hideous misery as a student of human life.' He blew his nose heavily.

'Of course, you feel bitter…but it has happened. It is a fact. But we are, all of us…*au fond*…friends.'

Lytton got up and went to the door, buttoning his coat. 'I'm going home. I can't look at you any more.' He went out, leaving the door open. Maynard, shaken, listened to his steps diminishing and then, going to the window, saw Lytton walk in a haphazard meandering manner across the road.

Duncan, in trousers held up by string and an open-necked shirt, leant on the foot of the bed in which Lytton was lying in a state of exhaustion.

'I never wanted to hurt you.'

'I should have refused to see you,' Lytton whispered.

'We're too close. We have to talk about it.'

Lytton pulled himself up into a sitting position. 'You know I feel as if I were a pocket handkerchief that somebody has dropped on the top of Mont Blanc.'

Duncan laughed, and Lytton became increasingly frenetic. 'But I have to tell you…it's going to annoy you…I can't take your affair seriously. Not seriously the way you do.'

'You seemed to take it seriously…'

'I don't think of Maynard as you do. If I did I suppose I would be in love with him, too.'

'But I don't see why you being besotted with him should prevent my liking you both as much as I always have…' Duncan came and kissed him affectionately on the mouth.

Maynard took a parcel from the postman and closed the door. He put the parcel on the hall table and opened it; three well-bound leather books and a letter were revealed. 'Dear Maynard,' he read aloud, 'I only know we've been friends too long to stop being friends now.' Duncan came out of the bedroom naked to the waist, listening. 'You must believe that I do sympathise and don't hate you and that if you were here now I should probably kiss you. Except that Duncan would be jealous, which would never do. I am taking solace in my friends.'

Virginia and Lytton were leaning against the pillars on the steps of the British Museum. Virginia watched as Lytton looked up from the *Cornhill Magazine* which he was reading. 'Your percipient piece of criticism gives me solace.'

Virginia smiled in relief at the praise. 'I thought you might pull it to pieces with your terrifying irony!'

'No. You are accurate, concerned yet detached. You restore my bruised faith in humanity.' He looked at her for a long moment, then spoke impulsively. 'Will you marry me?' He realised what he had said and shrank with shock. She was just as startled, and there was silence as they gazed at one another.

Virginia said, 'Yes!'

'Are you sure,' Lytton asked faintly. A bearded man collided with Virginia as he ran up the steps but she scarcely noticed.

'No!'

He regained his composure. 'You are not sure?' Virginia shook her head. He asked tentatively, 'You don't love me?'

'No. But I do admire you tremendously. And we have an enormous amount in common.'

'But perhaps not quite enough…'

'But quite enough for the most satisfying kind of friendship.'

'And as always, you are right,' Lytton replied gratefully. He took her arm and both appeared relieved as they walked down the steps toward the street.

Virginia and Vanessa stood close together in a corner of the bookshop, whispering. Browsers glanced up when their voices became too loud.

'He was probably terrified you would leap over the back of the sofa and kiss him!'

'He said he had a sudden vision of a paradise of married peace.'

Vanessa did an imitation of Lytton's shrill delivery. 'We're two clever people. We should marry and admire each other's work forever. We never need actually touch!'

'Shhh!' Virginia giggled. 'I could feel him shrinking away like a mollusc!'

'Hardly a mollusc. He's all shell.'

'He's afraid of being alone, Vanessa.' She picked a book and took it over to an assistant. Vanessa looked after her, her smile fading. Virginia was speaking of herself.

Clive and Vanessa were in bed. Clive was reading and Vanessa was lying down, her arms under her head.

'Are you jealous? That he proposed to her?' Vanessa asked.

'She didn't accept him.'

'She did for half a minute.'

Clive put down his book, an art book with colour reproductions under tissue paper. 'Then common sense presumably prevailed.'

'I sometimes feel she prefers female company. Not that it should get in the way. She does love Lytton, of course.'

'We all do. But not in the way required for marriage.'

'I'd feel relieved if she married. Not Lytton. Double problems, don't you think.'

'Your sister is a sexual coward.' He lent over and kissed her. 'Unlike yourself!'

Vanessa put her arms round his neck. 'Then she would have been safe with Mr Strachey. And she adores his mind. She would like to be married, Clive.'

'I wouldn't want to live with Adrian either!' He kissed her again, more passionately.

'Do you think it's all George's fault? Hands-up-the-skirt etcetera when Mother died. If only she was like me. Orgasms since I was two!' She looked ready to have another.

Sophy, in a black dress, white organza frilled apron and goffered cap with ribbons, opened the door to Virginia, Vanessa, Adrian and Clive. They were all in evening dress, unusually formal. Bright lights and murmured conversation and Sophy smiled with pleasure. Vanessa put a hand on her arm. 'It's lovely to see you.'

'And you, too, Miss Nessa. Mrs Bell I should say!'

Clive and Adrian went ahead, the girls lingered to talk. 'You *are* happy here, Sophy?' Virginia asked.

'Oh, Lady Margaret's very good to me. And I always did have a soft spot for Mr Duckworth.' She lowered her voice. 'More than you did, Miss

Ginia!' She paused. 'And I understand their ways.' Sophy helped Vanessa off with her cloak, and then Virginia.

'Bloomsbury ways were rather trying!' Virginia agreed.

Vanessa adjusted her hair in front of an ornate mirror, pleased with her glowing reflection. 'I'm more used to this kind of house,' Sophy said apologising.

'Of course you are!' Adrian and Clive joined them and Sophy opened the door to announce them.

'Mr and Mrs Bell...'

The formal dinner party was at the fruit stage. The dining room had Edwardian grandeur, it was candlelit and although the guests were relaxed, there was a sense of the conventional pomp that the Bloomsbury group had deliberately discarded. Virginia sat across from her cousin, Commander William Fisher, chief of the Admiral's staff on the battleship *HMS Dreadnought*. He was in his dress uniform and he was peeling a pear with his fruit knife and holding forth on the invincibility of the British navy. George Duckworth and Lady Margaret were sitting at either end of the table, and between them were Clive, Adrian and Vanessa, Mrs William Fisher, Aunt Adeline and Aunt Mary.

'I would say categorically that the *Dreadnought* has made England the undisputed mistress of the seas. Big guns, an auxiliary for anti-torpedo purposes...'

George said, 'Cost must have gone up no end. All this expansion.' On either side, Aunt Mary and Aunt Adeline concentrated on their fruit.

'I'll give you an example. In the year of Trafalgar the fleet had 120,000 officers and men. Cost - £15,035,630.' William gave a smile of smug satisfaction.

Lady Margaret said, 'What a wonderful memory for figures!'

'Today we're in the region of 450,000 officers and men – and I don't give an exact figure even at a family dinner table – around £140,000,000.'

Virginia said quietly, 'Surely the officers are men?'

Vanessa and Adrian looked at one another in delight. William appeared not to have heard and Aunt Mary had heard none of it. 'These grapes are delicious. So sweet.'

'We have acquired a splendid new greengrocer!'

Adrian asked, 'Keep the state secrets, eh, Willy?'

'Don't use that mocking tone, Adrian. It's not patriotic,' William said rather pompously.

'I hope I didn't seem to be mocking you. Good heavens, no. I firmly believe that even in peace our defence should be fiercely guarded.'

George gave Adrian a warning look. William took it at face value and nodded ponderously. 'I would say our security is at the highest pitch of efficiency.'

'Invincible, would you say?' Clive asked.

'Invincible!'

'My grandfather went to war in a frigate!' Aunt Adelaide said.

'In those days I'm afraid the enemy had superior vessels. But not now. Not now...'

Adrian whispered softly to Virginia, 'Invincible!'

Lady Margaret stood up. 'Shall we leave the gentlemen?' The women rose; Aunt Mary brushed off the crumbs and Aunt Adeline dropped her napkin on the floor.

In the drawing room of Gordon Square Virginia, with blackened face, false beard and moustache and dressed in an embroidered kaftan, was looking at herself in the mirror. She adjusted her turban and Duncan began to blacken his face. In the reflection Virginia saw Adrian in a false moustache and ill-fitting bowler hat, and Horace Cole in a dress suit and top hat.

'Invincible!' Adrian said.

'It won't work. Willy'll recognise us.'

'No, he won't,' Horace said. 'I pulled it off before with the Mayor of Cambridge. He thought I was the Mayor of Zanzibar's uncle. I had the full ceremonial treatment.'

Virginia turned from the mirror and faced him. Duncan was in the process of putting on garments from one of several boxes marked WILLIAM CLARKSON – FANCY DRESS AND CARNIVAL OUTFITTERS. Similarly dressed were Adrian's friends, Anthony Buxton and Guy Ridley, and a third friend, Tudor Castle, in his shirtsleeves, who was setting up a camera with a black cloth.

'The mayor wasn't your cousin whom you had dined with a week before. And you weren't trying to discredit the British navy,' Virginia said.

'My dear, no one could recognise *me*,' Adrian said smugly. 'I look like a seedy commercial traveller.'

'Come on Grant. Make your decisions! I want to take the picture.'

Duncan pulled off a waistcoat and pulled on another long, sleeveless, embroidered jacket. Anthony Buxton hung a gold chain round his neck and with a safety pin attached a star-shaped jewel. 'Chief Prince Makalen! I expect you to bow when I utter!'

Duncan rummaged and Horace was writing on a piece of paper. 'As soon as the train leaves, Castle, you're to send the telegram. I've written it out in capitals.'

'Move the chair over, Buxton,' Tudor Castle said. 'You sit in the front, with Miss Stephen on the sofa.'

Virginia sat down and arranged her robes. The others took up their position. Tudor Castle came forward to place them and Duncan closed the lid of the box with a flourish and took his place. 'The Foreign Office probably has code for its telegrams,' Virginia said. 'I think you're being foolishly optimistic.'

'It will be signed by the right man, Hardinge. Spelt with an "e" '

Duncan laughed. 'They'll be so bowled over by the honour they'll be scrubbing the decks all morning!'

'Has anyone actually seen the Emperor of Abyssinia?' asked Guy. Horace went under the black camera cloth.

Adrian said, 'Hopefully – no.'

'Nobody smile!'

'As your emperor, I can only say...*Bunga Bunga!*'

Tudor Castle pressed the button.

A naval officer was overseeing two porters laying down a red carpet. A barricade was in place, with a small group of sightseers already behind it and the station-master was fussing alongside. There came the sound of the Weymouth train approaching and then it stopped. The naval officer became fraught and officious. 'Leave the carpet, men. Stand to one side. Move those people back. Clear the way.' He almost ran as he quick-marched through the arch to the platform and the station-master took up a position just inside it.

The sightseers peered and murmured, doors slammed, couplings jangled. The shouted command, 'Present arms!' and the rifles clashed and there was a stamp of feet. Then Anthony Buxton appeared, walking majestically with the naval officer at his side. Adrian followed just behind with Horace Cole and Virginia, Duncan and Guy Ridley took up the rear. The station-master bowed low, and Anthony Buxton nodded graciously in his direction. A small boy was trying to climb over the barricade and the station-master sidled round the royal party.

'Control your child, madam.'

Anthony Buxton stopped and turned to Adrian and glared. '*Yembo inscala, milu berango scutala bunga astema havashi shemal.*' Adrian kept a straight face, and Virginia, Duncan and Ridley and Cole managed to turn their hilarity into nodding smiles.

Adrian replied in a German accent, 'His Highness asks me to convey his delight in the sight of a happy child.'

'Let the child come forward,' the naval officer said to the station-master. The small boy was pushed by his mother towards them and he started to snivel. 'Bow your head. This is a great honour.'

Anthony Buxton, running the Latin together, said, '*Heu-cuculus-nobis feurat bubga cantare-suetus?*'

'His Royal Highness says you will have a life blessed with happiness,' Adrian told the small boy. 'You may touch the hem of his robe.'

'Do as you're told, boy,' Horace said. The little boy, still snivelling, touched the hem. Virginia, Duncan and Guy Ridley smiled and applauded. Virginia, in a deep, growling voice addressed the boy. '*Nunc bunga bunga.*'

The small boy ran back to his mother, both proud and protective as she wiped her eyes. The navel officer turned to Adrian. 'Would you be kind enough to inform His Royal Highness, sir, that I have cabs waiting to take the royal party to the harbour, sir.'

'*Bloomsburyesque. Parisius bunga.*'

Anthony Buxton swept on, followed by his retinue and the amazed gaze of the sightseers.

The bo'sun piped Anthony Buxton aboard. The admiral and his officers who were lined up behind him, saluted. Virginia and Adrian managed to exchange a look of great apprehension and Horace Cole stepped forward. 'May I present the Emperor of Abyssinia, sir.' The admiral held out his hand and Anthony took it and pumped it heartily.

'*Alt aris domi ni bunga bunga bone rucco bunga.*'

'His Royal Highness wishes to say,' said Adrian in his German accent, 'what an honour it is for him to come aboard the great flagship of the noble British fleet.' He glanced nervously at William Fisher and the admiral bowed.

'Please convey that we consider the privilege to be ours. I would like to present the ship's officers.'

Anthony took a step forward and solemnly shook hands with everyone.

Dinner had been served in the railway compartment and Horace Cole, a little drunk, was leaning back against the antimacassar, a drink in his hand. He raised it. '*Bunga bunga*!' He roared with laughter.

Raising his glass, Guy Ridley said, 'The King!'

'The Emperor of Abyssinia.' Anthony Buxton turned to Horace. 'Cole, you're drunk. I hope you didn't disgrace yourself in the wardroom.'

'You're jealous, old boy, because you couldn't risk smudging the greasepaint.'

'Quick thinking, you'll have to admit,' Adrian said 'Religious beliefs. Impossible to touch food unless it is prepared in special Abyssinian ways.'

Duncan gave a sigh. 'It was painful and I was starving. And extremely thirsty.' He took a long swig.

'But your moustache was detaching in the sea breeze!' Virginia said, and they were all laughing and revelling in the reminiscing.

'Much miming before he pressed it back!'

'I did well, though, didn't I? Royal to the last salute.'

'But was it necessary to insist that the train waiters wear white gloves?' Virginia giggled.

'Oh, they love to feel inferior,' said Anthony. 'Anyway, it wouldn't do to drop the impersonation. Be in the papers in no time!'

Adrian was walking down the road when he came across a placard for the *Daily Mirror* – proclaiming 'Dreadnought Hoax'. He went into the newsvendor's shop and bought a copy and opened it up to read as he walked home. He was laughing along the street, and laughing when he went to the house and straight up to Virginia's sitting room. 'There is a full page photograph!'

'Who told them? The man from Clarkson's who brought the costumes? I thought he looked shifty.'

'The photograph has to have come from Horace! He has always longed for fame.'

'He denied it,' said Virginia.

'He didn't actually deny it. He just didn't admit it!'

The door opened and Vanessa came in, carrying the papers and the mail. 'Then you've seen them!' She put down the papers and handed the letters to Virginia. 'I told you it was a stupid idea. Now you'll be stuck for ever with the boring and bumptious Horace Cole'

'Adrian rather likes him.'

'He has a flair for spectacular pranks! You're so standoffish since you married, Nessa!'

Virginia opened a letter – an invitation – and gave a little scream. 'We've arrived! We're invited. Lady Ottoline must have seen the papers!'

'Everyone's seen them. Everyone must have recognised you.' Vanessa took the invitation and read aloud from it. 'Lady Ottoline Morrell requests the pleasure of the company of Miss Virginia Stephen and Mr Adrian Stephen...'

'The Morrells recognised us because Lady O has a gimlet eye for gossip. And she only lives across the square. After all Willy didn't see through our disguise and he even heard us speak.'

'And no names! Just a picture!' Adrian spoke in a German accent holding up the paper.

'Reporters aren't idiots,' Vanessa said. 'They're sleuths.' As if on a cue, the front doorbell rang and they all fell silent and they listened as the maid answered it. 'I told you. The gentlemen of the press. I'll go.' She opened the door wide and went out, saying over her shoulder, 'I can tell the truth.'

Vanessa stood on the doorstep and three reporters stood in the street.

'Were you one of the Abyssinians?' a small fat reporter said.

'Do I look like an Abyssinian?'

'We've been told on very good authority that a young lady went aboard the *Dreadnought*.'

'It certainly wasn't me,' Vanessa turned to go indoors.

'The naval gentlemen have given us to believe it was a tall young lady with classical features,' said the second reporter who was thinner and younger than the first one.

'I cannot be described as tall.'

Virginia appeared in the doorway behind her and Vanessa looked horrified. The reporters scribbled away and Virginia said, 'If it were me, gentlemen, I would say I was delighted to have been of help to my country. From now on the British navy will have to tighten up the regulations concerning official visitors. A simple telegram announcing an arrival will hardly suffice.'

The room had pale grey walls, yellow taffeta curtains and was sumptuously furnished. Glasses of champagne were being served and Lady Ottoline went among her guests, a dominating and extraordinary figure in emerald velvet, rows of pearls and pearl earrings. She was tall, with mahogany-red hair and a long neck, a long nose and an undershot jaw. Everyone was talking about the *Dreadnought* hoax. Lady Ottoline took the glass of champagne offered by her butler and joined a group with her husband Philip, Member of Parliament for South Oxfordshire, and Kitty Maxse.

'Of course I recognised them at once!' Kitty said.

'Questions are going to be raised in the House,' said Philip.

Bertrand Russell came across to them. 'Talking about the Great Hoax, are you? Does them good. I like to see authority take a tumble!'

'So do I, Bertie.' Ottoline took Philip's hand briefly. 'But Philip thinks it's all disgraceful, don't you, darling?'

'My wife doesn't take the state of the nation as seriously as she ought.' Ottoline made a face and brushed close to Bertrand Russell and gave his hand a quick squeeze as she moved away.

'Apparently the admiral was chased down the street by a horde of little boys all shouting "*Bunga Bunga!*" ' a young man said, amidst laughter. Augustus John came over and drew Ottoline aside as he caressed her arm secretly.

'Be discreet!' she whispered.

'You're looking ravishing tonight,' Augustus whispered back.

'I hope you received the lilies I sent,' Ottoline said in a normal tone of voice.

Augustus said, 'My son Romilly ate them up for breakfast.'

Kitty approached and overheard. 'Then you must starve him! I've come to be introduced.'

Ottoline said, 'And you shall be. Although of course you know who the notorious man is! Mr Augustus John, painter extraordinaire! Mrs Leo Maxse. Kitty.' Augustus John extended his hand and bowed over Kitty's.

'Is it true? You've really asked them here tonight?' Kitty asked Ottoline. 'I suppose you've heard that George Duckworth is denying he's related!'

Winston Churchill was talking to a small group, his back to Kitty. Ottoline, half-whispering to Augustus, said, 'Two of the Emperor's entourage are here. Disguised as Englishmen.'

'I'd like to shake the perpetrators of that hoax by the hand,' said Augustus in a booming voice.

Churchill overheard and turned, furious. 'A disgraceful breach of our National Security.'

Adrian and Virginia had just arrived and overheard as they approached. Ottoline's eyes sparkled at the outrageousness at what she was about to do. She stretched out her hands to them. 'Have you been introduced to our Home Secretary?' She turned to Churchill. 'I'd like to present Miss Virginia Stephen and Mr Adrian Stephen. Mr Winston Churchill.'

Churchill, unaware that he was talking to the hoaxers, inclined his head in a bow. 'A great pleasure. I knew your father! He put my father in his book.' He turned to put his hand on the arm of the woman next to him. 'Clemmie...Sir Leslie Stephen's children...'

On the benches of the House of Commons there were Winston Churchill and Philip Morell. It was the 24th February 1910. Colonel Lockwood was standing and there was a pause. 'I would like to ask the First Lord of the Admiralty whether a hoax has been played upon the naval authorities by the pretended visit of the Abyssinian princes; and if so, whether he will take steps to prevent such conduct in future?'

The Speaker raised his voice above the hubbub. 'Mr McKenna! Silence. Silence.'

'I understand that a number of persons have put themselves to considerable trouble and expense by pretending to be a party of Abyssinians, and in this disguise visited one of His Majesty's ships.' There was laughter and some cries of strong disapproval. 'The question is being considered...' his voice was raised above the din, 'whether any breach of law has been committed which can be brought home to the offenders.'

Mr William Redmond stood up. 'Will the Right Honourable gentleman include in his inquiry as to whether it is not a fact that these gentlemen conferred the Royal Abyssinian Order on the admiral, who wrote to the King to know whether he could wear it...and will he wear it?' Most of the members rocked with laughter. Philip Morrell was smiling but Winston was not laughing at all.

Another member of the opposition got to his feet. 'Would the First Lord of the Admiralty inform the House of the circumstances in which these reputed 'Abyssinians' were received by the admiral and officers of the ship with full naval honours? And whether by the admiral's orders they were furnished with a special train on the return journey to London? And is it not a fact that certain pairs of *white kid gloves* were actually purchased for the occasion? And can the Right Honourable say who will pay the expenses?'

'Hear, hear,' Churchill said loudly.

Chapter 3

When You Kissed Me I Felt Like A Rock

Vanessa was seated at a reception desk in the Grafton Galleries and Roger Fry stood behind her. He was the organiser of the exhibition. There was a pile of catalogues beside her and a pompous businessman stormed up to the desk and tore the catalogue he had bought in half and flung it in front of Vanessa. He jabbed his umbrella towards Picasso's *Nude with Flowers* and shouted, "Pornography! Filth! Purveyors of filth and you...a woman...sit there...degraded..."

'Ah...you believe that only men should look at pictures of naked women! Perhaps you would prefer it if I faced a naked man?'

Roger said gently, 'Sir, Señor Picasso is acknowledged as a very fine artist.'

'An artist? An organ grinder! An ice-cream maker! I shall forbid my wife to enter these doors.' He flung open the doors as he spoke and was almost knocked off his feet by Augustus John and Ottoline entering. She wore a hat with a swept-up brim and he had a velvet-collared jacket. Ottoline looked after the pompous businessman and said, 'An undoubted success!'

Vanessa put her hand on Roger's and he looked at her adoringly. 'The press was wonderfully outraged. Roger Fry is the best hated man in London.'

'At *my* exhibition they are all talking about yours,' Augustus said.

'At *my* exhibition they are all talking about yours!' Roger said dryly, 'I understand you described ours as 'a bloody show'!'

'Oh, he only said that to draw attention to himself, the dreadful creature,' Ottoline said with a smile. 'Otherwise he wouldn't be here for a second visit, would he?'

Two visitors swept out, affronted, as Lytton entered in his cloak, hat and greenish-yellow gloves. His eyes shone at the public reaction.

Augustus said, 'My first post-impression of the Post-Impressionists was taken – post-haste. One does not have to be charmed at the first viewing.'

'Charm is not the word one would apply.'

A matron, formally dressed, recognised Augustus and took him for an ally. She was followed by Duncan – as usual in an open-necked shirt, hair in disarray, eyes smiling. He shrugged as the matron spoke.

'Mr Augustus John! Now you are an artist! A great artist. Oh, your delightful' (affected French pronunciation) 'Provençal studies.'

'Madam, I am flattered. But I beg you to look again at the Van Goghs...'

She fixed her lorgnette on Roger. 'Is *this* Mr Roger Fry?' Roger nodded. 'Then Mr Fry, you should be locked up with your exhibits and made to look at them night and day. *Purgatoire!*'

Roger gave a little bow. 'Nothing would give me greater pleasure.'

She opened her bag and rummaged furiously. In the background could be heard Clive's voice angrily trying to convince people above general murmurs of disapproval. From out of her bag the matron pulled a pair of scissors and, in spite of her size, she moved with astonishing agility towards a Gauguin portrait of two Polynesian women in a landscape. There was a tremendous skirmish; a scream from Ottoline, a shout of encouragement from an older man. In the nick of time Clive grabbed her and wrenched the scissors away. The furore subsided, with Bloomsbury applause for Clive and spectator applause for the matron who was flushed and panting.

'That is what I think of your audacity to call the filth art. Art!'

Lytton replied loudly and piercingly, 'I think you will find the audacities of one age generally become the platitudes of the next.' She looked at him with hatred as she straightened herself and prepared to sail out.

'You're one of the Bloomsbury people, aren't you? Defend this rubbish if you choose. The "next age" will judge you as a criminal association, not an artistic one.' At the door Clive gave a little bow and handed back her scissors. She snatched them and exited, her head held high.

Duncan turned to Lytton. 'Thank you for defending us against the philistines.'

Lytton gave a slight smile. 'Especially as I don't much like the stuff myself!'

'If you sent Mr Fry a gilded turd in a glass case,' whispered Augustus into Ottoline's ear, 'he would persuade the Contemporary Art Society to buy it for the nation!'

Vanessa and Virginia, as Gauguin women, were being pulled on a float by wildly dressed art students at the Post-Impressionist Ball. A costumed crowd, as well as newspaper photographers and journalists, were pushing through the couples attempting to dance. Duncan was dressed as a Picasso cubist Spanish woman in a cardboard tube with breasts painted on it, a lace fan in his hand and a mantilla on his head. He was attempting to pull Lytton – the only person in evening dress – onto the dance floor.

'No, Duncan, I'm a literary person. Not a wild painter. And I want an ice cream like Ottoline Morell,' Lytton said. He looked towards Ottoline spooning ice cream from a glass dish. She was dressed as a grand Spanish doña in black taffeta and black lace, and Philip Morrell was beside her in a black velvet court suit. Their costumes were notably more expensive compared to the homemade Bloomsbury ones. Augustus John and his mistress, Dorelia, were both dressed as French peasants – she rather short with a large head.

Philip said, 'Is he going to marry his mistress now his poor wife is dead?'

'Oh, you don't understand at all. They were a ménage à trois. Between them they mothered his seven sons. Passion, not marriage is the important thing for Augustus John.' Ottoline's eyes followed him longingly as the waltz changed to a polka.

Philip observed Ottoline and patted her hand in a kindly fashion. 'My dear, you are so attracted by La Vie Bohème. Dorelia's such a dumpy little woman. How does he manage to paint her with a swan's neck?'

'I thought they were all going to be beautiful people here tonight,' Ottoline said. 'I thought we were going to see something quite Mozartian.' She broke off in horror. 'Just look at Vanessa Bell!'

In the cloakroom Vanessa looked at her reflection in the mirror above the wash basins. Virginia was applying greasepaint to her face.

'The ice cream was a mistake! I should have learned from being an Abyssinian,' Virginia said.

Vanessa sat down on a gilt chair. A prim, uniformed attendant looked disapprovingly at her bare legs as she cleared away the greasepaint-stained hand towels. The door opened and a woman came in. She was in an evening gown, stout and formal. Vanessa recognised her as the matron who had swept out of the art gallery.

'You were at the disgraceful exhibition!'

'And now we are both at the disgraceful ball!'

The woman turned her back and summoned the attendant who hurried into the lavatory where she could be glimpsed wiping the mahogany seat. Then she came out and did a semi-curtsey and the woman swept in.

Vanessa turned to Virginia. 'I *know* Roger is in love with me,' she said.

'Are you in love with him?'

'I feel very passionate about him. I admire him tremendously. So does Clive.'

Virginia asked slyly, 'Does Clive know about your being 'passionate'?' Two more women entered and caught the last word. They looked at one another in disgust.

'He doesn't know…yet. I haven't told him.'

'Will he mind?'

'How could he mind,' Vanessa said. 'He pursued you in Cornwall.'

'Fruitlessly.'

A young girl dressed as Columbine rushed in and put on lipstick in front of the mirror. Vanessa went on talking. 'That depends on one's situation! Fruitless in sexual terms for Clive, of course. Not so fruitless for you. The kind of involved flirtation you thrive on, digging out all those emotions. Fruitless for me? Rather fruitful, really.'

The woman came out of the lavatory and washed her hands at the basin beside Virginia. Vanessa raised her voice. 'Over the breast-feeding I came to terms with the idea of marriage being absolutely ridiculous in conventional terms! If one feels passion one must make love.'

The elderly woman could not contain her feelings. 'You are an affront to womanhood!' She dried her hands and stalked out and Columbine stifled a giggle. 'You give me heart - for art - and womanhood!' she said, somewhat shyly.

Vanessa lowered her voice and Columbine went into the lavatory. 'His wife's going mad. Roger's wife, I mean.'

'Like me?' Virginia said.

'Far, far madder than you. Mad forever.'

'I wish I felt passion – for anyone!'

'Only for the written word! Do you want to be married? Do you want to have babies?

Virginia paused. 'I want marriage, children and the freedom to write. The *ability* to be free. Like you.'

'Of course most of the men we know are married already, like Roger and Clive.'

'Or else they're buggers, like Lytton.'

'I know one who isn't either!' Vanessa replied.

Leonard was putting on his overcoat. 'I'm very glad you told me about the ball!' He smiled and took his gloves out of the pocket and pulled them on. 'I'm re-adjusting to the climate.'

'So you'll come with us?' Virginia said. 'Ottoline has a box at the Opera House to see Nijinsky – and Adrian is away.'

'If she'll accept a substitute.'

'She doesn't watch the ballet – she watches us! To make sure we're enjoying it!'

Nijinsky was alone on stage, dressed for *Carnaval*, taking his curtain call. There was tumultuous applause. Lytton stood, put his lips to Ottoline's ringed hands and tiptoed out of the door. Leonard looked after him anxiously and whispered to Virginia who shook her head The applause eventually died down and they went out of the Opera House and down Floral Street, but there was a huge crowd around the stage door. Nijinsky came out, and the crowd gasped and cheered and parted to allow him to walk to his car.

'There's Lytton!' Virginia said and as she spoke Lytton pressed a bouquet into Nijinsky's hands. 'He must have got it from the flower seller at the corner of the street – no wonder it's called Floral Street.'

Nijinsky stopped and spoke for a moment, and then walked past Leonard and Virginia to his car. There was a dark figure seated in the back in a Homburg hat and fur collar – 'It must be Diaghilev,' Virginia whispered excitedly – and Nijinsky got in. 'I told you Lytton didn't leave the box because he was feeling unwell!'

Virginia and Leonard were walking down a picturesque village street in Sussex. They looked about them with pleasure. Virginia was in a blouse and skirt and wore a straw hat and she and Leonard both carried sticks. A sign – Fresh Vegetables – on a slate caused them to pause.

'We must! Think of the London prices! And they'll taste so much better,' Virginia said.

Leonard smiled and nodded in agreement and held open the wooden gate for Virginia to go in. They didn't even knock at the door when an old man, ostensibly waiting behind it and peering out of the window, opened it and said, 'You've come for vegetables, madam? I'll take you down the garden.' He was wearing a flat cap, had gnarled hands, a weathered face and few teeth. He had a strong Sussex accent. 'What do you want then, madam and sir?'

'What shall we have? Lettuce, beans, peas…?' Leonard asked Virginia.

'Oh, I can't let you have no peas, sir. Them birds do so terrify the peas, I must put a net over them.'

'Terrify them?' asked Virginia.

'Oh, something dreadful.'

'Then we'll have broad beans instead!' Virginia said.

Carrying the vegetables in a woven basket, Virginia and Leonard were walking across the Downs. 'Life is so much simpler, so much better,' Virginia said.

'Because the beans cost less?'

'Because there's rioting in the Liverpool docks and soldiers camping in Hyde Park and rail strikes and fireman's strikes and to that man the most important thing was to put a net over the peas.'

Leonard smiled. 'In the scale of things, it is rather more important for working men to negotiate a living wage. No one lives on garden peas.'

'Oh, I know that, but here, on this wonderful hot summer day, I just feel I'm in the heart of England and here is where life really matters.'

'My father told me,' Leonard said, 'that the fortunate Jews are the ones born in England. He told me I was blessed. And I am. But freedom is relative and there's a great deal to be done here. If we are ill, we can call in a doctor. If we want to eat, we can manage the London prices. We were educated…even you, who felt thwarted because you didn't go up to Cambridge.'

'You make me feel selfish, only concerned with my own life, with writing my book…'

Leonard said, 'You were sufficiently concerned to teach working girls at…'

'But that was only an extension of myself, that was about writing and how I felt about writing, that isn't what you are talking about,' Virginia replied ruefully. 'Except that I gave up.' In a Sussex accent she said, 'Them women did so terrify the writer she put a net over herself.'

Leonard roared with laughter and took her arm.

After dinner, in the drawing room in Gordon Square Virginia, Leonard, Vanessa (pregnant again), Clive, Lytton and Morgan Forster were sitting and talking over coffee, very relaxed. 'They were delicious beans,' Morgan said. 'I'm glad the birds hadn't terrified them as well.'

'And when his wife came out to put all the things we'd bought into a basket, she said…' Virginia lapsed into the Sussex accent, ' "After the terrible storm all the flowers in my border were dishabille." She pronounced it as spelt!'

'Verbal relic of the Norman Conquest,' said Clive.

'My dears,' Lytton cut in, 'I know exactly how it feels to be *déshabillé*! After I had finally met Nijinsky at Ott's, I sent round a vast basket of very 'habillé' flowers. And they were actually delivered to him on stage!' Everyone laughed affectionately.

'But Mr Diaghilev keeps him on a leash,' said Clive.

'Alas!'

'Mr Diaghilev wears a very strong scent. Sold under the name of Mitsuko – but better known as Power!' Morgan interrupted him.

'Too cruel…'

It was a rainy afternoon. Leonard held an umbrella over Virginia as they hurried along towards the Woolf family house in Putney.

'Here we are!' said Leonard. He stopped at the gate of a large Victorian villa and Virginia looked at the heavily curtained windows. It seemed very gloomy and she looked at it apprehensively.

'Did you like growing up here? Which was your room?'

Leonard led her up the path. 'My room was at the back.' He smiled. 'I never thought about liking or not liking it.' He rang the bell.

'I knew I didn't like Hyde Park Gate.'

A maid answered and Leonard shook out and closed the umbrella and ushered Virginia in. They both wiped their feet on the mat before the maid closed the door.

Mrs Woolf, very much the matriarch, sat at the head of the table with a silver tea tray in front of her. An elderly aunt was the only other guest. Milkless tea in a glass was passed to the aunt by a maid and Mrs Woolf said, 'Pass Miss Stephen a sandwich, Leonard.'

'You like a nice sandwich?' the aunt inquired.

'Not ham. Potted meat. We don't eat ham, bacon or shellfish in this house,' said Mrs Woolf.

Virginia said, 'Not shellfish? Why not shellfish?' She glanced around the sombre room with the heavy sideboard, wine-coloured damask curtains and a couple of dark landscapes.

The aunt let out a groan. 'Huh...why not shellfish? Ask our Mr Josephs at the synagogue.'

'You can't expect Miss Stephen to know the laws,' Leonard said.

'Because it says in the scriptures that they are unclean creatures,' Mrs Woolf explained.

The aunt let out a sigh. 'Of course you are not Jewish yourself?'

'No. Not anything myself...' Virginia laughed nervously.

'Not anything! You sound like Leonard,' Mrs Woolf said. 'Well, do you like a sandwich which isn't ham?'

'It's nicer than ham.' Virginia took a bite.

'You come from a large family like ours?'

'You remember my talking of Thoby Stephen at Cambridge. Her brother.'

'You talked of this one and that one. Only one brother?'

'Two brothers, one sister.'

'I brought up nine children. A widow. On my own.'

'Mother!' exclaimed Leonard.

'Miss Stephen will know it wasn't easy. My first marriage, that was different. I had a set of sables. My trousseau came from Swan and Edgars. Happiness is never perfect. Leonard, cut the cake, Aunt wants a little slice – I've never found perfect happiness.'

'Perfect happiness would mean perfect boredom!' Virginia said. Mrs Woolf looked at her shocked.

Leonard leant forward and kissed Virginia in the shaded gas light. They were in Virginia's sitting room and, still holding her hands, Leonard led her to the sofa to sit down.

'You know that I've fallen in love with you.'

Virginia tried to smile. 'Even though I shocked your mother?'

'I am hoping that the love is mutual?' Virginia let her hands rest in his but did not return any pressure. 'Then it isn't,' he concluded.

'Oh, Leonard, I don't know. I mean of course I feel there is something permanent and growing. But...perhaps I can never fall in love.'

'I wanted you to have more time. I asked for an extension of my leave...' he gave a deprecating laugh. ' "To settle my private affairs". The

Governor of Ceylon has decreed that unless I elaborate on these "private affairs" the extension cannot be granted. That may mean my resignation, Virginia, I want to marry you. Very much.'

'I've often told Vanessa I want to marry,' she said in a desperate voice, 'and then I've felt I never can.'

'I must go back. Or resign.' Leonard took her in his arms and she relaxed against him but in an asexual way. 'God, the happiness I feel being with you. Just talking to you. I feel it is mind to mind, soul to soul. I like to think…when you've finished the novel…'

Virginia was touched by the understanding. 'I must finish my book…'

'It is the most important thing you have done in your life. Of course, I understand.'

'You know I could look on marriage as a profession.' She spoke urgently. 'Everyone always talks about the advantages for women. But I couldn't settle for being quite happy, having companionship, a busy life bound up with husband and children.'

'Darling Virginia,' Leonard said, 'if I wanted a wife – an inferior wife – satisfied with just that, I wouldn't be asking you to marry me.' He paused. 'Much as I love you, if I thought it would cause you any unhappiness. I'm cold and reserved to other people. I don't even feel affection easily. But with you, for you…apart from love, apart from desire, I'm fond of you in a way that I've never been fond of anyone or anything in the world.' He moved to kiss her and there was a frozen moment as if she was going to move away. Then she moved towards him and they kissed. When Leonard released her, Virginia got up and walked to her lectern, leaning on it. It was difficult for her to say what she intended.

'When you kissed me…I felt like…a rock. Desire will come between us, Leonard.'

'Physical love is only a part of it.' He paused. 'It will change.'

Virginia shook her head. 'It might not. I'm half afraid of myself. Oh, if I said yes, I'll marry you…I would have to be able to give you everything and if I can't, well, marriage would only be second best for you as well as for me.'

'I care for you so much.'

'Why should you?' She was rather fraught. 'I find it almost overwhelming. I'm fearfully unstable. I pass from hot to cold in an instant. Without any reason.'

'I find it loveable.'

Virginia found another excuse. 'Your being a Jew makes it even more difficult. You seem foreign.'

'Too long in Ceylon, you mean?' Leonard smiled.

'Your family's different. I haven't been in a house like that before. The furniture is hideous.'

Leonard was trying to calm her. 'You told me the furniture in Hyde Park Gate was suffocation.'

'Your mother, I know she has good qualities. She brought you all up, penniless, widowed. She kept complimenting herself on it. I counted. Nine times. Was that one for every child?'

Leonard said gently, 'Was that so foreign?' Virginia didn't answer, becoming increasingly overwrought. He came over to her. 'We like one another. We like the same kinds of things and people, we understand the realities that are important to us.'

Virginia said desperately, 'You said when I finished the novel...' He nodded. 'I want to go on as before. As we were before tonight. I want to be left free. I want to be honest...'

'I want you always to be honest with me,' Leonard said. 'When the time comes you will tell me honestly, yes or no.' He kissed her tenderly on the cheek and held her, and her eyes filled with tears. 'I'll see myself out.' He went out, closing the door gently behind him.

Virginia stood rigid for a few moments, then she pressed her hands together frantically, her breathing became shallow and she walked round and round the lectern. Then she began to write, agitatedly, speaking aloud. 'Work and love and Jews in Putney take it out of me...'

Vanessa's and Clive's new baby was asleep in the perambulator, and on the grass nearby in the park sat Vanessa and Adrian on a rug. Two-year-old Julian played nearby, running backwards and forwards between his mother and the pram.

'It's not really will she marry him, but should she marry him. Or rather,' said Adrian, 'should he marry her. Have you told him she has bouts of insanity?'

'Oh, she's not really mad. She just needs to have a rest. Leonard knows she's resting in the country.'

'But does he know...' Adrian paused for a minute, 'that she's been in the nursing home a few times before?'

'Adrian! He loves her. He said to me she's highly strung, very nervous and he knows when they're married he'll be able to keep her calm.'

'He'll be giving up his career.'

'He's not going back to Ceylon. He's resigned. Whether she decides to be Mrs Woolf or not. Julian!' Her voice rose. 'Come here. You'll wake the baby.' She turned to Adrian. 'Actually he sleeps like a Bell, not a Stephen. Heavily.'

'So you're not going to discuss it with Leonard any more?'

'What do you want me to do? Give him the doctor's reports? She's all right anyway. She'll be far better off with Leonard than with Lytton. That would have been a bloodless liaison.'

Adrian laughed. 'A marriage with two wives!'

'It's only headaches and acute nervous tension. It's not as if she's like Roger's Helen, locked up in an asylum for life!'

There were two easels standing in the long grass side by side in a Sussex field. In a close embrace Vanessa and Roger Fry lay side by side on the ground and Roger said, 'The surroundings aren't exactly hospitable!'

'Consider we're in a Matisse painting – we need only consider the things that really matter!'

'Doesn't Clive really matter?'

'Clive has chosen to have his own life, Roger.'

'And have you had your own life?'

Vanessa whispered, 'Not until today…' Roger lay on top of her and kissed her passionately.

Vanessa, Clive, Duncan and Roger were sitting round a large wooden table in the farmhouse kitchen and Duncan was eating an apple. Closely watched by Vanessa, Roger was decoratively painting a garden flower pot with quick strokes. He turned it triumphantly round so that they could see it all.

'There you are! You don't need art galleries to enjoy art.'

Vanessa leapt to her feet and rushed across to the sink and grabbed a frying pan. She came back to the table and took up Roger's brush and tried to paint the pan.

'Why not frying pans? If the paint would only go on…! There! A flower! Wouldn't you rather fry eggs in a frying pan with flowers on it?

Why should anything be hideous any more? Art in the kitchen! Art everywhere! Our whole lives permeated by art.' They all laughed, but there was an air of excitement.

'Think of the employment for penniless artists who can't sell their pictures,' Roger said.

'Like this penniless artist!' Duncan sighed with exaggeration.

'Absolutely nothing pretty,' Clive suggested, 'Nothing refined, nothing tasteful.'

They chorused their agreement. 'And I would suggest nothing too expensive,' Duncan added.

Roger nodded. 'Of course not! This is applied art for the people. We'll have to raise the money for a shop. How about being our business director, Clive?'

Clive shook his head. 'I'll leave all that to you and Vanessa. You'll manage everything beautifully together.' His smile intimated that he knew about their affair and Vanessa smiled at Clive, understanding and affection between them. Julian ran in and Vanessa scooped him onto her lap. At the same time Duncan was carefully taking the pips out of his apple core and planting them in a pot of geraniums on the windowsill.

'But I am an expert at giving advice. I'll certainly help with the fund-raising. Should we involve Maynard, do you think?'

Duncan looked up from his planting. 'Too busy feathering his own nest!'

'Ottoline should be good for a hefty commission.'

'Ah, yes! Our aristocratic supporter of the arts!' He wandered back to the table and set the geraniums in front of Julian, who smelt the flowers and wrinkled his nose. 'This is in case our plans don't work out. I'm going in to the apple-growing market.'

'How can it fail?' Roger remarked. 'Post-impressionism will cut a swathe through the homes and wardrobes of England. It will be the last word in style!'

'What shall we call ourselves?' Vanessa said.

'Last word! I didn't say that for nothing! The Omega Workshops!'

Vanessa was impressed. 'How can you be so decisive about anything as important as a name.' She paused. 'Clive. I think we should change the baby's name. I don't think Gracian's right.' Clive looked up questioningly, amused. 'Adrian feels it is too fanciful.'

'What do you suggest?'

Vanessa looked pleased. 'Claudian! What do you think? Claudian! I think it's a lovely, lovely name.'

Lytton, carrying a parcel of books, walked up to the door of 38 Brunswick Square and rang the bell. A maid opened the door and Lytton went in, still holding his parcel, took off his hat and hung it on the coatstand.

'Who did you wish to see, Mr Strachey, sir?'

'Who is in?'

'I think everyone is in this morning, sir.'

'Then I shall see everyone.' The maid bobbed politely and walked down the hall. Lytton knocked at the door opposite him.

'Who is it?' Maynard called out.

'I'm not a creditor.'

'Hold on!'

Lytton took out a copy of his first book, *Landmarks in French Literature*, and proffered it in readiness. Maynard opened the door, dressed ready to go out and Lytton said, 'An offering of total forgiveness. First copy of my first book.'

Maynard held it up. 'Your name on the cover! You just beat us to it!'

'All of you!' Lytton smiled.

'At least I'm at the printers. Congratulations. And *multo grazi*.'

Lytton took out another copy and craned to see into the room. 'Is Duncan in?' Maynard closed the door and put on his coat, slipping the book into his pocket.

'Went out early. If you feel like poker this evening, we're organising a game.'

'Then I shall call on Adrian!' As Maynard put on his hat and took his umbrella, Lytton was already half-way upstairs. On the landing he knocked at the door and it was opened by Adrian without a shirt. On the bed behind him, pulling on his socks, Duncan looked up. Lytton took out a second copy of the book and held it out as he entered. 'Darling! You are like God. *Omnipresent!*'

Virginia was in her sitting room, almost identically furnished as the one in Gordon Square. She stood at her lectern writing, crossing out, writing again. She was smoking. There was a knock on the door and Virginia called out, 'Come in. If you must!' Lytton came in and Virginia looked surprised.

'I thought it was Adrian who's sworn not to disturb me…' She saw the book in Lytton's hand. 'You've got it! Oh, Lytton. How wonderful. Let me see it. Let me smell it. Oh, that wonderful smell of new paper! I'd know by the smell it was written by you.' She took it to the window, opened it and turned the pages. 'Victor Hugo…Balzac…Molière… oh, heavenly. And I know that everything you've written will be *right*.'

'Just a textbook for students, my dear.'

'Lucky students, to be guided and instructed by Mr Lytton Strachey.'

'And your book, Virginia?'

'Revised and revised and revised. I think I shall rival the cow elephants with the length of my pregnancy. Seven years.'

'But almost finished?' said Lytton.

'Yes. Almost finished. And so am I!'

'You owe it to posterity to save yourself until you have written the last word.' They smiled at each other – mutual affection and support.

Lytton climbed the stairs again for the last time, one book left in his hand. Leonard's work was spread on the table, books piled on the chairs and a tobacco jar on the floor. He smoked his pipe and the room was full of smoke. Lytton removed a pile of books and sat down. 'This house is a warren of creativity!'

'I'm afraid my *oeuvre* isn't what you'd call creative – just making a fiction out of the Ceylon experiences. Life in a jungle village.'

'Far, far better than being there.'

'Well…I wonder. I was at least of use in that small society. Here… I see the mistakes being made and there is nothing much I can do about it.'

Lytton lowered his voice conspiratorially. 'I rather feel a mistake has been made downstairs. I discovered Duncan chez Adrian! In a state of semi-dress!'

'There is much activity on the lower floors!'

'And up here? Are you sleeping with Virginia?'

'None of your business.' Leonard paused. 'Alas, we are the only two occupying separate rooms. We are perfectly proper. I have suggested we remain proper by marrying. She merely collects my rent.'

'Which is…? I'm most curious.'

'Thirty-five shillings a week. Maynard pays two pounds because he has half the ground floor.'

'And he's richer.'

The door opened and Virginia came in, pencil and list in her hand. 'It's the cheapest way of living, if you want a house and servants. If you choose the inmates carefully.' She turned to Leonard. 'I'm going to the butcher. My creative flow was destroyed.' She gave Lytton a glance. 'What do you want on your tray tonight? If you have any influence with Duncan beg him to remember to put his empty trays in his hall.'

'I'd rather take you out to dinner.'

Virginia was pleased. 'Good! Then it's only chops for Maynard and something for the maids,' and she went out.

'If only,' Leonard said, 'she could make up her mind to marry me.'

'She knew within seconds that she did not want to marry me. Is that a comfort?'

Leonard managed a smile. 'No. I feel rather desperate. Am I going to live forever in this unmarried house?'

'Why don't you go away for the weekend to the country? Take my book, plan your future – either way...'

Leonard, dressed in country clothes and with a stick, walked with letters in hand towards a rural post office. As he posted his letters a young farm worker came out of the post office, a three-year-old child on his shoulder, following a mother holding a baby. They radiated love and companionship and Leonard watched for a few moments, and made up his mind. He walked purposefully into the post office and filled in a telegraph form. *Will you marry me...*

Virginia opened the telegram. She unfolded it and read it and as she did so she nodded her head. She spoke aloud. 'Yes, yes – oh, yes!'

It was pouring with rain and a violent thunder storm raged. George Duckworth and Lady Margaret ran from their car, an umbrella held over them by the chauffeur who was getting soaked. At the same time a cab drew up. Leonard, his brothers and sister emerged and Leonard got wet as he paid the driver. Duncan and Saxon Sydney-Turner, in long raincoats hurried along the pavement, trying to keep close to the buildings for what little shelter there was. They all converged as they went into the St.Pancras Registry Office.

The thunder could be heard throughout the ceremony.

'Place the ring on the bride's finger, Mr Woolf.' Everyone craned to watch Leonard do so. George Duckworth sighed. Lady Margaret glanced at him sympathetically – an unsuitable marriage! George and Lady Margaret were dressed as if for a society wedding, while Vanessa was in a loose, bright dress. Leonard's brothers were dressed, like Leonard himself, in dark lounge suits, and his sister was wearing a sedate silk dress.

'Repeat after me, I call these persons here present…'

'I call these persons here present…'

'…to witness that I, Leonard Woolf…'

'…do take thee…' The registrar peered at the paper… 'Virgellia…' Vanessa let out a giggle.

'…do take thee, Virginia…' Leonard stressed the 'n' and they looked at one another amused.

'…to be my lawful wedded wife.'

George whispered to Lady Margaret, 'At least Bell is a member of the Christian church.'

There was a sudden stir and George and Margaret looked round startled. Vanessa was pushing her way forward, and addressed the registrar. 'Before you hurry us all out…'

'MADAM!'

'I need to know how to change my son's name,' Vanessa said. 'I registered him as Gracian but I've decided to change it to Quentin. Would you be kind enough to tell me the procedure?'

Clive expostulated. 'Vanessa…!'

'Please do not interrupt the ceremony, madam.'

Vanessa looked at him, astonished, then looked round. Duncan was smiling, but George and Margaret were horrified and the registrar was scarlet with anger. 'But I thought they were…oh! I'm sorry. Sorry Ginia, sorry Leonard.'

Virginia was laughing, Leonard was amused. George came forward and took Vanessa's arm, drawing her back.

'My god, I'm terribly sorry, I thought it was all over. I thought when Leonard said she was his lawful wife and all that…'

The registrar said in a booming voice, 'May I continue?'

'Please,' Leonard said.

'Repeat after me, Miss…er…Virgin…ia…'

'And I wonder,' George said under his breath, 'just what kind of honeymoon Mr Woolf and his Virgin will have!'

It was a simple room with rough white walls and a polished wooden floor with a rug. A crude Madonna and Child was framed above the bed. 'If you were given a guess you would guess it was Spain,' Virginia said.

Leonard's jacket and tie were carefully draped over the back of a rush-seated chair and Virginia stood looking out of the window. Leonard came up behind her and put his hand tenderly on her shoulder. She turned to face him, panicking. 'Virginia! Virginia darling...' He drew her to him and began to kiss her face and hair. 'You have made me so happy.'

She put her hand to his hair in a determination to respond. 'I do love you, Leo.'

He kissed her on the mouth passionately – then gradually released his hold. 'You mustn't be afraid, my darling.'

'I know, I know...oh, I do want to make you a good wife...'

Leonard held her a little away. He began slowly to unbutton her blouse. She stood rigid but didn't try to stop him. Leonard took off the blouse and unpinned her hair. She wore a white camisole and her hair covered her shoulders. Still with great tenderness Leonard led her towards the bed.

Virginia and Leonard, tanned and well, stood at the rail of the cross channel steamer from their honeymoon in Spain. A high wind was blowing and Virginia clutched at her hat to prevent it being blown overboard. Leonard put his arm around her shoulders and kissed her in a brotherly fashion on her cheek. She looked at him lovingly. 'Have I failed as a wife, Leo?' Virginia asked.

'Oh, my dearest! No. You are the wife I wanted. The wife I want.'

Virginia's eyes filled with tears. Leonard took out his handkerchief and wiped them away.

'It's just the wind.' She paused. 'I am going to support you. I am going to be with you to do important things...'

Leonard nodded, deeply moved at her words.

They were dressed against the winter weather in an East End street. 'I think this is the one,' Virginia said and she waited a minute and then knocked at the door. At last a woman came and answered it.

'I suppose you'd better come in!' She closed the front door and led the way down the narrow hall.

The room was a general living space. The walls were damp and peeling and the furniture minimal. The grate was empty and a baby cried in a cradle made from a box. Virginia sat on a wooden chair at a table on which there was a tin plate containing a few boiled potatoes. Leonard stood, as did the young man and his wife who were the tenants of the room. The young man was strong, proud and resentful and his wife was pale, ill-looking and subservient towards her 'betters'. Both of them were wearing worn and patched overcoats against the cold. 'So don't you have any coal?' Virginia asked.

'He manages to pick up bits sometimes, lady, down by the docks…'

'But you must at least have a fire. The baby will be ill.'

'Don't you mean die, lady,' the man said harshly.

'I shall put forward your case to the Care Committee,' said Leonard, 'I'm sure they will look favourably on…'

'Is that what they do? Look favourably? Put down their knives and forks, do they? Give a bit of their roast meat to the pet 'ound, do they?'

'Oh, Jim, don't…'

The man replied hotly, 'Don't show me feelings.'

'No. No…not to your betters. They come to 'elp us.'

The man clenched his fists and shut his mouth. Leonard said, 'We will help…'

'Oh we're ever so grateful, sir,' the man said sarcastically, ''ow can we thank you, sir, for coming into our poor dwelling and offering to…'

'I am well aware that whatever we do will scarcely touch your needs.'

'But my husband will do everything he can,' Virginia said.

'Thank you. Thank you both. Don't take any notice of him.' The man turned away, bitter at having to accept and Virginia was agonized. 'We're very grateful to you taking the time to come here.'

The Omega showroom was in startling contrast to the squalor of the room in the East End. There were murals, chairs, cushions, nursery furniture, fabric screens and decorated boxes. Leonard spoke to Roger Fry and to Ottoline who was dressed in hat and furs. In the background Vanessa was displaying to two women customers an oyster-coloured satin cloak, hand painted in brilliant colours by Duncan. 'Our business is to dispense charity. We are only supposed "to give relief, if the case is deserving". Relief! I tell you, I would rather live in a hut in a Ceylon village than in the poverty stricken, sordid, dilapidated, godforsaken hovels of Hoxton. My God, standing in those grim rooms, speaking to people in the depths of hopelessness... I tell you, nothing but a social revolution, a major change, could deal with it. I resigned from the Care Committee.' He looked down at an elaborately decorated cradle and set it rocking with a fierce movement.

'But resigning, Leonard...they depend on charity. We more privileged people really do have a duty,' said Ottoline.

'I'm joining the Socialist Party. I think it has to be tackled on a somewhat wider scale,' Leonard replied.

The women customers thanked Vanessa who showed them to the door. Ottoline called to Vanessa, 'Walk about, darling. It is amazingly beautiful. Who painted it?'

'Duncan,' said Vanessa.

Ottoline turned to Leonard. 'Really? Oh, the Socialist Party.' She wasn't really interested.

'Only we don't tell anyone,' Roger explained. 'One name for everything. Just Omega!'

'Just Omega!' Ottoline was excited.

'You know we're doing a room for the Ideal Home Exhibition. So you'll just have to hurry up and order your chairs, Ott,' Vanessa said.

Duncan came in from the street in an open shirt and shivering with cold, the *Daily Mirror* in his hand. Ottoline said, 'You've arrived just in time to protect me from this forcible little sales girl! In her dowdy cape!' And she gave a shrill laugh.

'Help me off with it, someone. I'm terrified of spoiling it before it's sold.'

Ottoline helped her with great care, revealing Vanessa in walking shoes, skirt and a woollen jumper. Duncan opened the paper, holding it so that Roger could see a photograph of himself and two of the showroom. Duncan began to read. ' "Would you like your house fitted with Post-Impressionist furniture, carpets and hangings? If you would go to the Omega Workshops, Fitzroy Square and Mr Roger Fry will do the rest." '

'Wonderful. What with the new exhibition we are doing excellently! They're very upset by Picasso!'

Duncan continued reading. ' "This is the kind of room in which you would live if your nerves could stand it." ' He turned the paper round so that everyone could see it.

' "This shows Mr Roger Fry thinking out some futurist nightmare." Oh, I hate the press,' Vanessa said.

'Don't you mean presstitutes!'

Leonard laughed. 'If we are to go by the picture, the nightmare seems to include reproductions of Byzantine mosaics! I must take a copy home to show Virginia.' He walked toward the door and Vanessa hurried after him.

'How is she?' Her voice was low.

'Very upset by the Hoxton visit. She does it to support me, but it's harder for her.'

'Headache?' Leonard nodded. 'But the book?'

'I think…she might even finish it…this year.'

Virginia put down the pen at her lectern and burst into tears. Leonard took her in his arms. 'Oh darling! You've done it!'

Virginia laughed through her tears. 'All these years…writing, writing, writing…' Her laugh became uncontrollable.

Leonard tried to hold her but she broke away.

Sir George Savage was seated behind his desk, very much the pompous Victorian medical man in frock coat, perfect cravat, pince-nez in the top pocket. The room was high-ceilinged with a bookcase full of weighty medical reference volumes. Leonard faced him, straightforward and anxious about the advice he was seeking. 'You've known my wife since she was a child, Sir George. And you know the family history. You know there are problems. Would you advise us against having a child.'

'Let me put it this way, Mr Woolf,' Sir George said. 'Are you a country boy?'

'No!'

'My dear fellow, like the female of all species, a woman's body is made for childbearing.' He gave a patronizing smile. 'There is no happier sight in the world than a bitch with her litter!' Leonard was repelled by the image. 'Gets on well with her sister's children, don't she?'

'She loves them very much. But she sometimes finds being with them a stress.'

Dr Head was a much more accessible man, younger, without preconceived ideas. His consulting room was lighter and brighter and he and Leonard were standing. 'One must consider that her delicate mental balance is a form of ill health. How much does she want a child?'

'We both want one.'

'I understand you are of the Jewish race, Mr Woolf.'

'Yes…'

'No offence,' Dr Head said. 'Just an observation. The English aristocracy and the Jews – keenest of all to carry on the line.'

Leonard said firmly, 'But not at the expense of my wife's emotional health.'

'In my opinion, you would be well advised not to start a family. It might be dangerous for Mrs Woolf to undergo the strain.'

They were all lunching together at Duckworth House, George, Lady Margaret, Virginia and Leonard. The view through the window was of spacious country grounds. Sophy was serving the meat course.

'Liverpool, Manchester and Bolton,' said Leonard.

'And Glasgow? All in ten days? Weren't you exhausted, Virginia?' asked Lady Margaret.

'I did very well, didn't I, Leo? I wore sensible clothes and stout boots and tramped from one co-operative hall to the next.'

'Weren't you frightfully depressed?' Lady Margaret went on.

'Depressed and impressed,' Leonard said. 'It is an inexplicable miracle that human nature can remain as nice as it is in a Manchester slum. You wouldn't think there is much resemblance between the wife of a Lancashire textile worker or a Durham miner and a Singhalese villager. But I think the days and months and years I spent talking to alien women in the Kandyan hills helped me to get in touch with Mrs Barton and Mrs Harris.'

The meat course was now served and Lady Margaret began to eat and the others followed.

'I have great respect for the Women's Co-operative Guild. The aim is to educate the women members, advance co-operative principles and to obtain proper recognition for women's interests. Vital progress, though it may sound dreary.'

'It doesn't sound dreary at all,' Virginia broke in. 'How can you say it does?' She cut her food into very small pieces, put a portion onto her fork but didn't eat.

George said, 'All these worthwhile causes do. That's not to say they are, what?'

'And they are not,' Virginia continued. 'We met women…you'd call them ignorant…and they know they are, they have an extraordinary native, intuitive understanding of their own problems and the problems of their class and they long passionately, they passionately desire education. And they argued for it…'

'I'm sure they argued! With all the female logic at their disposal!' said George.

'One of the most gross, vulgar errors is that women are more emotional than men!' said Virginia.

George looked at Leonard and smiled and Leonard looked at Virginia. 'Never met an emotional woman, have you?' George said.

Leonard kept it on an even keel. 'These northern women are immensely tough.'

Lady Margaret spoke brightly, attempting to change the subject. 'And what about your book? Are you still writing it?'

'Didn't I mention it?' asked George, 'Going to be published by the family firm. And I hear they think it's rather good.' He turned to Leonard. 'You married a clever wife!'

Virginia cut her meat smaller and smaller. Lady Margaret said enthusiastically, 'Oh, how splendid. I can't wait to read it. You seem to have been working on it forever. What is the title?'

'It's called *The Voyage Out*,' Leonard said.

'What an interesting title. Out to where?'

'She's always written!' said George, 'When she was four or five, always scribbling away. We used to call her Billy Goat. I remember mother saying, "Our Billy Goat's scribbling again."'

Virginia began to laugh. 'Do you remember…Do you remember George…' As she laughed she knocked a piece of meat off the plate onto the linen cloth. '*The Experiences of*…what a precocious child I was. Leo, you should have known me them! *The Experiences of a* …' she laughed wildly, '…*a Pater Familias*.'

Leonard was very controlled. 'Was that the name of a book?'

'I scribbled that, didn't I, George? *The Experiences of a Pater Familias*. About…a loathsome baby called Alphonso.'

Lady Margaret said faintly, 'Alphonso!'

' "A" for Adrian, you see. I must have hated Adrian. Did I hate Adrian being born?' With her knife she flipped a piece of meat up into the air and the meat landed in front of Lady Margaret's plate and she gave a little gasp. Virginia laughed in a state of excitement and she flipped the meat more and more wildly from her plate. 'Is there great significance in an "A", do you think? Apostles.' She could hardly speak for laughing. 'That's significant. Ask Lytton.'

George half rose and Leonard held up his hand to indicate he should stay seated.

' "A" for angel. Oh, George, when you first became engaged. Not to you, Margaret! The *first* engagement.'

Leonard stood and went round to Virginia. He talked to her calmly and quietly. 'I'm going to take you upstairs for a rest,' he said.

'George fell madly in love with an 'F' not an 'A'. Lady Flora. Lady Flora. I sent a telegram about Lady Flora, I said she was an angel.' Leonard helped Virginia to her feet. She seemed not to notice as he led her to the door and she went on talking and laughing. Very concerned, Sophy opened the door for them. 'Signed Goat... She is an angel. Goat. But when it arrived...it read...it read she is an aged goat...and the engagement was broken off... Lucky for Margaret...perhaps not. Lucky for George...'

Daylight was showing through the curtains in Virginia's bedroom. She lay in bed in a deeply depressive state. Her eyes were open and she stared into space away from Vanessa who sat close, but Virginia was aware only of the pounding waves growing louder and louder in her head. Vanessa approached the bed. 'Is your headache worse? Is there anything you want?'

'There is nothing I want, Mother.'

Leonard sat in Sir George Savage's consulting room. 'It is not only the headaches, but the depression. And then the violent bouts of euphoria...euphoria, no other word can describe...'

'Only rest and good food...she always responds. It takes time, but it always works.'

'She loses touch with the world,' Leonard said, 'she has terrible delusions...'

Sir George sighed. 'I know her symptoms.'

'I have been keeping a diary...' Leonard took it out of his briefcase and opened it and attempted to hand it to Sir George who waved it away.

'My dear fellow, always ups and downs. Neurasthenia follows a pattern.'

'I have talked to various people and I know that manic-depressives...'

'You must leave the diagnoses to us chaps in the know. Your wife is not suffering from the manic-depressive insanity. Total rest. Total rest, darkened room if necessary. And wholesome food, plenty of milk.' A telephone rang outside the room. 'Infernal ringing! I'm afraid I am very pressed for time. See that she drinks fresh milk, Mr Woolf. No more visits to the Russian ballet. No more parties. Not until I'm satisfied...'

A secretary came into the room. 'I'm sorry to interrupt.'

'I'm in consultation, Miss Parker. Is it urgent?'

'I'm afraid it is. It's Mrs Bell for Mr Woolf. Mrs Woolf has tried to kill herself.'

The ambulance approached. Virginia was being violently sick. Vanessa was heaving Virginia off the bed and Sir George Savage and Leonard forced her to walk while she vomited. She collapsed onto the bed and her breathing was loud, snorts and snores. Eventually Leonard and Vanessa went downstairs and waited exhausted, sleeping fitfully in armchairs. It was dawn before they woke, and Sir George was bending over Leonard. 'Mr Woolf! Mr Woolf! She's out of danger. I'm going home to sleep. I'll arrange for nurses. She must not be left alone.'

'I don't know how to thank you.'

'By keeping the veronal locked up, my friend. Another time we might not be so lucky.'

A nurse approached with a breakfast tray. She was middle-aged, short, brusque, grey-haired. She entered the bedroom and Virginia was lying in bed in the darkened room. The nurse put down the breakfast tray and drew back the curtains. It was raining and the nurse said, 'It doesn't look very nice.'

'Listen to the birds singing, Mother. They're speaking Greek! I think it's Aristophanes. It's a lovely day. The sun is shining and I can barely look out of the window.'

The nurse took up the tray. She put it on the table in the corridor and called to Leonard. He took a minute to respond as he was still sleeping, and then he rushed up the stairs.

'I took the tray away, Mr Woolf. I can't seem to stop her talking.'

Leonard went into the bedroom. 'Mother, it wasn't true. I said to 'Nessa, who do you love the best, and she said Mother. It seemed to me so grossly unfair to exclude Father, I said he was the one I loved the best. It wasn't true.' Virginia began to cry. 'It wasn't true.'

He attempted to take Virginia's hand and she snatched her hand away. 'It wasn't true.' He stroked her forehead, and she sat bolt upright. 'The groaning was terrible. Listen. Listen. Can you hear it? Like a walrus, grunting and groaning at the zoo.' Virginia imitated terrible groans. 'Oh, Father is dying. He heaves himself up in bed. Groaning. They want fish, you see. They have extraordinary beaks. Beaks of brass. Tears flesh. Pierces brains.'

Leonard put his hand on her shoulder, but she strained away from him. 'Such fishy thoughts, brains coiled in oil. It made Thoby strong, of course, but Adrian was thin as string. Play with him. Play with him. Don't leave him out. Don't disappoint him. George! George!'

Dr Head was taking Virginia's pulse as she talked on wildly, her eyes open but unseeing. 'Never bear children. Such vanity. Such faults. Worms in the meat. Feed, feed, consuming the gut. Three-and-sixpence or three-and-seven. Far too expensive for us!' and she laughed wildly.

Virginia talked on. The dawn was visible through the drawn curtains. Leonard was slumped in a chair but he was awake. Two nurses stood looking down.

'I wouldn't have believed it!' said one of the nurses.

'Dying in the fish, I can't hear, I can't hear, I can't hear,' Virginia said.

'You ought to go and get some sleep, Mr Woolf,' said the other nurse. Leonard shook his head.

Leonard stood outside the bedroom with Dr Head. From inside the bedroom Virginia's voice carried on monotonously. 'She doesn't know me, she doesn't hear me. No matter what I say. I cannot understand how her clear and logical mind…'

Simultaneously Virginia's voice rang out. 'Books. The Leonardo. Post. Post. Tears. Absolutely not.' Her voice rose to a scream. 'Get out. I know what you're plotting. Get out.' The nurse came hurrying out, very flustered, and Dr Head went in.

Shaved and refreshed, Leonard waited for Dr Head in the corridor outside Virginia's bedroom. He came out smiling. 'All she needs now is good food and rest. Problems over. Out of her system.'

A nurse came up the stairs carrying a tray, with a flower in a vase, pretty china set out on a tray cloth. 'I'll take it, nurse,' said Leonard.

'I'll be in tomorrow. Plain sailing now.'

'Thank you, doctor,' Leonard said gratefully. And he carried the tray into Virginia's room.

Virginia sat against the pillows, her hair combed, pale but rested. She caught sight of the nurse and doctor but Leonard closed the door. 'I've brought you some lunch,' he said.

'I'm not hungry,' said Virginia.

'Let me do the pillows,' Leonard said, gently rearranging them and adjusting the bedjacket around Virginia's shoulders.

'I'm not eating eggs,' Virginia said.

'I don't want you to eat eggs,' Leonard replied, patiently. 'I've brought you beef tea.'

'They disguise them,' said Virginia, 'they take off their shells. They hide them in custard.'

Leonard smiled as if she were joking and put a spoon into her hand. He put the tray in front of her and sat down beside the bed. Virginia made no attempt to eat, not even looking at the food. 'You can't trick me into it,' she said, 'I can see the blood.'

'Look at it, Virginia,' Leonard said firmly, 'You're imagining things. I want you to look.'

Slowly, fearfully, Virginia looked down at the cup of broth. Then she recoiled, pressing back against the bedhead in terror and disgust. Suddenly she leant forward and heaved the tray at Leonard, catching him full in the chest.

Chapter 4
I Think I Trust Lloyd George

Virginia's sanity was temporarily restored: first she had four nurses, then two, then one – and then just Leonard. They were walking along the coast with their dog and Virginia picked up a stick and threw it, and the spaniel rushed after it.

'Are you really going for a swim?' Virginia asked.

'It's such a beautiful afternoon. And what do you think I've brought a towel for?'

'To swim!'

Leonard went behind a bush and came out with his bathing costume on. He said, 'I won't be long,' and the dog ran into the shallow water, barking. Leonard swam towards a safety raft and he hauled himself up and waved to Virginia and she waved back, keeping an eye on his clothes. He dived into the sea and swam under water for a minute and came face to face with a large, red-faced man. He trod water and panted; he was very breathless.

'Damned Kaiser. Do you know there's going to be war?' he asked. Leonard looked shocked. The large man puffed and blew. 'Oh yes,' he went on, 'no doubt about it. I'm here on holiday and today I get a telegram calling me back. There's going to be war.'

Leonard and the man swam side by side. 'Who sent the telegram?' Leonard queried.

'It was official. They wouldn't recall me unless it was going to be war. I'm from London. A bobby. A copper. A member of His Majesty's Police!'

Leonard wondered how to tell Virginia.

Bertrand Russell was walking with a colleague deep in conversation as Maynard collided with him, rushing along with a briefcase and a small suitcase.

'Forgive me. Apologies.'

'Europe is racing towards destruction,' said Russell.

Maynard was impatient. 'Possibly…' Into view came Maynard's brother-in-law, wearing a leather coat, helmet and goggles, pushing a motor cycle with a sidecar, '…on my brother-in-law's motorcycle. Have to get to London.'

Russell spoke with distaste as the goggled man approached. 'Couldn't you go by train?'

Maynard hurried on and climbed into the sidecar. 'No time. Banks are panicking at the prospect of war. There's a run on gold. The whole economy could collapse.' He balanced the suitcase upright on his knees and the engine revved noisily.

Over the roar Russell shouted, 'You're defending Mammon rather than man!'

'England, Bertie, England!'

'You disappoint me, Keynes.'

Maynard sat in the side car as his brother-in-law drove him to London and the Treasury. At a crossing where the motor cycle slowed down Maynard saw a newsvendor and read the headlines… FINANCIAL CRISIS. TREASURY PREPARED TO TAKE ACTION.

'Can't the Treasury take action without you?' asked his brother-in-law.

As they moved off again, Maynard said, 'Let them try.'

Maynard sat at his desk surrounded by papers. He was deep in reading and he did not look up when his male secretary hurried in with some more papers, and Maynard took them without lifting his eyes from the page. He sat there until it was night and three senior officials from the Bank of England joined him – many years his senior. They were tired. Maynard had his jacket off, ties were loosened, the ashtrays were full and the room was thick with smoke.

'Bank rate up to ten per cent…no, no, no, we must not suspend the gold standard before it is absolutely necessary,' said Maynard. 'We must convince the Chancellor.'

One of the bankers replied wearily and resentfully, 'What do you suggest, Mr Keynes?'

'The alternative would be disaster…'

Leonard and Virginia were standing outside the Lewes post office with an anxious crowd of about twenty people. An official came out of the building and pinned up a short hand-written notice. AUGUST 4TH 1914. BRITAIN IS AT WAR WITH GERMANY.

A fire was burning in the drawing room at Gordon Square. Lytton, wrapped in woollens, sat close to it, knitting a khaki muffler and opposite him, much more lightly dressed, was Morgan Forster.

'I expect by the time I've finished it,' said Lytton, 'the war will be over.'

'It has scarcely begun.'

'Instead of one of our brave soldier lads wearing the muffler, I'll have to give it to Duncan.'

'I'm sure Duncan will be very pleased with it.' Morgan paused. 'It's deuced warm in here, Lytton.'

'And I feel quite chilly. I always do. Never mind. We won't build up the fire again.'

'Good!'

'Come along. Test me some more.'

Morgan picked up a German phrase book which was lying on the arm of the chair. 'Learning German is ridiculous. And very unpatriotic. The Royal Family may come from Germany but we're not allowed to say *kindergarten* any more.' He flicked through the book, found a page and bent the spine flat.

Lytton said, 'My dear, one has to face realities. It is very possible we shall be over-run by the marauding Hun. No point in my going on learning Italian, melodic as it is. I want to learn some good German words!'

'It would be more useful,' Morgan said, 'if you served with the Red Cross. That is what I intend to do if the need arises.'

Clive Bell was in bed with Mrs Raven-Hill. Married to one of the illustrators of *Punch* magazine, Mrs Raven-Hill had seduced Clive at the age of eighteen and their affair had continued intermittently even after

Clive's marriage to Vanessa. Moving sensuously Mrs Raven-Hill attempted to arouse Clive but his mind was elsewhere.

'I can't. I'm sorry,' he said. 'Not much use tonight, am I? I'm too wrought up about this bloody war. We can't just sit back and be ruled by the militarists. When I read of their ranting and shallow optimism... My God, I'll have to forsake art criticism and write something against the war.'

Mrs Raven-Hill stroked him affectionately. 'Darling,' she said softly, 'we just have to tell ourselves we're going to win.'

'That's just what we don't have to do,' said Clive. 'We just have to persuade the powers that be that war is monstrous and destructive and benefits no one. We need peace at once.'

'Oh Clive, no one agrees with that,' said Mrs Raven-Hill, planting kisses on his chest, 'The Germans need a lesson.'

Inside his Treasury office Maynard sat smoking, drinking coffee and writing furiously. Signing and blotting the memorandum he handed it to the waiting secretary. 'To Mr Lloyd George, immediately. And may it do some good,' Maynard said as the secretary hurried out.

At the corner of Russell Square Leonard read a newspaper placard: REDUCTION OF BANK RATE. BANKS AT WORK AGAIN. He bought a paper and walked along, reading it. 'Good old Maynard,' he murmured under his breath.

Virginia was making a bed under the table with pillows and rugs – a makeshift air-raid shelter off the kitchen. Leonard, in dressing gown and pyjamas, pillow and books under his arm, was about to climb onto the table which was spread with newspapers. The lights were out and there were candles burning.

'Here, have a blanket...' She threw a blanket up to him and it landed onto the spread of newspapers on the tabletop. Leonard picked it up and saw the headlines underneath. 'And Maynard is still boasting he saved the county's economy!'

'He probably did. And if he didn't, no doubt he will.' There was the sound of a distant Zeppelin engine and Virginia stood up to look.

'Lloyd George took credit of course. Still, he must trust Maynard. Otherwise he wouldn't have him permanently in the Treasury. And it's comforting to have someone *we* trust close to the seat of power!'

The Zeppelin became closer. Virginia extinguished the candles and the pale glimmer from the new moon was the only light coming through the basement area windows. She crawled into bed and drew up her knees to make room for Leonard. The door opened and the maid rushed in, in dressing gown and curlers, terrified.

'Oh, madam. . .oh, sir!'

Leonard said, 'Calm yourself. Get under the table with Mrs Woolf.'

The maid, trembling violently, sat under the table with Virginia. 'Them wicked Germans. Oo'd believe they'd find a way of killin' us in our 'omes. My dad says it's not like a proper war...'

There was a sudden crashing explosion and some of the windowpanes were blown in. The maid screamed.

'Are you all right?' Leonard said after a pause. He went to the basement window and looked up as the room was increasingly illuminated by the red flickering light of the fire. 'I wonder how many people are being killed tonight...'

In the Omega workshop showroom Vanessa, Roger Fry and Duncan were sitting on the nursery furniture beside a cut-out paper elephant. Vanessa was flushed with indignation. 'As if Clive was a traitor or something. The Lord Mayor *ordered* Clive's book to be burned. And he was only pleading for peace.'

Roger said wryly, 'There will probably be a black market in copies.'

'Don't make stupid jokes.' Vanessa was furious and stood up. 'It's terribly upsetting for Clive.'

'It was courageous of him to write it,' Duncan said.

'Yes, it was. And you've no idea how people are attacking him. War, war, war, that's all people seem to want. Even his stupid father has cut off his allowance.'

'Well, patriotism is stirred, Vanessa,' said Roger. 'You've read Chesterton's attack on Clive in *The Nation*?'

'Yes, I did read that disgusting attack. And don't defend it...'

'I have no intention of...'

'...just because you're too old to enlist, you don't have to champion the Rupert Brookes and all the other mad patriots...'

Roger stood up and walked away. 'If you insist in misinterpreting everything I say. . .'

Duncan looked up at her and in a motherly fashion Vanessa planted a kiss in his hair. 'If they want to fight, let them. But I don't believe in it and neither does Clive. Or Duncan. Do you?'

'No!' He kissed her hand. 'I can't bear to fight anyone. Ever.'

'In fact, I think we should all spend the war in Cornwall with a huge studio and absolutely no newspapers until they have all come to their senses.'

'Paint and make love.'

'And we can all forget about the perfidious Adrian and the horrible girl he married. You can find someone new to be in love with...' Duncan laughed and hugged her and Roger's unhappiness showed.

Vanessa was in a large high bath. There was plenty of steam and her hair was tied on top of her head. She was soaping her arms and neck with a sponge and the door was opened and Duncan walked in.

'You want a bath and I want a shave and there's only one bathroom.' He went across to the washbasin. 'Where's Clive's razor?'

'In the medicine cupboard.' Her eyes showed that she loved him.

Duncan opened it and took out a shaving mug and a cut-throat razor. Vanessa lay back in the water, watching him. He opened his shirt neck wider, soaped his face and stropped the razor. In spite of her nakedness, he had no sexual reaction. He started to shave.

Garsington Manor, a Tudor house built in Cotswold stone, had garden statues lining the formal terraces and a swimming pool converted from a pond. In the shadows from the trees a screaming peacock in full display was in pursuit of a peahen. Dora Carrington and Mark Gertler were kissing.

'It's too noisy here to kiss,' Carrington said, releasing herself. Round the trees came Ottoline, chasing the peacock. She was wearing a bottle-green velvet suit trimmed with swansdown and a large feathered hat. Two pug dogs were following her.

'You've stolen the peacock's tail!' said Mark.

'I think you look like a cockney *elegante* on Hampstead Heath!' said Carrington.

'If those birds don't behave themselves,' Ottoline smiled, 'we shall have to eat them for lunch!' They walked on, Mark making energetic runs at the peacock. 'And talking of lunch...' Ottoline turned to Carrington, 'I've put you next to Mr Lawrence. With Frieda on his other side. I don't want him being moody again. You must charm him.'

Carrington shuddered, 'That fierce, black, scowling man...'

The dining room was panelled, with a low ceiling, but the panelling was painted sealing-wax red and hung with pictures by Augustus John, Duncan Grant and Mark Gertler, as well as with a variety of earlier Italian artists and various pieces of bric-a-brac. From the central beam a cardinal bird in a lacquered cage was suspended over the long trestle table. Several pug dogs snuffled around the table, and under it. Ottoline gave them titbits of food; she was sitting at one end of the table and Philip Morrell at the other. D.H. Lawrence, brooding and bearded, sat between Carrington and Frieda and next to Carrington were seated Maynard Keynes and then Lytton. He did not speak but his eyes and ears were alert, and he looked from one to another in a kind of horrified joy. On the other side of the table were Duncan, David (Bunny), Garnett (Duncan's new friend), Vanessa and Mark.

'Oh, but there won't really be conscription, will there?' said Carrington

'I'm afraid Mr Lloyd George is in favour of it. He doesn't seem to grasp the economic repercussions.' Philip nodded gloomily at Maynard's words.

'Well, I think artists should be let off,' Vanessa said. 'I think it wrong to make any artist fight.'

Lawrence sighed. 'You are sentimentalising artists, Mrs Bell.'

'How can you say that? When you're a writer.'

'But he is also a painter, too,' said Frieda in her German accent, 'Yes?' (Duncan looked across at Maynard and half-smiled.) 'He paints...very physical.'

Carrington looked round. 'I think we all do!'

Ottoline shot her a warning look. 'Carrington and Mark have just left the Slade,' she explained.

'Out in the real world now!' said Carrington.

'You don't know what the real world is,' Lawrence sneered. 'Aesthetic ecstasy! Significant form! Did they teach you that at art school?'

'What's wrong with them?' Mark said. Philip said simultaneously, 'There's plenty of room for all kinds of art. Right, Keynes?'

Maynard smiled. 'As long as they're negotiable securities.'

Vanessa looked furious and Bunny, Philip, Ottoline and Lytton laughed. Under the table Lawrence gently kicked one of the pugs away and Bunny pressed his leg against Duncan's. The conversation split.

'Carrington is a strange name,' said Frieda.

'I don't use the Dora.'

'So strange. Why?'

'Because she's a crophead.' Vanessa smiled as she said it.

'Crophead?' Frieda looked puzzled.

'We all cut our hair,' Carrington shook her head and her fringe bounced.

At the same time Ottoline said to Maynard, 'You should tell that to the Prime Minister.'

'I'm told that 840,000 men can be spared from civilian occupations. The Prime Minister isn't in favour of it. It's Mr General Public, he claims.'

Bunny gave a little smile. 'War fever! There will be conscientious objectors.'

'Well, if it happens, I will give any artist who wants it 'essential work' on my farm,' said Ottoline.

Vanessa lent across Bunny to Duncan. 'There you are, darling! Ott's going to be your saviour.' She caught sight of Duncan's thigh pressed against Bunny's and of one of the pugs making overtures to Lytton's shoe as he struggled to release it. 'And Bunny's of course…'

After lunch the guests relaxed in the garden, Frieda and Ottoline were secure in a close relaxed friendship. 'You must not forget when he attacks your artist friends that he is the son of a miner of coal!' said Frieda.

A distance away from them Mark Gertler sat avidly reading *The Voyage Out* by Virginia, and Lytton, walking with Bunny, passed Philip asleep in a deck chair. Lytton said, 'For once I couldn't utter. I could hardly distinguish people from pugs…all through lunch… one pushes them down in vain.'

Vanessa, Maynard and Lawrence were sitting round a garden table and as Lytton and Bunny reached them Vanessa turned fiercely on Maynard. 'I blame you. We all know perfectly well you are helping to keep the war going,' she said.

'Yes, Maynard, my dear,' said Lytton, 'we rather wonder why you are still at the Treasury?'

Maynard turned and saw Lytton, and Lytton sat on the arm of Maynard's chair. Lawrence watched, his fury mounting.

'Oh come along, Lytton. I'm saving the country millions of pounds a week. I'm bloody good at my job and you know it. Do you want England to go down the financial drain?'

Vanessa said, 'Do you believe in fighting, or don't you? Either you do or you don't.'

'I don't believe in conscription. No one should be ordered to fight,' Maynard said.

'Freedom of choice.' Bunny smiled.

'Either you're going to be a conscientious objector or you're not. You're a hypocrite, Maynard,' Vanessa said, accusingly.

Maynard appeared somewhat hurt. 'I am not a conscientious objector but I will certainly conscientiously object to compulsory service.'

Carrington ran by in a bathing robe, waving to them.

Lytton said, 'Two masters perhaps? Conscience – and government?' Bunny looked after Carrington, smiling. She reached the swimming pool and threw off the robe and jumped in.

'Trust Carrington to make a splash!'

Lawrence rose to his feet in a towering rage. 'You Bloomsbury... you Bloomsbuggers make me mad with misery, hostility and rage! You make me dream of black beetles!'

Vanessa reacted with a half-giggle of shock and amazement. Lawrence stood over Maynard. 'You're corrupt, Keynes. You're fucking unclean. Homosexuality has fucking sterilized you. Your class doesn't know what life's about.' He stormed off. For a moment they all sat, stunned.

'The lady doth protest too much methinks...!' said Lytton.

Carrington called, 'Why don't you come in, it's glorious!'

They took no notice of her. Maynard was unhappy. 'You know I'll do all I can to help my friends,' he said quietly

It was the Council Chamber of Hampstead Town Hall and Lytton's sisters were already seated in the front row, all plain young women with a distinct family likeness. Bloomsbury supporters were pushing in through the doors and filling the public seats – Virginia and Leonard, Duncan, Adrian and his wife Karin, Bunny, Ottoline, Mark Gertler, Vanessa and Clive and Saxon Sydney-Turner, Carrington and Morgan Forster, plus two or three others (two 'cropheads' with hair like Carrington) and a handsome boy, no doubt the friend of one of the men. At the tribunal table on a low dais were eight council members, visibly weary. This was the last case of the day and the clock above their heads showed seven-thirty. The members included a woman, two military men with red tabs on their shoulders and four civil servants. Their chairman was a J.P., a pompous establishment figure. He had a typed list and he stopped Philip Morrel, who was carrying a light blue inflatable cushion and asked, 'Mr Giles Lytton Strachey?'

'No, no, no.'

'Please take a seat, sir.' Phillip sat at the front of the court and in front of him was an empty chair for the applicant.

On the tribunal table a civil servant lowered his voice. 'Last one.'

One of the military men, a major, didn't bother to lower his voice. 'Thank God. Had enough of these degenerates!'

Lytton entered, carrying sheaves of papers and a tartan rug. The policeman announced him and the tribunal looked at him with a mixture of derision and disgust.

'Here, I suppose,' Lytton looked around and saw the chair. As he approached Philip handed him the air-cushion and Lytton placed his papers and rug on the chair and solemnly blew up the cushion. He stopped, a little breathless, smiled at his sisters, and then put his lips back to the valve, finished the inflation and then put the cushion on the chair and sat down cautiously and slowly, arranging the rug round his knees.

Virginia whispered to Leonard, 'Piles.' The tribunal members looked amazed and then the chairman recovered and looked at the papers in front of him.

'Are you Mr Giles Lytton Strachey?' Lytton nodded and smiled. 'Please answer yes or no.'

'Yes,' answered Lytton, still smiling.

'Please stand.' Lytton looked astonished. 'Are you an invalid, Mr Strachey?'

'Semi-invalid. Yes.'

'You appear to be able to walk unaccompanied. Would you please stand.'

Lytton let the rug drop to the floor and slowly stood, making great play with his papers.

'You are here, Mr Strachey, because you have refused all forms of service on the grounds of conscientious objection. Is that correct? Wasn't your father a Major General?'

'Yes. Oh…' Lytton dropped his papers. Philip Morell came forward and gathered them up for him and handed them back.

'It is up to this tribunal to decide in this time of national emergency,' said the chairman, 'whether it should be deemed proper for you to serve in His Majesty's forces.'

'Might I sit down again? I am feeling most unwell.' The tribunal looked at one another and one or two whispered.

'Very well.' With the same commotion Lytton seated himself carefully on the cushion. 'The tribunal may decide that you should be directed to such other forms of national service, on the land or elsewhere, as may be thought appropriate, as laid down under the terms of the Military Service Act now in force. Should you, however, continue to refuse service if so directed, then it is within the power of the tribunal to commit you to prison without further ado and for an indefinite period, or for such term as may be decreed under the Military Service Act. Do you understand?'

Lytton said, 'I have here medical letters…'

'Do you understand, Mr Strachey?'

'Completely.'

'Very well, you may state your case.'

There was a disturbance at the door. A messenger had arrived and was talking to the policeman. The policeman nodded and made his way through the spectators to Philip Morrell and whispered to him.

'I have to interrupt. Please excuse me…'

'This is out of order.'

'Philip Morrell, Member of Parliament for Burnley. I am here as a character reference for Mr Strachey, but I have been summoned to the House for Division.'

'Very well, Mr Morell.' Philip made his way out and the chairman turned back to Lytton. With a sigh he said, 'Please state your case.'

Lytton looked through his papers, and up at the tribunal. 'I cannot, on moral grounds, take part in acts which assist in perpetuating the war. Further I consider the use of force to be repugnant and wrong.' He read from his papers, 'My convictions have been conscientiously reached by an examination of the ethical and philosophical concepts involved. I am…' he puts down the paper, 'you might say, a pacifist.'

There was applause from the Bloomsbury supporters. 'You do not object to being branded a coward, Mr Strachey?'

'By whom?'

'By every decent man and woman in the land. By every young soldier prepared to die for England. The country which has nurtured you in the freedom you are not prepared to preserve.'

'The freedom I understand you wish to remove from me.'

'Very clever, Mr Strachey!' said the chairman. 'And do you object to all wars?'

'Oh, no, not at all,' Lytton replied shrilly. 'Only this one.'

The lady member was angry. 'I suppose you have heard of the white feather?'

'Indeed. And I find it rather attractive.'

The Major almost burst with rage. 'You have lost your character reference sir, but I think I can assess it. I want to ask you a question. What would you do if you saw a German soldier raping your sisters?'

Lytton turned and looked at the five sisters, and they looked back at him. He looked at the Major and their eyes met. There was a long pause, then Lytton answered gravely, 'I would try to place my body between them.' There was a burst of laughter from the Strachey sisters and the Bloomsbury spectators. The Major swept out, fuming.

Virginia and Vanessa were walking and talking. 'No one in their right senses would have put Lytton into uniform. But Duncan's different. He can't turn up with an air-cushion. Oh God, Ginia, if they make Duncan fight, gentle Duncan, he couldn't survive. I don't just mean physically...' Vanessa paused. 'I can't paint without him. I can't exist without him. Could you exist without Leonard?'

'No. I couldn't. My doctors don't think so either. I was too mad at the beginning of the war even to know he wanted to volunteer. Leo isn't a pacifist. Not totally, like the others. His moral choice was between his country or his wife! I don't feel guilty that he chose to look after me. Just thankful.'

'Did he feel guilty?'

Virginia paused. 'When he heard his brother was killed, and another wounded, with the same German bullet? Yes, he did feel guilty.'

'For not being slaughtered with the rest of England's young men?' Vanessa was bitter.

'When he was conscripted they turned him down. His health, not mine.' She smiled wryly. 'Saved by the shakes!'

'Duncan doesn't even shiver when he's cold. He's so horribly fit.'

'You've worked for the Council of Civil Liberties. You must know of some way round it.' Vanessa shook her head. 'Think, Nessa, there must be someone we know who could help.'

Outside the Ipswich Town Hall Maynard, carrying a large, locked bag with the royal cipher on it, asked the policeman on duty the way to the tribunal court.

Inside the Council Chamber, smaller than the Hampstead one, Duncan and Bunny sat on a bench facing the tribunal, once again composed of eight members, this time all male, one of them an army officer. The chairman of the tribunal called upon Bunny to stand up and give an account of himself.

Bunny stood up. 'I come from a family of pacifists...' he began nervously, 'My mother went to Russia and visited Tolstoy...'

'I don't care which town or country your mother visited Mr Garnett,' the chairman said brusquely, 'We are here to discuss your exemption from military service. You may sit down.' Bunny sat down looking distressed and anxious.

Maynard entered the court, somewhat breathless, and took a seat unseen by either Duncan or Bunny.

'Duncan Grant,' called the chairman, as if Duncan were outside the room.

Duncan stood.

'Do you have anyone to appeal on your behalf?' the chairman asked, without looking up from his papers.

At the back of the court Maynard stood up. Duncan and Bunny turned to see who it was, gratitude and relief on their faces at the sight of Maynard.

Maynard announced himself to the tribunal. 'John Maynard Keynes. I am here on behalf of both Mr David Garnett and Mr Duncan Grant. May I ask that the cases are heard as expeditiously as possible since I have to return to London to work of some national importance to the Treasury.'

The chairman looked impressed as did the rest of the tribunal. 'What is your position there, Mr Keynes?' the chairman asked.

'I am head of the department dealing with external finances.'

'Please proceed, Mr Keynes,' said the chairman.

Less than twenty minutes later the chairman, having briefly conferred with the rest of the tribunal, rose to announce the verdict.

'Mr Duncan Grant, Mr David Garnett, the tribunal grants both of you exemption from military service on the grounds of conscientious objection on condition that you undertake work on the land…'

Outside the town hall Vanessa rushed to embrace Maynard while Duncan and Bunny looked on, beaming, under the gaze of the policeman. Duncan moved close to Maynard and whispered, 'We'll kiss you later…'

Vanessa cycled up the muddy lane to view Charleston, the 17th-century house in Sussex where she was to live for the rest of her life. The house was built of flint and brick with a pond and orchard. She parked her bicycle and took a labelled estate agent's key from the basket and let herself in by the front door. At a first, cursory appraisal, the house seemed to Vanessa as perfect on the inside as it had seemed from the outside.

Vanessa was deep in discussion over a hedge with a neighbouring farmer. 'If I take the house, would you give employment to my two gentleman friends?'

'What they call conchies, are they?'

'One is a writer and the other an artist.'

The farmer was without much comprehension. 'Be they then?'

'And very keen workers!'

'Maybe, we'll see how it goes,' the farmer said without much enthusiasm.

Duncan was making love to Vanessa, kissing her breasts and throat. 'I've wanted this for so long. So much…I do love you…do you love me more than Bunny?'

'Differently from Bunny,' Duncan said after a pause.

'But I am the first woman…'

'Someone tried to make me have a tart in Paris…but it didn't work!'

'You're so beautiful,' Vanessa whispered. They kissed passionately and were so totally immersed at first they did not hear knocking at the front door. Duncan rolled off Vanessa. The knocking grew louder and Duncan jumped out of bed. As he reached the window a handful of gravel hit the glass and he peered out. There was Bunny, suitcase in hand by the front door, looking up, handsome, waving. Duncan turned from the window, smiling delightedly.

'Bunny!' as he hurried out, naked, to let Bunny in, Vanessa was resigned and saddened.

'Bunny!' she echoed flatly.

It was pouring with rain and Duncan and Bunny were working in a field, sacks over their heads. Duncan asked, 'Would you prefer the trenches?'

'I'd prefer a drink!' They looked round for the farmer and he was nowhere in sight and they ran back to Charleston and took their boots off outside the back door. 'It's good to be home.'

Vanessa and Maynard were sitting at the kitchen table when they walked in. Paintings by Vanessa and Duncan were on the walls and canvasses were stacked on the floor.

'You're spending more than you're earning,' Maynard said. 'Let me invest your capital for you... I could increase your income to two hundred a year...'

'We'd like a drink!' Bunny gasped, 'We don't think we can work in the rain!'

Duncan, in shabby corduroys and jacket, was wandering in the Ministry of Finance offices, looking at the names on the doors, a catalogue in his hand. He saw the door he was looking for, knocked and entered without waiting. Maynard was sitting at his desk and the secretary looked up, astonished at the interruption. He hurried forward to eject Duncan. 'I'm sorry, you cannot come in here like this. I must ask you to leave at once.'

'It is all right, Jessop,' said Maynard. Duncan went forward and put the catalogue in front of Maynard with a flourish.

'We can't let it go,' said Duncan.

Maynard turned to the secretary, hovering uncertainly. 'You can leave us. Come back in...'

Duncan was excited. 'Half an hour!'

'Half an hour.'

The secretary left a little reluctantly. He looked worried as he closed the door.

'Where did you get it,' asked Maynard.

'Roger's studio.' Duncan turned the pages of the catalogue. 'See what they've got. Delacroix, Cézanne, Manet, Gauguin… We have to buy them for the National Gallery. You've got to go to Paris. You have got to get them.'

'With whose money?'

'You can get it! Convince the Treasury, talk to the Trustees.' He stood. 'We can't let them all go to the Louvre. The Germans might get them.'

Maynard thought for a second. 'As a matter of fact, I do have to go to Paris around the end of March. The Inter-Ally Finance Conference…'

'You can do it!'

'They'll fight the expenditure.'

'You'll fight harder. The opportunity, Maynard. A cultural investment!'

Maynard smiled suddenly and reached for the telephone. He asked for the number and said, 'Mr Maynard Keynes. I need an urgent word with the Chancellor of the Exchequer.' He turned to Duncan. 'Stay in town and have dinner…Ah Chancellor. I have just had word of an extraordinary sale of paintings in Paris…yes, I know there is a war on…'

Vanessa sat in her nightgown taking her hair down in front of the mirror. In the mirror she saw the door open and Bunny came in. He closed the door and paused. 'You are *so* beautiful, Vanessa!' He came behind her and put his hands on her shoulders, slid them up her neck and under her hair.

'Oh, Bunny! Don't start! You know I'm going to say no.'

'We're three strands. You love Duncan, he loves you and me and I'm half in love with you. And Duncan's in London.'

Vanessa said, 'And the boys are in the next room.'

'Asleep. And it wouldn't matter if they woke.' He tried to kiss her. 'They're your children. They understand life.'

'And I want Duncan's baby.'

Bunny let her go, surprised and not unpleased. 'Duncan's baby! What about Clive?'

'I know he wouldn't mind. Oh, Bunny.' She stood up. 'I want his baby more than anything in the world.'

Bunny sat on the edge of the bed and pulled Vanessa onto his knee. 'I don't think I'm jealous. Of either of you.' He kissed her on the cheek. 'Yes.

I think you should. Duncan's baby. Well, well. Have you told him?'

She smiled. 'Not yet.'

The barrel organ was playing 'The Last Rose of Summer'. Leonard and Virginia crossed Farringdon Road, avoiding city workers and a few servicemen and they walked past the barrel organ which had a monkey on top. Virginia opened her purse and gave a few pennies to the organ grinder while Leonard talked to the monkey. Although it was chained, it had just enough leeway to jump onto his arm as he petted it. The organ grinder lifted it and put it back on the top of the organ. Both Leonard and Virginia looked well and happy and they walked on, looking briefly into shop windows. They stopped outside the Excelsior Printing Supply Company and gazed in. There was a small hand printing press and they looked at one another in eager anticipation. The barrel organ began 'Goodbye, Dolly Gray' and they went into the shop.

'I should suggest something a little more elaborate, sir,' said the salesman, 'like this one…!'

Leonard shook his head. 'I think we have made up our minds.'

'Absolutely made up our minds…' said Virginia.

Leonard wrote the cheque in his rather shaky hand for nineteen pounds, five shillings and five pence. Virginia stood looking excitedly over his shoulder as he handed it over to the salesman. As they were waiting for it to be wrapped up Virginia whispered, 'Hogarth Press!'

Vanessa, Duncan, Bunny and Clive were seated round the Omega table at Charleston, finishing supper. A sixteen-year-old maid, Grace, was clearing the plates. She wore a plain dress and an apron and was tall and good-looking. Vanessa said, 'Who wants pudding? Clive?'

'What kind of pudding?'

Grace replied shyly, 'Bread-and-butter pudding, sir.'

'Grace made it. Her mother's recipe, isn't it?' Grace nodded and smiled and went out to the pantry to fetch it. 'And you're to say you like it even if you don't…' said Vanessa.

The door opened and Maynard came in wearing a hat and coat and carrying a case. He took off his hat and threw it on an empty chair. They looked at him, astonished. Grace returned with plates and the pudding and stepped back at the sight of Maynard.

'You're just in time for Grace's bread-and-butter pudding,' Vanessa said.

Maynard smiled and put down his case. He spoke very casually, enjoying the impact. 'Austin Chamberlain gave me a lift in his motor. By the way, there's a Cézanne down the drive. Behind the hedge. Hadn't enough hands to carry it.'

Duncan jumped to his feet and embraced Maynard. 'You did it!'

Maynard nodded and smiled. 'I really did it. Channel was murderous. Came across in a destroyer.'

'Come on!' Vanessa, Duncan, Clive and Bunny rushed out and Grace stood in the middle of the room holding her dish. Still in his coat Maynard sank down, exhausted.

Vanessa threw her arms round Maynard. The others put the package on the table, pushing the meal aside. Grace jumped back, still clutching the dish. 'Absolutely all your venal sins are forgiven,' Vanessa said.

Clive unwrapped the paper. 'I got the Treasury to fork out 550,000 francs.' Maynard laughed. 'They said it was the first time I'd been in favour of spending.'

Clive gasped. 'It really is a Cézanne.' They stood back and admired the still life of apples.

'And in the suitcase a Delacroix, an Ingres and several charcoal drawings by Degas. For less than £500. The prices were unimaginable in Paris. We could hear the guns. No one wanted to stay longer than they needed. Naturally I took full advantage!'

Grace still hovered with her dish. She said in desperation to Maynard, 'Here, sir?' Maynard stretched out his hand and took it from her.

'I'll eat it straight from the dish, I'm starving!'

Grace looked horrified. Clive said mockingly, 'The gentry never behave as well as your class, Grace, as you'll soon discover.' He took the Cézanne off the table and put it on a chair. 'Don't shock the servants, Maynard. Come and sit over here.'

They all sat at the table, Vanessa beside Maynard. 'Come on, Nessa, tell me all the Bloomsbury gossip since I've been away.'

'It's not exactly gossip.' She paused. 'I'm having a baby.' Maynard looked first at Clive and then at Duncan. 'And if it's a boy I shall call it after you, Maynard. Because you are back in the fold.' She gave a sardonic smile and Maynard laughed.

Lydia Lopokova returned to the stage in the Coliseum at the end of her performance. The applause was continuous. Maynard leant across to be heard. 'I think she's a rotten dancer. She has such a stiff bottom!' They went round to the stage door and asked their way to Lopokova's dressing room.

There was a clutter of costumes, flowers, telegrams and champagne and Lopokova sat at her dressing table, her back to the mirror. As Ottoline came in followed by Lytton and Maynard, Lydia beamed and threw open her arms. 'Ah…! You like? You like?' She had a strong Russian accent.

'Darling, we like. Very much.' She kissed Lydia and drew Lytton and Maynard forward. 'You have met… Maynard Keynes, Lytton Strachey. Miss Lydia Lopokova.'

'Of course, we met. Your beautiful party.'

Maynard kissed her hand. 'Miss Lopokova. A breathtaking performance.'

'Congratulations. Enchanting.' Lytton said.

'Ottoline, such beautiful flowers!' She indicated an enormous lavish bouquet among smaller tributes.

'It is wonderful to have the Diaghilev Ballet back in London.'

Lydia pouted. 'But everyone say, where Nijinsky. Not without the great Nijinsky. No one say, very good we still have Lopokova. No?'

'And where is Nijinsky?' Lytton asked casually.

'There, you see! Where Nijinsky. Nijinsky with his wife. Very big scandal, big scandal when Mr Diaghilev learn Vaslav married man. He kick him out. Never dance for me again.' She untied her ballet shoes and took them off, wriggling her toes as she talked. 'Why not we have champagne. Mr Lytton, you look strong man, you open champagne.' Lytton took the champagne bottle and opened it as Lydia continued. 'Anyway, now Diaghilev has new boyfriend. But he don't get over.'

'Understandable,' Lytton said. The cork popped, Lydia shrieked, and he poured the champagne. 'Those muscles were irreplaceable.'

'All dancers have wonderful muscles.' She stretched out her legs and Lytton put a glass beside her. 'Feel muscle. Like bullet.'

Lytton smiled and handed a glass of champagne to Ottoline. 'Feel!' he said to Maynard wickedly. Maynard looked startled, then shyly knelt down and gently pinched Lydia's calf.

Flags hung out the window in Brunswick Square. Virginia was watching Adrian heaving sandbags away from the basement wall and civilians and servicemen were running and dancing and waving Union Jacks. Leonard was at his mother's house waiting for his brother Philip to come home. He was standing at the front door when Philip pushed open the gate and limped up the path. Leonard embraced him and his mother, with tears in her eyes, embraced him, too.

'I wish there were two of us to come home,' Philip said with tears in his eyes, too.

'You survived. We are grateful for that.'

As he went in Philip took his tin hat and knapsack from his shoulders and hurled the hat into the hedge.

There was a cake decorated with Allied flags in the garden of Charleston. Maynard was talking to Clive in the light of a huge, crackling bonfire and Julian and Quentin, very excited, were running round and round trying to drag a laughingly protesting Virginia with them. Vanessa, very pregnant, was dispensing mulled wine to Leonard, Bunny and Duncan. Leonard said, 'Not unmixed rejoicing! We start the peace with so much loss.'

Bunny raised a glass. 'To their memory!'

'All three quarters of a million of them.'

'Well, Rupert Brooke, unlike the rest of us, you will never grow old.'

Leonard sighed. 'This celebration is making me increasingly melancholy.'

Virginia arrived, gasping and breathless, the little boys now concentrating on eating large slices of cake. She overheard Leonard and sensed the reason for the 'increasing melancholy'. 'You were honestly exempted from fighting. There is nothing to be ashamed of in being alive, Leo.'

'Oh, you're right. And my mother would agree,' Leonard replied sharply. 'One son dead, one wounded, but one with shaking hands unharmed.'

Vanessa was very grave. 'My sister couldn't have survived the war without you!'

'Nor could the labour movement,' Maynard said as he approached. Quentin and Julian returned for Virginia and dragged her off again.

'Come on, come on,' Julian shouted, 'we're going to cook sausages in the fire.'

Virginia, her voice raised, 'And if you stay at the Treasury you won't survive either!'

It was winter. A fire was burning in the grate in Moore's room in Trinity College and he was pouring out sherry for Russell, Maynard and Lytton. 'Do I understand you are going to Versailles, Keynes?'

Maynard looked gloomy. 'The Peace Conference hasn't even begun and I'm already exhausted negotiating with the French. And they're supposed to be an ally. Could you top up my glass!'

'Well, the armistice has saved me from a second spell in prison.' Russell laughed. 'Towards the end they tried to call me up for military service and couldn't find me. The idiots forgot they had me in Brixton Prison for advocating peace!'

Lytton laughed. 'Maynard could have wielded power again. A familiar figure at tribunals.'

'He couldn't have saved me even if my principles allowed it. I'd have been back behind bars.'

'Oh, the great human lust for punishment and revenge. We're baying for Germany now,' Moore said. 'I suppose you heard the First Lord of the Admiralty here in Cambridge?' He imitated him. ' "The Germans are going to pay back every penny. They are going to be squeezed as the lemon is squeezed. Until the pips squeak. My only doubt" ' (Lytton joined in and they quoted together) ' "is not whether we can squeeze hard enough but whether there is enough juice." '

'I sometimes feel I work for a government I despise for ends I think criminal.' Maynard paused. 'I'm afraid they are determined to have their pound of flesh. I only hope to persuade them to moderate their demands.'

The train was crossing France and in the carriage Maynard was playing bridge with a British and two American delegates. A steward brought coffee and sandwiches and the players had their ties and jackets off. Scoring was on improvised pads made from the backs of official papers.

'Two hearts,' said Maynard.

'Two spades,' said the first American.

'Three hearts,' said the second American.

'Four hearts,' said the Englishman.

'Double!' Maynard cried.

It was dawn and the game still continued but now there was wine, bread and charcuterie on the table. 'Game and rubber!' said Maynard laying down his cards and making himself an open sandwich. The train was slowing down and they all looked out of the window. Maynard took a large bite and the train passed a Red Cross soup kitchen. There was a line of threadbare and hungry Germans queuing for food and as the train came to a halt, jolting and creaking, the first American said, 'Extraordinary feeling to be on German soil!'

At Treves six international financiers boarded the train, among them, walking a little apart, the German Dr Melchior who was small, very well dressed with a brilliantly clean white collar, grey cropped hair and dark, sorrowful eyes. They entered the carriage and everyone bowed stiffly and there was some confusion as to whether to shake hands. They began to seat themselves, the Allies on one side of the table, the Germans on the other; very congested, crushed and awkward. The train began to move and a number of the men began to smoke, offering the cigarettes around.

'Everyone understands English?' Maynard asked. A murmur of '*Ja*,' 'Go ahead,' 'Continue please.' 'Then in the simplest terms I shall put forward the Allied proposal. That in return for adequate food supplies, Germany surrenders all ships of her merchant fleet.'

'Before we continue along these lines, Mr Keynes,' a French delegate said sharply, 'we would like to establish the gold in the Reichsbank is transferred to the occupied territory.'

'In order to keep it safe from Bolshevism!' The American delegate smiled.

Dr Kaufmann, who was elderly and had nervous eyes and a sense of defeat, said 'Impossible! As representative of the Reichsbank I wish to state categorically that I consider this entirely unnecessary.'

'I believe it is possible that America would furnish us a loan.' Dr Melchior was quiet and serious. 'We must purchase our food supplies.'

'I am afraid that in our official view that is out of the question,' Maynard said.

'Mr Hoover does have large stocks of bacon...' said an American delegate.

'We have been defeated, but we do not have to lose all our dignity. A loan would enable us to feed our people until the next harvest, to buy what we need which...' (Dr Melchior gave a gentle smile) '...may not necessarily stop at bacon.'

'A loan has been discussed but is considered impossible,' said Maynard.

'A loan is necessary. We must have credit,' insisted Dr Melchoir.

'Your fleet would provide it,' the Frenchman said.

Maynard looked sympathetically towards Dr Melchior.

'But, gentlemen,' Kaufmann put in, 'Article 26 of the Armistice Agreement states, and I quote, "the supplying of foodstuffs to the German people in such measure as might be recognized to be necessary." '

'That is a very high price to pay,' Dr Melchior said.

The American muttered, 'Christ! We're getting nowhere!' Maynard heard the remark and looked very concerned.

Dr Melchior stood alone in his hotel room, smoking nervously. There was a knock at the door. '*Ja?*'

Maynard entered and at once Dr Melchior crossed to the door and locked it. He made a stiff bow.

'Thank you for seeing me in this way,' said Maynard.

Dr Melchior looked at the window, gave a nervous start and hurried across to draw the curtains. 'You have my word that no one will know of our meeting. It is better when we are against the rules. *Nein?*' He gave a slight pause. 'Do you wish to be seated?'

Maynard sat on the edge on an upright chair beside the bed. 'We are in accord, I think, Dr Melchior.'

'I would like to think.'

'Forgive me.' Maynard took out a cigarette. 'I am somewhat emotional and exhausted. We both know it is essential we do not delay the food supplies.'

'It is urgent.'

'Believe me, it is in our interest that your government survives. You must trust me that our intentions are honourable. The British and American delegates...'

'Ah, yes,' Dr Melchior said, 'the British and Americans. But the French prefer to obstruct.'

Maynard spoke passionately and he trembled slightly as he inhaled his cigarette. He stood up from the chair. 'I am sincere. I know that you are sincere. Secure a little latitude from the Weimar, keep them from pressing for a loan for the time being and I will do my best to urge Lloyd George that it is not in our best interests.'

Dr Melchior was doubtful. 'Lloyd George is a politician!'

'He is being pressed hard not to yield. But I have faith in him.'

'I will do my best to…how do you say it…play for time. I have my Jewish pessimism to overcome.'

'There is a chink,' Maynard said. 'If you and I do not work to widen it, I fear it will be extinguished.'

'You are right. If we are to save Germany we cannot wait for all the arguments. For myself, I expect my country to collapse and civilization to grow backwards.'

Maynard took Dr Melchior's hands. 'Let us at least try to civilise the peace.'

'Unless we are given nourishment soon, there will be no one left to pay any reparations.'

'I will do everything in my power…'

Lloyd George was standing and speaking in full flood with all the passion of the Welsh orator. This was a 'summit' meeting; President Woodrow Wilson of America, President Clemenceau of France, Foch, Flotz, General Smuts and other French, Italian, Japanese, American and British delegates – among them Dr Melchior and Maynard taking notes, seated round a horseshoe table. They were identified by name cards and national flags, and in the background were other secretaries and advisors, passing notes, hurrying to and from senior delegates, in and out of the room.

'I urge with all my might,' Lloyd George said, his voice rising, 'that steps should be taken to revictual Germany. Our honour is involved. Under the terms of the Armistice, the Allies gave an undertaking that food was to be let into Germany. On this understanding, the Germans accepted our Armistice conditions. And they were severe conditions.' Maynard looked up from his notes, his eyes on Lloyd George full of admiration and relief. 'But so far, so far, gentlemen, not a single ton of food has been sent into Germany. Are we really going to let German men, women and children *starve*, while hundreds and thousands of tons of food are lying now at Rotterdam?'

'Well, now Keynes…Not doing too badly, are we?' Lloyd George and Maynard were in the washroom, Lloyd George washing his hands and Maynard at the urinal stalls.

'Not too badly at all, sir! The French needed that humanitarian onslaught…'

Lloyd George nodded. 'And I gave it to them with all the Welsh passion at my command…'

'You did, indeed. Especially when you accused them of furthering Bolshevism by starving the Germans.'

'Oh, the Germans will get their food now, Keynes.' He was delighted at his success and was emanating great personal charm.

'What I would like to suggest, Prime Minister, if you will allow me...'

'You want me to make sure they don't have to consume Mr Hoover's second-grade bacon that the Americans seem so anxious to part with!'

'I want to refresh your memory on the Treasury view,' said Maynard seriously, 'of what is a realistic sum to be paid by the Germans.'

'Oh, I have my notes on the recommendations, Mr Keynes...'

Maynard overrode him. 'Our view at the Treasury, sir, is that two or three billion pounds would be feasible...' he paused, emphasizing, 'but not more!'

'Ah! But my advisor, Lord Sumner, does not agree with you!'

'Sir, Lord Sumner, with all due respect, is not cognizant of the full situation. Twenty-five billion pounds is a monstrous figure.'

Lloyd George walked across to the roller-towel and dried his hands as he spoke, his charm replaced by blustering. 'Oh, no doubt we'll find some compromise...'

Maynard turned to face Lloyd George. 'If Germany is to be milked, Prime Minister, she must not first of all be ruined. We need a healthy Germany for a healthy Europe. We may well learn that by sucking her dry now, she will never forgive us.'

Lloyd George was pacifying. 'You have had your way on the food issue...'

'Three billion, with payments limited to thirty years,' Maynard persisted. 'Whatever the crimes, no one should be made to pay forever.'

His charm turned on again, Lloyd George said, 'No promises, no promises. But you may be assured I will give the keenest attention to the points you have made, believe me.' Maynard was relieved. He did believe.

Maynard knocked at the door of Dr Melchior's room. There was a pause before Dr Melchior answered it and he drew Maynard into the room and shut the door quickly. They shook hands.

'The conference is not yet over,' Maynard said with a note of warning.

'I know. But if we lose, Herr Keynes, you will be feeding us to the Bolsheviks.'

'I am doing my utmost to make reason prevail!'

'With compassion, I am sure,' Dr Melchior said. 'Thank you.' His gratitude had a note of despair.

Maynard's confidence was not complete. 'I believe I have my Prime Minister's support…'

Clemenceau was on his feet in the conference chamber hammering his points with Gallic fervour. 'We must have retribution. We have suffered, our land has been raped, the flower of our youth killed. If we feed Germany, Germany must pay. To pay what she can afford is not a punishment. Germany must pay the full penalty, 26 billion, and must go on paying until her debt is honoured…' Maynard was listening with increasing despair and disgust, his hopes being destroyed. President Woodrow Wilson, was speaking. 'There is no question of allowing Germany to be released from paying pensions to discharged military and to their families, and to war widows, and to orphans…'

Lloyd George said, 'I must reluctantly agree with the President of the United States. We have previously held that there should be a time limit of, say, thirty years, for Germany to pay her reparations. I am not advocating 'an eye for an eye', but I believe we cannot envisage the sum of twenty-five billion being repaid within that period and that in this vital treaty we must leave open the length of time.'

Maynard put his head in his hands at this ultimate betrayal of his advice.

In the dining room at Charleston, Maynard banged his fist down on the Omega table. 'Politicians! They are the greatest frauds on earth.' He picked up a newspaper with a photograph of Lloyd George smiling and holding up a document with a headline LLOYD GEORGE PROMISES GERMANS WILL PAY. Vanessa (and nine-year-old Julian, who was listening with almost adult intensity) was no longer pregnant. She now had a daughter, Angelica, who was asleep upstairs in her cradle. Half the table was taken up with Maynard's battered typewriter and the first draft of *The Economic Consequences of the Peace*. On the other half Julian had been eating his tea.

'Oh, Vanessa, the amazing complications of psychology and intrigue and greed. Our Prime Minister gave in because he was afraid of being crucified in parliament.'

Julian interrupted him. 'I should have thought Lloyd George would have been on your side, Maynard.'

'Because you are innocent, as yet untouched by the wickedness of human life,' Maynard said. 'Yes, he was on my side but he wasn't prepared to be honourably driven from power by holding fast to what he knew was right. Which is why I resigned. Worn out by disappointment, rage and despair.'

'Is that what you've been writing all day?'

'Yes. Because unlike Lloyd George, your mother is good, loyal and true, and she gives me space on her beautiful table for my typewriter whenever I ask for it!'

'When will the world by told?' Vanessa said after a pause.

'Can't be soon enough,' he said.

Maynard moved the papers to one side. 'Have you damned everyone?' asked Vanessa.

'Everyone who deserves it.' There came the sound of Angelica crying upstairs as he spoke, and Vanessa lifted up her hand to listen.

Julian said, 'She's not going to stop, mummy.'

'No, I don't think she is. Clear your plate Julian and give Maynard more room.'

Julian sighed and took his plate and got down from the table, as Vanessa hurried out and Maynard continued to type furiously.

In the bedroom Vanessa lifted Angelica out of the crib and soothed her, and the crying gradually stopped. 'Was it a dream? Did you have a bad dream?' Bunny, passing the open door, paused and entered.

'How could anyone as young as Angelica have a bad dream.'

'Oh, I'm sure they do…'

'Just a device to be held in your arms.'

'Probably,' Vanessa said dotingly.

Bunny stood beside her and put his arm round her. 'Aren't you going to feed her?'

'I told you, it was a dream, not hunger. Anyway, I like to feed her alone. Just her and me, Bunny. Without you gawping at my breasts.'

He laughed. 'More than her daddy does!' He paused. 'Are you going to tell her that Duncan is her father?'

'One day I expect. But for now all the world thinks she's Clive's.'

Bunny put out a finger for Angelica to hold. 'You have the two most attractive parents in the world. I don't know which is the most desirable!'

Vanessa became irritated. 'Leave her alone and she'll go back to sleep.'

'Look…she likes me.' He addressed Angelica. 'You're getting more beautiful every day. If I can't persuade your mother to love me, I shall just have to wait for you to grow up.' Angelica clutched Bunny's finger and smiled up to him.

Maynard was typing again; he finished a page and took it out of the machine. Julian stood beside him, watching. 'May I read it?' Maynard picked up the page and handed it to him. Julian studied it for a moment and then read it out loud in a non-comprehending treble with occasional stumbling over words. While he read Vanessa re-entered the dining room and listened. 'Nothing can delay for long that final civil war between the forces of re-action and the despairing convulsions of revolution, before which the horrors of the late German war will fade to nothing, and which will destroy, whoever is the victor, the civilization and the progress of our generation.'

'Well?' said Maynard. Julian handed back the sheet of paper.

'I don't know what it means, really.'

'It means as sure as eggs are eggs we will have another war. It means that boys like you will have to fight another war when you grow up.' As he spoke Maynard's eyes met Vanessa's. She looked quickly away towards Julian, in a moment of terror struck by Maynard's words.

Chapter 5

The Girl's Gone Up The Spout

Virginia was printing, wearing a bright blue overall with a cardigan over it. Her hair was escaping in wisps and she was smoking as she worked, peering through steel-rimmed spectacles. On the wall was a calendar – December 12, 1919 – and on the table the printing press and a pile of books. She pulled the handle of the printing machine and Leonard entered the door, dripping with rain. He deposited a heavy, wet, brown parcel on the table, hung his raincoat, still dripping, on the back of the door, and extracted from it a book – *The Economic Consequences of the Peace*, by Maynard Keynes. He held it up.

'It's out. Wait till the government reads this one!' He slammed it down triumphantly on the table and Virginia snatched it up.

'We should have published it!'

'He didn't ask us! He paid for the printing himself, he was in such a rush to get it out. People were snatching it up like starving…'

Virginia smiled, 'Wolves!' She glanced towards the window as Lytton and Carrington's legs appeared walking briskly along the pavement, and then descended the area steps. Lytton held an umbrella over Carrington and he had Maynard's book under his arm. 'Here's Lytton and his shadow.' Still holding the book, she went to the door and let them in.

'Actually, you still owe me five shillings on my woodcuts,' said Carrington to Leonard. She picked up *Two Stories* by Virginia and opened it at the illustrations.

'Come into my sanctum and I'll pay you!'

Virginia said, 'Your woodcuts *sold* the book.'

'It was your story! I think it is wonderful.'

'Why is the girl so modest?' Lytton asked.

'Go on, Carrington, follow him into the larder! He'll open up the cash box for you.'

She followed Leonard into a small room off the main basement area. While they were gone Virginia and Lytton talked in low tones.

'Virginia, my dear, that woman dogs me. She won't let me write.'

'Ottoline says you'll end up marrying her,' Virginia said with a malicious glint in her eyes.

'God, the mere notion is enough. I will never marry anyone because you turned me down!'

Leonard's voice reached them. 'Two shillings, two and sixpence, three, four, five. There. Sign here…'

Virginia thought of Carrington, youthful, enthusiastic, her hair shining. 'I believe I'm sometimes jealous,' she said.

'Inconceivable!' Lytton replied.

'You don't like her better than me, do you, Lytton?'

'I like you better than anyone.'

'But you kissed her!'

'That was years ago.' He smiled. 'Everyone else was at the front. It was only because she looked like a boy!'

Carrington was sitting cross-legged on the bare floor in Mark Gertler's studio, hands around a mug of tea. He paced the room, full of nervous energy, his eyes burning with intensity, running his fingers through his shock of dark hair. There were finished and unfinished paintings around the room, and jars of brushes and bottles of turpentine were on the table covered with newspaper, together with a bottle of milk and a pot of tea under a knitted cosy.

'I need you, I want you, I love you passionately. I beg you, I implore you. Marry me or live with me.'

'Oh, Mark, you know how I feel!'

'Well, when?' He sighed. 'You always put me off. Next summer, next autumn, when it's winter…'

Carrington gave a little smile. 'In the spring.'

'Oh, for God's sake, I'm an artist. I need a woman like I need food…'

'Then find a 'woman' who'll do what you want. It can't be difficult.'

'You know I didn't mean…' Mark said, 'I love you, my work is stultifying. I suppose I'm not used to your type of woman…oh, that's insulting, isn't it! Lady. To your kind of *lady*. And I'm just an East End boy.'

She held out her cup. 'You're just being silly. Pour me another cup of tea. You know I care for you more than anyone else.'

Mark began to pour the tea, then set the cup down wildly, spilling it.

'More than Lytton Strachey? You're always traipsing about with Lytton Strachey.'

'Of course not!' Carrington giggled. 'He's a horrid old man with a beard. He kissed me.'

'He doesn't kiss *women*!'

'What are you talking about? I told you. He kissed me.'

Mark spoke deliberately. 'He kisses men, Carrington.'

She was genuinely innocent. 'I don't understand what you're trying to say.'

'H-O-M-O-S-E-X-U-A-L.' She looked blank. 'Like Oscar Wilde.'

'I never really understood about Oscar Wilde.'

He threw up his arms in a typically violent gesture. 'Then I shall have to tell you. I can't believe…oh well.' He pulled forward a chair and sat astride it, his arms on the back. She got up and finished pouring her mug of tea. 'The penetration is anal, not vaginal. It takes place between "gentlemen".' Carrington turned to look at him, her mouth open in amazement. 'Lytton Strachey is known for his sexual activities with members of his own sex. Which is why, even if he did kiss you, it was nothing but an experiment. He probably felt curious to know what it was like.'

She took this in, her eyes burnt with indignation growing into anger. 'I'm very glad you told me, Mark. I shall take my revenge.'

'Are you going to be like Delilah and cut off his hair?'

'Yes!' she gave a girlish shriek. 'His beard!'

In the studio Mark and Carrington were lying on the cushions among the paint pots and he went to kiss her.

'Don't, please. We've had such a lovely evening. Do you remember how lovely it was when we first met?'

'I'm more concerned with the present. I want you to stay here tonight.'

'Oh, you do keep on so.' Carrington sat up. 'Mark, Mark! I swear I love you. But not with my body!'

'I love you with all of me. What's wrong with making love. It's wonderful.'

'But it isn't to me,' Carrington replied guiltily. 'I just…well, I don't like nakedness. I'd kiss you. But you always seem to want more.'

'You let me "do more" once, didn't you?'

'It made me feel ashamed.'

Mark got up and walked across the studio and looked at a portrait of Carrington naked to the waist. 'You are so bloody beautiful.'

'I hate being a girl.' Carrington was anguished.

'Don't you find me attractive?'

'Lytton does.'

He was furious and frustrated. 'Huh! What draws you to that man?'

'He's kind and safe and clever and he doesn't ask me for anything and is just pleased with what I give. I can't understand what he's saying…and that is wonderful…' She gave a sudden giggle. 'And I love his knees!'

The orchard at Charleston was in full bloom and Carrington was bathing the blisters on Lytton's feet. His toes were in a tub of water and the manuscript of his new book was on his knees…the knees that Carrington loved so much. 'Oh Lytton darling, I don't know what "eminent" means. I know what "Victorian" is, of course,' she added quickly.

'It means remarkable and distinguished. But I use the word somewhat slyly. My "Eminent Victorians" will be revealed as people… What do you know about Florence Nightingale, Carrington?'

She paused. 'She was a good, kind, wonderful nurse…'

'Saint Florence Nightingale! The time has come to cut these idols down to human size.'

Duncan was lying asleep on the grass in the sunshine, shirt off. A little further away was an easel with Carrington's half-finished portrait of Lytton on it. Lytton re-arranged his pages and started to read; ' "The history of the Victorian age will never be written: we know too much about it. For ignorance is the first requisite of the historian – ignorance which simplifies and clarifies, which selects and omits, with a placid perfection unattainable by the highest art." '

Carrington looked at his heel. 'You really have got the most horrid blister... sorry... go on...'

' "It is not by the direct method of a scrupulous narration that the explorer of the past can hope to depict that singular epoch. If he is wise he will adopt a subtler strategy. He will attack his subject in unexpected places; he will fall upon the flank, or the rear..." '

She lunged forward and kissed Lytton's thigh. 'Only you're sitting on your rear...'

' "...he will shoot a sudden revealing searchlight into obscure recesses hitherto undivined!" ' He and Carrington both laughed at the double entendre.

'Go on, go on, it's important and it's serious and I want to hear.'

' "He will row out over the great ocean of material and lower down into it, here and there, a little bucket, which will bring up to the light of day some characteristic specimen, from those far depths, to be examined with careful curiosity. Guided by these considerations, I have written the ensuing studies. I have attempted through the medium of biography, to present some antediluvian Victorian...!" No!' He scored out a word and then backtracked, ' "...to present some Victorian visions to the modern eye." '

Carrington looked up sharply. 'Is that the end of it?'

He put down the manuscript. 'The end of all I intend to read to you today.'

She remained silent for a few minutes. Finally she said, 'I think it's all very masterly.'

'No, you don't. You are more concerned with my feet!' He took his feet out of the bowl.

'They can dry in the sun, can't they. I want to finish my painting before tea.' She paused. 'I will dry them for you if you want.'

'Do your worst with the brush. Capture my likeness.'

Vanessa and Grace came out of the house carrying laden trays. With them was Maynard, who wore a white floppy hat. Julian and Quentin followed.

'It will have to be after tea,' said Carrington who waved to Vanessa who was prodding Duncan with her foot.

'Wake up, you lazy thing.' Vanessa and Grace put the tea trays down on the ground, and Duncan stretched and smiled.

'Lytton's been reading us the new book.'

Lytton smiled at Maynard. 'And she pronounced it "very masterly"!' He nudged Duncan with his wet foot. 'An ill omen! Duncan slept through it all.'

Maynard sat down in the chair beside Lytton. 'I'm sure it is masterly!'

'Offer the bread and butter, Julian,' Vanessa said. She knelt to pour the tea, and handed the cups up to Grace who gave them to Carrington, Duncan and Maynard. Julian followed with the bread and butter and Quentin with the jam, spoon and plates.

'Are bare feet the latest Bloomsbury fashion?' asked Maynard.

'Carrington has been ministering! I am old, debilitated and floating. She has soothed my summer.'

Maynard smiled. 'Some of us have been thinking she should soothe your winter too.'

'Alas…Quentin, don't disappear with the jam… pecuniary shortcomings impel me to spend the winter with my parents and my sisters.'

'Those of us with less shortcomings propose to put twenty pounds apiece to allow you and Carrington to rent a country house.'

Carrington was beaming and it was clear from her expression she knew of the plot. Lytton was touched although he covered with his usual nonchalant manner. 'Generous of you, Maynard. I do find London more and more disagreeable in which to work. And Carrington wants to be in the country. So it appears on the whole to be a reasonable project.' He paused and then he said in a heartfelt voice 'Thank you, dear fellow.'

Carrington dropped her bread and butter on the grass and threw her arms round Maynard.

Mark and Lawrence sat in the shade on the terrace at Garsington. The peahens idly pecked for food and the peacock had spread his tail and was strutting between their chairs.

'She's incapable of real love. Like that dull little hen,' said Lawrence, pointing.

'But I adore her.'

'Like most women, she hates men. She hates the active maleness in a man. She wants passive maleness. Disgusting passive maleness. What Carrington probably wants is power – not love.'

Mark spoke desperately, 'I thought she loved me. When we were at art school…'

Lawrence leant forward. 'Can you not feel the repelling energy she sends from the body, Mark? By herself she can achieve nothing. She only wants a man to stand between her and all the others… she has the energy of *evil*.'

Mark jumped to his feet. 'Carrington? Evil?' He was almost hysterical. 'I think you're crazy, Lawrence. You sound like one of your own characters. I need help. I don't know what to do.'

Lytton and Carrington came out of number 38 Brunswick Square. It was night time and they walked along the pavement. 'So if I'm there before you,' Carrington said eagerly, 'I'll have had all the fires lit and I'll cook something lovely like a rabbit stew…'

Out of the shadows came a dark figure – the drunken Mark Gertler; he hurled himself on Lytton, giving a cry of hatred and rage and punching wildly with both fists. Lytton attempted to fend him off, made his own ineffectual punches while Carrington screamed. Maynard ran from the still open front door and grabbed Mark's arms from behind and Mark instantly collapsed, sobbing.

'I love her…' Overcome with remorse, Carrington stroked his face, and Maynard let him go. Lytton dabbed his split lip with a handkerchief.

She said, 'Don't be unhappy, it's the way things are… Mark… Mark…'

'I know you're living with him.'

Maynard turned to Lytton and said in a dry voice, 'You'd think it was a sin!' Lytton managed a painful smile.

The Bloomsbury-ites were all reading *Eminent Victorians*. In prison a warder heard laughter coming from one of the cells and he walked towards the sound. He looked in through the spyhole and there was Bertrand Russell roaring with laughter as he read.

Virginia was wearing glasses and reading by a poor light. Leonard lent over her shoulder and said, 'Come to bed!'

She looked up from the page. 'I don't find it altogether interesting but it will make Lytton famous.'

'And possibly rich. Stop reading now or you'll have a headache in the morning…' He took the book gently out of her hand and marked the page.

In Duncan's studio a screen concealed Lydia and Duncan stood by his easel on which there was a recognisable portrait of her in a costume from *Les Sylphides*. Maynard had Lytton's book in his hands. 'While you paint I shall continue to read. Is anyone the better, the kinder or wiser for a book that destroys the halo of at least three of England's heroes?'

Lydia stuck a leg out from behind the screen and waggled her foot. 'That's the Russian for *no*,' said Duncan.

'Biography will never be the same again.' Maynard was satisfied. 'And he's going to make so much money he'll be able to pay us back the rent!'

Lydia leapt out from behind the screen in a *grand jeté*, ending in the balletic pose of the portrait. Duncan picked up his brush and Maynard looked down at his book.

Lytton stood in the post office in the village of Tidmarsh where they had rented The Old Mill House. Carrington was waiting to be served, and while she waited she was reading *Eminent Victorians*. In front of her was a blimpish military type wearing tweeds. As he received his stamps he turned round and with his stick he made a jab at the book.

'The bounder who wrote it should be flogged. Book's only fit for the sewer.'

As she moved to the counter she managed to give him a blow in the stomach with the book and Lytton turned away, hiding a smile.

'Four penny stamps,' she said, very pleased.

Carrington was in the raspberry cages picking fruit which she dropped into a bowl. Through the mesh she saw Lytton ensconced in a rocking chair, a panama hat on his head, cutting out reviews from newspapers and magazines. She called out, 'You aren't feeling chilly, are you?'

Lytton smiled. 'I'm basking in the warmth of the book's reception.'

'I know, and I don't feel cold at all, but you're sitting still.'

Ralph Partridge, in Major's uniform, came round the corner of the house. He was large, powerfully built, with a high-coloured complexion and light blue eyes – about twenty-four. Lytton turned his head to see what had taken Carrington's attention and he sat bolt upright, smitten.

Ralph smiled, a little apologetically, and held out his hand towards Lytton. 'Sorry for bursting in unannounced like this. My name is Ralph Partridge. I've come to see Dora Carrington.'

Slowly Carrington emerged from the raspberry cage, still holding the bowl.

'You probably don't remember me. I'm an army friend of your brother's.'

'I remember you. This is Mr Lytton Strachey. I'm going to make a summer pudding. Why don't you stay for supper?'

'I'd love to,' said Ralph, 'if you're sure I'm not intruding.'

Lytton smiled. 'Not at all, dear boy.'

They were eating the summer pudding. Carrington poured cream over Lytton's and then passed the jug to Ralph. He was continuing an argument; 'No, I have no objection to being killed fairly and squarely and honestly by an enemy.'

'But,' Lytton asked, 'could you kill?'

'If the cause is right… yes.' Lytton rolled his eyes.

Ralph was chopping wood, strong muscles bulging and Lytton watched with a muffler round his neck. 'You're metal for the Olympics.' Ralph stopped, rested and smiled.

'Too lazy. Couldn't stand the hard work.'

'Oh! Imagine being fit enough to have the opportunity – and then to turn it down!'

Ralph swung the chopper again, split a log and spoke with amused self-mockery. 'Theme for a sad ballad, do you think.' He burst into song. 'Why am I not a rowing blue, eyes to match, and only twenty-two.' Although, of course, I'm twenty-four.'

Lytton, unwell, was sitting up in his single bed reading aloud to Carrington and Ralph. He was reading a Shakespeare sonnet. Ralph's eyes were drawn to Carrington whose eyes were feasting on Lytton. From time to time, at significant moments, Lytton glanced up at Ralph who was really not listening.

' "Crabbed age and youth cannot live together:
Youth is full of pleasure, age is full of care;
Youth like a summer morn, age like winter weather;
Youth like summer brave, age like winter bare." '

Carrington silently reached out for the pill bottle by the bed and put two in her hand, then replaced the bottle.

' "Youth is full of sport, age's breath is short;

Youth is nimble, age is lame;

Youth is hot and bold, age is weak and cold;

Youth is wild and age is tame" ' (Ralph watched Carrington's every move, adoringly.)

' "Age I do abhor thee; youth I do adore thee." ' (Lytton looked quickly at Ralph.)

' "O! my love, my love is young;

Age, I do defy; O! sweet shepherd, hie thee,

For methinks thou stay'st too long." '

Lytton put the book face downward on the bedclothes. Carrington handed him the pills and then poured him a glass of water from a jug with a muslin cover.

'I feel a hundred!' said Lytton.

'Don't let Shakespeare depress you,' said Carrington. 'Poor man, he must have suffered personally to have written anything so sad. He must have been deeply in love with someone very unfeeling. A horrible, unfeeling girl.'

'Or boy,' Lytton said. 'What do you think, Ralph?' He took the glass of water and swallowed the pills.

Ralph tore his eyes away from Carrington. 'About what?'

'I don't think Ralph was paying proper attention.' She took the glass from Lytton.

He said meaningfully, 'We'll educate you yet, Ralph Partridge.'

Carrington completely misunderstood. 'Yes, because next month you'll be working at the Hogarth Press with Virginia and Leonard – and they're very literary.'

Lytton smiled, amused and affectionate.

In the orchard at Mill House Carrington drew Ralph in the nude. He was lying in the grass in a muscle-flexing pose. 'I'm not doing very well. Your legs and thighs have got me in a flux.'

'Then for God's sake, marry me, Carrington. I'm madly in love with you.'

'Oh, Ralph, you know I won't leave Lytton.'

'Well, he's hardly going to marry you. Or desire you.'

'He gives me the most love anyone could want.'

Ralph held out his arms. 'No, he doesn't. Give in to the flux.' He smiled, slowly. 'Youth and youth, darling…'

She hesitated a moment longer, then put down her sketch book and went towards him. 'So you were listening, then!'

It was in the basement and Virginia's face peered through a window from the corridor leading to the Hogarth Press. Leonard, a spaniel seated near his feet, stood at the dresser totting up a sheet of figures. A distant telephone rang and stopped and Ralph – now an employee – was at a desk correcting galleys. Virginia opened the door and wandered in, ash dropping from her cigarette. 'Another telephone call to ask us if we're publishing *Ulysses*.'

'Perhaps you should have done so,' said Ralph.

Leonard looked up briefly. 'No.'

'Joyce is a queasy undergraduate scratching his pimples. Don't let any of this talk convince you otherwise,' said Virginia. She looked over Leonard's shoulder and said slightly jealously, 'I thought you were going to see Forster. I thought you couldn't be late.'

Leonard did not answer and continued to tot his figures. 'Twelve copies of the Katherine Mansfield, twelve of the Gorky at a discount of thirty-three per cent...take a look at this for me when you've a moment, Ralph. I can't seem to account for two and threepence halfpenny on the Bumpus sale...' He looked up at Virginia. 'I am. And I won't be late, Virginia.' He shuffled the paper together and as he did so, syncopated dance music began – faint but audible – from the hotel next door.

Virginia said, 'They must be tea-dancing in the hotel!'

Leonard put the spaniel on a lead and spoke to Virginia as he went out. 'I'll go into Dunhills for some tobacco on my way back.'

When he had gone she went over to the new Minerva printing press and completed setting a line. Suddenly she said to Ralph, 'Do you dance?'

He turned round from his galleys. 'Love it!'

Virginia gestured towards the wall and the music. 'That kind of dance?'

'Every kind of dance.'

She held up her hand. 'I see them circling, don't you? A kind of syncopated minuet.'

'The rhythm isn't compatible with circling.'

'No, I suppose not.' She listened. 'What would you call that?'

'The Big Apple.'

Virginia giggled wildly. 'Show me how it goes. Go on!'

Ralph pushed back his chair, pulled her towards him and launched himself into the dance. She followed clumsily and said breathlessly, 'It feels quite liberating!'

'It does rather.' He stopped.

'I shall think of you three at the Mill House, dancing the Big Apple.' She became carried away by the image – and typically spiteful. 'Lytton tea-dancing! Lapsong – in the thinnest china of course – steaming gently in his long fingers. If Carrington hasn't broken all the thin china by now!'

'Virginia! What am I going to do about Carrington. I'm so desperately in love.'

She turned and looked at him intently, her eyes bright for gossip. The music from the hotel stopped. 'I thought once Lytton went to Italy she'd make up her mind to marry me,' he said desperately. 'She says she objects to marriage in principle. She says I don't really belong to "her world".'

'Which of us does?' said Virginia.

'She is the most wonderful, extraordinary girl. Why won't she marry me? We're living together anyway. It won't affect her life.'

'Then why do you want her to?'

Ralph paused. 'Because I am tortured. I don't want to take her away from Lytton. We'll go down to the Mill House every weekend, it's more or less what we've been doing anyway. I can't go on like this.'

'You're in love with Carrington. Carrington is besotted by Lytton and Lytton's besotted by you. You care about him...' Virginia was firm '...so marry the girl at once. Give her the choice. Marry you. Or you'll go away for good.'

'But suppose she says go...'

'Then *go*!'

Ralph said helplessly, 'Go where?'

She said promptly 'Sheep farming in Bolivia!' Ralph gave a groan of anguish. 'Lytton doesn't want her for life, you know. Why do you think he's gone to Italy? To make the break. Can't you see he's nervous. Carrington's making claims.'

'Did Lytton tell you that?' Ralph sensed a glimmer of hope.

'Lytton doesn't have to tell me anything. It's a wonder to everyone that he's put up with her for all this time. I mean, what on earth can they find to do when they're alone.' Virginia smiled. 'Maybe you'll be best out of it, too.' She paused. 'Life in Bolivia is said to be very bracing.'

Sitting in leather chairs in Morgan's club, Leonard leant forward and said, 'You must go back to India, Morgan. You must accept the opportunity.'

'Mother doesn't want to go, needless to say.'

'Virginia and I want to publish that Indian novel. You know in what esteem she holds you.' Leonard leant forward. 'Your criticisms of her work matter more to her than anyone else's.'

'I may not be given time off from my official duties…' Morgan gave a sigh. 'I've got to dine with my Aunt Roselie in Putney…' He heaved himself out of the chair.

'You have to catch the English rule as it is,' said Leonard. 'Whatever they say, it won't go on forever. But the relationships, the meeting of cultures…there's more sociology in novels than text books. More in *War and Peace* about the Russian social order than in…' Leonard stood, too. 'You are going to go, aren't you? To India, not your aunt!'

'I shouldn't be sorry to leave Weybridge, mother and the aunts are already fussing.' He smiled. 'You have enthused me, Leonard.'

'India! I envy you! Then I hope you have a smooth passage…and of course to Putney…'

Virginia sat back in her chair. She had been listening to Leonard's account of the meeting. She paused before she spoke. 'Well, it won't be easy for him to come back from India to that ugly old house in Weybridge and that exacting mother.' She paused. 'The middle-age of buggers is not to be contemplated without horror. Even Lytton…'

In a café among workmen tucking into steak pie and two vegs Ralph and Carrington sat with mugs of tea. Ralph looked haggard and tired – he had not slept – and Carrington was guilty and concerned. Ralph spoke in a flat unnatural voice, 'I know you are not in love with me. But I think your affections are strong enough to make me happy.' Carrington put her hand on his arm. He went on, 'I cannot, I absolutely cannot go on any longer in the uncertainty and pain. If you really will not marry me, if you cannot come to that decision, I will go away.'

Carrington gasped. 'But not forever?'

'I will have to begin a life somewhere else. Start again in another country. I think you should hear what Virginia told me. Lytton is frightened you will become dependent on him. He wants to break the pattern.'

She was shocked. 'A permanent limpet? Oh Ralph, I never...' Two workmen with huge beer bellies pressed past them.

'You can't marry Lytton, Carrington.'

'I know,' she whispered.

'He will never want you physically.'

'Oh, I know...'

'He will be happy and relieved to know you are going to marry me.'

'Relieved!' The idea sank in. Tears rolled down her face. 'My poor darling Lytton. I will marry you, Ralph. I will!'

Carrington lay in bed awake and at her side Ralph, happy at last, slept. She got out of bed, covered Ralph carefully and tiptoed out of the room. Bare-foot, she went down the stairs, pausing anxiously, then went into the kitchen and sat at the table. She opened the drawer and drew out a pencil and paper kept for recipes. There were plates of uncovered food on the table and the sink was full of unwashed dishes. She was writing to Lytton.

"Darling," she wrote. "All these years I have known my life with you was limited. I could never hope for it to become permanent. After all, you are the only person whom I have ever had an absorbing passion for. I shall never have another. I know we'll be better friends, if you aren't haunted by the idea that I'm sitting depressed in some corner of the world waiting for your footsteps. So in that vile city of Reading I said I'd marry Ralph." Carrington was aware that there were tears pouring down her face. "You never knew or ever will know the very big and devastating love I have for you..."

It was at a street café in Florence that Lytton sat alone reading the letter from Carrington. The envelope was open by the plate where he had just finished eating zambocco. "Say that you'll forgive me for this outburst and always be my friend..."

A handsome young man in tight white trousers and a shirt split to the waist approached and saw Lytton and smiled. "Say that you'll forgive me for this outburst and that you'll always be my friend. Ralph is such a dear, I don't feel I'll regret marrying him. Though I will never change my maiden name that I have kept so long..."

The young man put his hand on Lytton's shoulder and he looked up, startled. It took him a moment to recognise him. Lytton could hear

Carrington's voice. '...so you mayn't ever call me another name but Carrington!'

Lytton got up and smiled – although not with his eyes. He paid for his meal, and the young man put his arm round Lytton's shoulders.

Lytton was walking up the path to the Mill House and Carrington burst out of the front door followed by Ralph. Lytton took Carrington in his arms and Ralph put his hand on Lytton's shoulder – it was a moment of incredibly tender friendship. Then Ralph went to the gate and picked up Lytton's suitcases covered with foreign labels and they all three went together into the house.

T.S. Eliot was staying at Monks House, the Woolfs' Sussex home. They were going for a walk to the river and Virginia, Leonard, a spaniel and Tom passed a cemetery that lay between their garden and the river. Tom was pale, fine-boned, with bright eyes under hooded lids. His hair was slicked back, he had a folded handkerchief in his top pocked and a very slight American accent.

'If you don't walk after Sunday lunch you sleep,' Leonard said.

'You've been here long enough now, Tom, to talk about the new poems!' said Virginia.

'If he wants to keep them to himself you must give him the privilege.' Leonard turned to Tom. 'She has the metaphorical pin to prise the winkle out of its shell.'

'I don't mind talking. You're going to publish them.'

'Well, do it!' Virginia told him.

Tom had a slow smile and a slow drawl. 'I had a kind of personal upheaval after writing Prufrock. I want to disturb externals. I really want to do a verse play. I want to take four characters from the Sweeney poems. In fact, I have to ask Leonard...' He looked round and Leonard's head and shoulders were the only things that were visible. He was urinating in the bushes and Tom hastily looked away. Virginia waited and Leonard came out of the bushes and joined them.

'Tom was about to ask you something. And you were gone!'

Tom was staring straight ahead and deeply embarrassed. 'Don't look so shocked,' Leonard said, 'I was only relieving myself. We all do it!'

'In privacy.'

'We could only see his head!' Virginia smiled.

'I couldn't possibly have done what you did.'

'Because you are a well-brought-up American. You shouldn't let convention bind you.'

'I can't shave in the presence of my wife.'

Virginia was fascinated and amazed. 'No wonder you work in a bank!' she said.

Leonard, Virginia and Tom were sitting around the table at the Hogarth Press discussing the forthcoming publication of *The Waste Land*. The proofs were spread out and Leonard had a copy of the American edition in front of him.

'Oh, your format is better. I like the size and quality of the paper.'

Leonard nodded. 'As a matter of fact I'm pleased with it myself. I got it at an excellent discount. How many copies do you think we should print?'

Tom tapped the American edition in front of him. 'They had a run of a thousand for each of the two editions.'

Virginia made a face. 'And about the same number of misprints.'

'I guess I don't spend enough time proof reading.' He gave a rueful smile.

'We all think you should spend time on matters pertaining to your creative work!' said Virginia.

'Man cannot live by verse… at least, unknown poets can't.'

Leonard met Virginia's eye, a difficult moment. 'I don't want you to take this amiss. As your publisher you can say I have a vested interest. It is not a charity…'

'What Leo is trying to say is that we've organised a fund to release you from the bank.'

Tom froze with discomfort. Leonard said, 'Three hundred a year to give you freedom to write.'

There was a long awkward silence and Tom looked out of the window. 'Does it carry with it the moral obligation to leave the bank?'

'That is its purpose.'

'I couldn't possibly consider leaving the bank for under five hundred pounds a year.'

Lytton was dressed as Virginia in a blue overall, a wispy wig, steel-rimmed spectacles and holding a drooping hand-rolled cigarette six inches long.

He looked about him in a bewildered manner. There was applause and laughter in the drawing room at Gordon Square as Ottoline, in an extravagant party dress, made an announcement. 'So allow me to present, ladies and gentlemen, the first performance of... Much Ado About the Hogarth Press!'

As she finished Lytton-as-Virginia moved centre stage and Virginia, in a silk dress with beads and brooches, hooted with laughter. The audience sat on chairs, on the floor (and on each other) in a haze of cigarette and cigar smoke. Clive poured refills of white wine into glasses held out to him. Lytton-as-Virginia spoke. 'We should have published Maynard!'

Maynard, with hair combed like Leonard's, carried a stack of papers and a toy spaniel, and Ralph joined Lytton-as-Virginia on stage. Lydia, clapping her hands delightedly, called out, 'Maynard! *Ya lublu*! I love you.'

Saxon Sydney-Turner, Vanessa, Ottoline – now seated by Philip Morell – Bunny, Duncan, Roger, Adrian, Karen and Mrs Raven Hill were among the audience.

'I'm pleased to say,' Maynard-as-Leonard spoke, 'I got a very good discount on this paper.' He paused and took out his pipe and juggled with the paper and the toy spaniel. 'My work is appallingly heavy,' he paused, 'only one interesting letter from Freud.' He tried to light his pipe. 'I may as well divide up the profits for the last five years.'

Lytton-as-Virginia pushed Ralph in front of her, a line-up of two, with outstretched hands. 'Ralph, here is three and sevenpence for you. I am deducting ninepence you will argue... argue...'

Leonard laughed delightedly as Carrington ran onto the stage area wearing overalls. The four of them came together and sang to the tune of "Widdicombe Fair",

"Imagine yourself in the Hogarth Press
All along, out along, down along, lea;
Where paramours, poets and printers digress
With Virginia, Lytton Strachey,
Dora Carrington, Ralph Partridge
And old Uncle Leonard and all
And old Uncle Leonard and all..."

The chauffeur opened the door of the Rolls Royce for Vita Sackville-West and her husband, Harold Nicholson. They walked towards the front door. Vita was dark, handsome, full-bosomed and wore a long flowing cape. Harold was about the same height, round-faced and with a moustache. The front door opened, the light fell upon the step and laughter and applause from within. Grace, having hung up Vita's cape, knocked on the drawing-room door and Harold and Vita walked in. Maynard-as-Leonard said to Lytton-as-Virginia, 'Whatever you do, do it quickly, before the aristocratic Rita Sackcloth East gives you another novel.' The audience recognised Vita and applauded her perfectly timed entrance. The actors bowed and Vita made a flourishing bow in return.

Leonard was muttering over a ledger, Ralph poured tea into an assortment of cheap white cups and Virginia was painstakingly leaning over the printing press. Vita entered and they all looked up. She wore boots, cape and a scarlet sombrero and she swept between the desk and the table.

'I'm not going to disturb you.' Her cape brushed papers off the desk as she sailed over to Virginia. 'In spite of the wicked sketch, I've just come to have a word with Mrs Woolf about the new book.' Virginia's eyes lit up and Vita held out her hands. Virginia hesitated, then allowed her outstretched hands to be taken.

Duncan and Vanessa were sitting at the table, breakfast over. Both were wearing espadrilles and Vanessa a painting smock. 'Virginia has always had these sapphist tendencies,' Vanessa said. 'Clive believes that's why she turned him down. He's never got over being rejected!'

'What do you think about Mrs Harold Nicholson?'

'I don't think she could ever be Bloomsbury. She's too… overpowering.'

Maynard, in dressing gown and slippers, came through the open door. 'God, don't tell me breakfast's over.'

'In this house nothing is ever over,' Duncan said. 'We're analysing Virginia Woolf!'

Vanessa got up, took two eggs from a bowl and put them on to boil. 'I didn't even hear you arrive last night.'

'I'm going to marry Lydia,' Maynard said. Duncan and Vanessa looked at him simultaneously.

'Oh… *don't!*' Vanessa was horrified.

'But I have every intention of it!'

'But she's so frivolous.'

'And she talks of ballet…'

Vanessa said wryly, 'She'll be a very expensive wife. She's frightfully extravagant. She'll make you poor.' Maynard laughed.

Clive and Angelica passed the window and came in. Angelica was about six and was treated by Clive as his daughter. She carried a small basket of mushrooms. 'Daddy and I had breakfast hours ago. We've been mushrooming.'

Clive poured himself a cup of tea and sat down and Angelica showed the mushrooms to Maynard and Duncan.

Vanessa gave a sigh. 'Maynard says he's going to marry Lydia.'

'Good God,' exclaimed Clive. 'Think about it, think about it.'

'Do you really think you would be happy,' Duncan said, 'tied to one person…'

'Do you mean to one woman?'

'We all know each other so well there's no need for this kind… the point is, Maynard, we have a very intimate society and bringing in a new partner will alter it, inevitably.'

'Because you are all happy and settled in your ways it is not going to stop me from making my own life happier,' Maynard replied. 'Anyway, Lydia is almost one of us already. You all like her.'

'We all like her as your mistress. If that is what she is,' Vanessa said.

'Duncan liked her enough to paint her.'

'A painting she has removed from this house – and kept!'

' "Oh, come along, Nessa." ' Maynard imitated a Russian accent with affectionate accuracy.' "Vanessa gave me drawing of me. I look like Scotch whirlwind so much activity and not only the legs – everywhere!" '

'I did not give it to her. She asked if she could borrow it.'

Maynard said, 'It has been insured by me and is on my bathroom wall.' He paused. 'And my eggs will be like stones!' Vanessa rushed to the pan which had almost boiled dry and spooned out the eggs. Angelica decorated the plates with some mushrooms.

'Of course you must marry her if you are sure it is what you want. But just remember Carrington and Ralph's disaster,' Clive said, 'he rushed into matrimony. And now he's in love with someone else!'

Outside the window of Lytton's bedroom it was a winter's morning. The fire was lit, and Lytton, dressed, lay on the bed, books and papers around him. Carrington leant over the foot of the bed gazing at him in anguish.

'I don't know quite how we'll manage about chopping wood,' Carrington said, 'Don't abandon us altogether.'

Ralph turned to face them. 'I'm not abandoning you. Just admit it, Carrington. We can live as brother and sister but not as husband and wife. I cannot be married to a woman who really loves somebody else.' He paused. 'I'm sorry, Lytton. We didn't tell you before because we thought we could sort it out for ourselves.'

'I have not been unaware that your affections have been elsewhere.'

'I told you!' said Carrington.

'So, as a matter of fact, have Carrington's,' said Ralph.

'And so, as a matter of fact, have mine,' said Lytton. 'But that is the way we function together.'

Carrington spoke with passion. 'Like a starfish, all those tentacly bits shooting out. It's in the middle we matter.'

Ralph said, 'Frances matters to me. If you're trying to dismiss her as a tentacle, just remember I intend to live with her. The trouble with you is you've always wanted your own way and that has to be different to everyone else's.'

'So have you always wanted your own way,' Carrington spoke sullenly.

There was a long pause, then Lytton replied calmly, 'I'm afraid that on our own Carrington and I will be constantly exposed to all manner of domestic disasters.'

She gave a wail. 'I told you. If you go, Lytton will leave me, too!' She burst into tears and Ralph, after a moment's hesitation, went across and put his arm round her.

'We can't exactly set up as a *ménage à quatre*, can we?' He spoke gently.

Lytton looked horrified. 'No…that wouldn't do…'

'You see, you see. I'm going to be left alone on my own.' cried Carrington. 'He won't want me, or the house…our lovely, lovely house…' Ralph looked over Carrington's head at Lytton and in Lytton's eyes too there was a sense of despair.

'I don't want to desert. I'm perfectly prepared to spend every weekend here. Frances understands, it's Carrington who won't see sense…'

Lytton had a look of relief on his face. 'I don't see why we shouldn't manage rather well.' Ralph released Carrington, gave a sigh of relief and ran his hand through his hair. She smiled rapturously through her tears and gave a half laugh, half sob.

It was dusk and Ralph and Lytton at the dining-room window watched Carrington running hysterically round the garden, leaping across flower beds and over a pile of chopped logs. As she passed she waved wildly. 'I would never have left her,' said Lytton, 'The girl's gone up the spout!'

Virginia's room was a glorified shed in the Monks House garden. She was writing and simultaneously a gramophone record was playing in the house – the *Cavatina* from Beethoven's *B Flat Quartet*. Leonard came out and went across to the garden room, the spaniel at his heels. Music poured from the open window, Leonard opened the door and went in, followed by the dog. Virginia had a board on her knee, and the board held an inkwell. There were books and a sofa and a dog basket and Virginia looked up. 'Now that's the music I want you to have played at my funeral, Leo. You know I detest hymns.'

'It's time you came in, darling. The air is quite damp.'

'I'm putting Vita in my diary! Close the door. Listen.'

Leonard smiled and closed the door and leant against it and Virginia began to read. ' "Vita Sackville-West has the subtle ease of the aristocracy but not the wit of the artist. She writes fifteen pages a day." ' She looked at Leonard. 'Fifteen pages a day! And I take seven years to write a book.'

'And it shows in both your work!'

Virginia smiled maliciously.

In country tweeds, hat and pearls Vita was buying biscuits from a display arranged in glass-lidded tins in front of the counter. The grocer, in a brown overall – red-faced, jovial yet deferential in manner – weighed her selection on scales with brass weights. The two Nicholson boys, aged seven and ten, were larking about almost knocking over a pile of canned fruit. Vita turned sharply and spoke irritably to them and gestured towards the shop window. Harold and Leonard were in conversation outside and Virginia loped round the shop and peered into a jar of aniseed balls. She was trying to think what she could write about Vita – "she shines in the grocer's shop with a candle-lit radiance, stalking on legs like beech trees, pink, glowing, grape-clustered, pearl-hung. What is the effect of all this on me? There is her maturity and full-breastedness, her capacity to control silver, servants and chow dogs; her motherhood – but she is a little cold and off-hand with her boys – her being, in short, what I have never been, a real woman." '

The grocer showed Vita and Virginia and the boys out of the shop. Leonard and Harold were waiting with their dogs and Harold said, 'Oh, the FO's not concerned about Mussolini particularly.'

The grocer gave a semi-bow. 'I'll send it all up with the boy this afternoon, madam.'

'It's time for luncheon. Come on boys, stop mucking about.' They all set off on the road to their houses.

'I've promised Leonard we'll mate the dogs and give them a puppy,' said Harold.

'What do you think? Shall we have one?' Leonard asked Virginia.

Virginia said coyly, 'The Woolfs and Nicholsons will be forever linked. Their dogs will correspond.'

Virginia and Vita were walking ahead and talking intimately about their husbands. 'It isn't the doctors who have kept me out of the asylum, but Leo. I couldn't have survived without him.'

'Oh, Harold and I have absolute understanding. Absolute understanding between a man and a woman. But it can never be that total understanding achieved between women. Don't you agree?'

'I am very close to my sister...' Virginia said.

'I'm not talking about sisters,' Vita spoke firmly, 'I don't have any – only child – but the relationship would preclude the kind of friendship I'm talking about.' There was a thrill in her voice. 'A friendship between two women is so secret and private compared with men. Don't you agree?' She linked her arm through Virginia's, walking her forward so that the men were left behind.

Wearing a yellow silk dressing gown, Lytton lay on his bed looking frail and pale. Carrington was bathing his forehead with cologne.

'That is immensely soothing.' Lytton paused. 'All the bird books and flower books are yours.'

'Why?' She put down the bottle of cologne and looked frightened.

'Because you enjoy them. After I am dead it would be important.'

'All my pictures and objects are yours after I am dead,' she said defiantly. 'Anyway, I think it's stupid to talk about dying. You've just got colitis. Both doctors say so.'

'I know. I am getting better.' He smiled comfortingly at Carrington. 'I feel quite well again this morning. Just a temporary sinking back into buzzing ineptitude. I'm afraid my health is becoming the Grand Bore of Christendom.'

She cheered up a little. 'Then perhaps you should go into a monastery.'

'What a splendid notion! But you'd be jealous of the monks... wouldn't you?'

'Oh, Lytton...' She hugged him.

Leonard and Virginia were walking up the path to the front door of the Mill House and Carrington in breeches and sweater, opened it. The hall was low-ceilinged and white-panelled and her picture of the Mill House was on one wall and her portrait of Lytton was on another. Before they could speak Carrington burst into tears and she said, 'You can't see him!'

Ralph came from a room opening onto the hall and Virginia closed the front door.

'We heard he was better,' Leonard said.

Ralph paused. 'He is, a little.'

Virginia embraced her. 'Then you mustn't cry!'

'He can't eat. Oh, God...he can't eat...'

'You really mustn't give way like this. It certainly won't help Lytton recover and you'll end up ill yourself,' said Leonard.

Ralph said, 'That's what I keep telling her.'

'I'd lend you a handkerchief but I've got a cold.' Virginia gave a little smile. 'We both have. We've run out. We've been using *newspapers*.'

Carrington gave a weak smile. 'I've got one...' she fished in her jersey sleeve and eventually found one and blew her nose. 'I'm sorry. What a greeting. When you've come all this way.'

'Well, we'll come back again. I've brought him a copy of *The Waves*. I don't know if you've heard about it, my latest novel.' She gave it to Carrington who took it.

'I'll take it up now in case he's awake. Oh, Virginia if he dies...' She broke down again.

Ralph said firmly, 'He's not going to die. It's bad colitis, that's all. We've had a second opinion.' Carrington shook her head and mopped her eyes. When they reached Lytton's room she opened the door, Virginia's book in her hand. Lytton was lying asleep, his beard combed over the sheet, his complexion alabaster. Virginia and Leonard looked at one another and Carrington tiptoed in and put the book beside the bed.

In the kitchen the large nurse was preparing a tray for Lytton – medicine bottle, spoon, milky drink – amongst Carrington's chaos. She picked up a tea cloth between finger and thumb and dropped it in the sink, poking it down into soapy washing water with the handle of a wooden spoon. Then she picked up the tray and walked out straight into Lytton's bedroom. He was propped up against his pillows with a pencil and paper, managing to write. The nurse put down the tray and took the paper away as she spoke. 'Now then, what are you doing?'

'Attempting to write a poem.'

The nurse poured a spoonful of black medicine and held it under his nose. 'If there's any poetry to be written in this house, I'll write it.' Lytton's mouth dropped open, half amused, half annoyed. She put the spoon into it. 'What's more, I've been reading your *Eminent Victorians*, Mr Strachey. If I'd known your opinions of Florence Nightingale I'm not sure I'd have taken the job.' She removed the spoon as Carrington came in. Lytton gulped and swallowed.

'I've come to read to you.' The nurse gave Carrington a disapproving look and went out.

'Just sit with me. I don't need to be read to. I just lie here and think about literature. All morning I thought about Shelley.'

'I know I don't read very well. But you haven't even begun Virginia's new book. What are you going to tell her when she comes to see you?'

Lytton gave a mock groan and Carrington took it off the pile of books. 'I haven't had the courage to dive into the waves!' Carrington smiled, then laughed and Lytton put his hand over hers. 'But I have been reading Leonard's book *After the Deluge*.'

They laughed together. 'Oh, Lytton! Was it a little dry?'

There was a huddle of three black-jacketed doctors in the middle of the dining room. They were looking distinguished and important and Ralph and Carrington stood together anxiously. The first doctor said, 'On the plus side, Mr Partridge, heart and lungs and pulse are doing well.'

'Come on, what's the prognosis? I feel I'm back in the trenches.'

The second doctor paused and then spoke. 'We feel confident that the original diagnosis was wrong. Mr Strachey has paratyphoid. The main risk is perforation and the danger period could be as lengthy as the illness itself. The critical stage gives no warning of its approach, I'm afraid.'

'But you don't think we should give up hope,' Ralph said.

Carrington was tearful and fierce. 'Of course we aren't giving up hope. You don't think Lytton is going to be defeated, do you?'

The doctors were moving towards the door. The first doctor shook hands with Ralph. 'It's a case of whether he can withstand the prolonged high fever...'

The third doctor said to Carrington, 'I understand your feelings. I'd quite dote on that chap myself if I saw much of him!'

Carrington sat by the bed and held Lytton's hand. He was delirious and his mouth formed some unheard words. She put her head close and he whispered, 'I always wanted to marry Carrington and I never did.' She cried silently.

The microphone at Broadcasting House was on the table and behind it sat Virginia. She was reading from a sheaf of closely written pages, nervous and breathless and rather dressed up for the occasion. 'Even words that are hundreds of years old have this power; when they are new they have it so strongly that they deafen us with the writer's meaning...'

Carrington was curled up in an armchair by the wireless, and Virginia's voice was distorted. '... and it is them we see, them we hear. That is why our judgement of living writers is wildly erratic.' Ralph appeared in the doorway behind her and she turned to look at him, horror in her eyes. He held out his hand to her and together they went up to Lytton's bedroom. He was lying in the bed, his eyes tightly shut and a nurse beside him. His eyelids suddenly snapped open and he looked straight at them. 'If this is dying, I don't think much of it.'

He became still and stopped breathing and Carrington collapsed on him. There were a few moments and then Ralph closed Lytton's eyes. In the sitting room the radio played to an empty chair. 'Only after a writer is dead,' Virginia's voice said, 'do his words to some extent become disinfected, purified of the accidents of the living body.'

It was evening and Virginia and Leonard were getting out of the Singer car. A plume of dark smoke rose from behind the hedge of the Mill House and Virginia looked anxiously at Leonard and hurried through the gate. He followed. There was a raging bonfire and Carrington was putting Lytton's pyjamas and then his spectacles into the flames. Silent tears were running down her face. Virginia froze, horrified, and then moved forward to stop her. Leonard put his hand on her arm. 'She needs to do it,' he whispered. Lytton's spectacle frames twisted, red-hot, and fell into the embers.

Lytton's bed was neatly made, the cover pulled up. Everything was in its place and Virginia's copy of *The Waves* lay on the table as before. She picked it up and opened it. The pages were tight and clearly unread and she cracked the spine and put it down. Carrington sat hunched in a chair wearing Lytton's yellow-silk dressing gown and Virginia walked over to the window and stood with her back to it, still huddled in her coat.

'If I could just sit here alone,' said Carrington, 'holding his clothes in my arms I would feel better.'

'He wouldn't have approved.'

'I know my feelings are bad. But they are my feelings. I can't help it. There's no one to talk to.'

Virginia paused. 'You have so many friends. You and Lytton.'

'No one else has ever mattered. No one else has ever understood him.'

'You weren't ever lovers, were you?'

Carrington turned her head away. 'He was more completely all my life than it is possible for any person to be.' Virginia was moved by compassion and shame at her interest. Carrington got up and took a book from the bedside table. 'I don't read very well. Lytton sometimes made me read to him but I liked to listen to him.' She coughed and began reading a poem.

'The spring is past and yet it has not sprung;
The fruit is dead, and yet the leaves are green;
My youth is gone, and yet I am but young;
I saw the world, and yet I was not seen;
My thread is out, and yet it is not spun;
And now I live and now my life is done.'

She finished and her arm dropped to her lap, still holding the book. Virginia put her arms round her, stooping in an ungainly way.

'Your life isn't done. You have so much ahead of you.'

Carrington moved out of Virginia's awkward embrace. 'I want to be left alone,' she said.

'I don't think you should be alone.'

'There's nothing left for me to do.' Carrington burst out crying. 'I did everything for Lytton. But I've failed in everything else. People say he was selfish to me. But I hated my mother. He was like a father to me. He taught me everything I know. He read French to me.' She controlled her tears. 'What will I do?' She gave a long pause and then she whispered, 'Should I do it, Virginia?'

She didn't answer and they looked into one another's eyes. A tentative knock at the door broke the spell. There was a moment before Leonard came in and he said kindly to Carrington, 'I see you've been gardening. All ready for spring.'

Carrington and Virginia looked at one another and Virginia said, 'I've asked her to come and see us in a few days.'

'Good. Will you come? Or not? Just as you like.'

'Yes. I will come.' She paused. 'Or not.' Leonard and Virginia pressed her hands and left.

Carrington looked at herself in the wardrobe mirror and slowly opened the wardrobe door. She took out a shotgun and positioned the barrel against her side.

Chapter 6
Before Lunch... Or After

In Lytton's bedroom Carrington looked at herself in the wardrobe mirror. She was wearing Lytton's yellow-silk dressing gown and the shotgun barrel pressed into the side near to her heart. The shot rang out and she fell. Blood oozed through the dressing gown and seeped into the sheet she had spread over the rug. Ralph and Bunny rushed into the room. They stood over Carrington and Ralph at last whispered, 'She's dead.'

There was a piece of paper lying on Lytton's bed and, with tears pouring down his face, Ralph took it. He could hear Carrington's voice. 'I hope you will marry and have children. Put my ashes next to Lytton's...under the laurels.'

Leonard held a letter in his hand as he and Virginia walked by the pond. Virginia stopped and looked at the water. 'All that gardening.' She spoke with horror. 'She was preparing her grave.'

'We must have been the last of her friends to see her that day.'

Virginia stared into the pond. 'She knew. She knew what she was going to do.'

Leonard looked straight at her. 'Virginia...did you?'

She paused. 'I wondered. The house was so cold.' She sat down beside him. 'She was like some small animal left behind.' She paused again. 'She was right to do it.'

'To make her own end? I don't know. Lytton died of cancer, but Carrington...'

'Carrington died of invisible wounds.'

'Of a very visible wound. She blew half her side out.'

'She died when Lytton died,' said Virginia. 'She was a part of him. In a way Lytton was to blame. He took her over.'

Leonard paused. 'She wanted to be 'taken over'.'

'There are no such things as spells.'

He was half laughing. 'Ask Freud. These things are not imposed, they're self-generated.'

'I know about spells, Leonard. Vita put a spell on me!'

A dove-grey Daimler Landaulette could be seen approaching Knole. Vita and Virginia were in the open rear portion of the car both wearing big hats and Virginia's hat and coat were in black astrakhan. She was gesticulating excitedly.

'Oh, the oaks, Vita! Fourteenth century? Fifteenth? The roots must go down into the heart of England. Who planted them? The first Lord Sackville?'

'Earlier!'

'Earlier than the first Lord Sackville? Who then? Who owned the house before your ancestors? Why is it called Knole?'

'On a grassy knoll. Of course, of course. The marvellous simplicity of the English language.' She giggled.

The car came to a standstill outside the north west front and the chauffeur, in grey uniform with peaked cap and gaiters, descended and opened the door for Vita and Virginia. Virginia looked all around her, enraptured, and flung her arms wide. 'My dear! An enchanted place! I am under its spell!'

Vita and Virginia and two chow dogs were running in the park. Virginia leant breathless against a massive tree trunk.

'As a child? Did you play extraordinary solitary games?'

'Rough, dirty games,' Vita said. To the dog she said, 'Get down!'

'But did you play alone? I see you alone, Vita…like a Kentish gypsy. Wild and imaginative, your dark hair marvellously tangled…' She laughed as she spoke.

'I was lean, plain, unsociable and unattractive. My mother despaired. I terrorised the neighbouring children and wept because I wasn't allowed trousers. I carried a pocket knife.' Vita tussled with one of her dogs over a stick and, having won, threw it. Virginia watched her, entranced.

'We were such pale fair children. They said in Cornwall that we looked as if we had been 'grawed i' the lewth.''

'What the hell is lewth?'

'Dark. As if we had been raised in the dark!'

Vita came close to her and looked intently into her eyes. 'Dark?' she paused. 'Virginia – you are all light!'

Vita was taking Virginia on a historical tour of Knole. In the portrait gallery Vita said, 'Thomas Sackville, first Earl.'

'Looks like you!'

'Robert Sackville, second Earl! And that is a portrait of Chaucer! Oh, my dear, don't miss Jane Seymour…and my Spanish gipsy grandmother and my beautiful illegitimate mother, glorious Gloria…who really didn't care for me very much!'

Virginia looked at her, amazed. 'Not care for you…? How could she not care for *you*…?'

Vita laughed breathlessly. 'Lionel Sackville, seventh Earl. Heraclitus. Democritus…'

They ended up in the old billiard room. 'And you end up taking it all for granted,' said Virginia. 'Your unquestioned birthright! To think that Leonard and I couldn't afford a bathroom in Monks House until last month! A triumph! My American book sales bought us a bath.'

'I see you rising from the soap suds like Venus from the foam.'

Virginia was startled. She blushed and moved quickly to look out of the window and giggled. Then turned back to face Vita who picked up a billiard cue and thrust it toward Virginia like a sword.

'Circa Charles the First!'

'Did he play billiards well?'

'Not as well as I do!' Vita spun round on her heel to face the antique billiard table and placed her cue. 'Do you?' There was an unmistakable tone of arch flirtatiousness.

'I only play word games.'

Vita hit the ball and the ball gently struck another. 'A move known as The Kiss, Virginia.' She put down her cue and Virginia shrunk away. Then she relaxed and took a step towards Vita and Vita took a step toward Virginia. Their eyes were locked. 'So do I play games. Both verbal…and physical,' said Vita.

Vita was kissing Virginia. She was sitting in an armchair and leaning forward and cupping Virginia's face; Virginia sat on the floor beside a blazing fire and on the table behind her were framed photographs of Harold and the boys.

'Why doesn't he resent me?' asked Virginia.

'He understands. Leonard understands, doesn't he? Why else would he have gone to London so conveniently for two days?'

'But Leonard and I...'

Vita stood up and said, 'Relationships are the only things that matter. Yours and Leonard's. Harold's and mine.' She paused. 'Yours and mine.' She took down a rapier from the wall and took up a swashbuckling posture.

'Perhaps no relationship should last more than five years.' Virginia dodged her head as Vita made a mock thrust with the rapier.

'Marriage included?'

'I don't believe I could survive a week without Leonard. I would sink to the bottom of the pond.'

Vita put the rapier down. 'Have you ever lived with anyone else?'

'Not since fate pushed me out of the sibling nest,' Virginia said mockingly.

'I meant physically.' She looked down on her.

'No.'

'And how physically with Leonard?'

'Not very physically with Leonard.'

Vita touched Virginia's head tenderly and stroked her hair. 'Because you are far too brilliant and far too fragile for masculine love!'

The milk was already on the step when the postman delivered the morning mail to Monks House. The dogs ran out barking and Louie, buxom and rosy, took in the milk and letters. Virginia was sitting up in bed in the garden room writing feverishly. Paper was all over the bed and floor and she looked up and out of the window. Leonard was taking a tray from Louie at the door of the house and walked with it across the garden. Virginia could see his breath in the cold morning air. He reached the door of the garden room and, balancing the tray, went in. Virginia looked at Leonard with shining eyes. 'I've been writing all night, Leo. About Orlando! About Vita.'

'Don't overtax yourself.'

'You know I can't help it!'

'You must keep calm,' Leonard said calmly. 'You must not excite yourself.'

Louie was dusting Leonard's study and the door to the landing was open. Virginia was in the bathroom and Louie could hear Virginia murmuring and gradually her voice grew higher and higher. 'Orlando has always been a woman. Orlando is at the moment a man.' She muttered and giggled. 'Orlando was a woman until the age of thirty…'

Louie looked towards the window and she could see Leonard gardening and the dogs nearby. Duster in hand she went to the door and stood listening, shaking her head. Virginia's voice went on… '…when he became a man and has remained so ever since.'

She was in the new high bath, her hair was pinned up and was escaping in damp wisps. As she spoke in the steamy bathroom she imagined she was her fictional creation, Orlando, who through the centuries changed from man to woman and was based on Vita. Orlando emerged from the steam in Elizabethan doublet and hose, a romantic, handsome young man. 'No human being since the world began had ever looked more ravishing. His form combined in one the strength of a man and a woman's grace…' murmured Virginia. The image of Orlando slowly metamorphosed from man to woman. Orlando undid his shirt laces and pulled it over his head to reveal full breasts, then untied his hair which fell loose over his shoulders. Virginia giggled and she threw up her wet streaming arms. 'Truth! Truth! Truth! We have no choice but confess he was a woman.'

In the garden room, her own hair loose, Virginia sat with the writing board on her lap, ending one page and beginning the next without looking up. 'Her sex changed frequently,' she said aloud. 'For the probity of breeches she exchanged the seductiveness of petticoats and enjoyed the love of both sexes equally.'

In the chemist's shop Vanessa paid for her purchases with a ten shilling note and waited for change from the till. Her eyes were fixed eagerly on Virginia and she said in a loud voice, 'But do you really like going to bed with a woman?' The chemist, eyes down and deeply embarrassed, handed

Vanessa her change and her purchases. She took it without moving her eyes from Virginia's face.

'Your voice is as loud as a parrot's!'

'And how do you do it?'

The chemist scurried away into his back room and Virginia and Vanessa went out into the street.

Angelica, aged ten, stood on the table dressed in the costume of a Russian princess. She wore glittering fake emeralds and pearls and Vanessa was arranging the skirt. Duncan was taking pictures with a new camera on a stand and Vita was fussing around her very pregnant dog.

'There's the sunshine,' said Duncan pointing to the window. 'Quickly. Out of the way, Nessa. Stand absolutely still...there.' He took the picture.

'Let me see, let me see!' Duncan moved away and Virginia put her eye to the lens. 'Oh, you look perfect, Angelica!'

'I don't even know who I'm supposed to be.'

'You're Sasha. And Orlando loves you!'

'Who's Orlando?' Angelica asked.

'Come over here. I'll show you.' Virginia looked at Vita and their eyes met. She moved the camera so that Vita was in its range and she let Angelica take her place. Vita laughed and turned her attention back to her dog, rolling it on it back and examining its nipples. Angelica looked through the lens, still puzzled.

'Who *is* Orlando?'

Virginia moved away from the camera. Duncan said, 'Your aunt's latest literary creation.'

'I know that...'

'Orlando lives for four hundred years and sometimes he's a man or sometimes he's a woman.'

'He can't be a woman, Ginia...' Angelica laughed so much that the filet of pearls on her head slipped and was caught by Vanessa. Vita looked up from the pregnant dog.

'I think the dates may be wrong. Her teats are enormous!'

Virginia was writing furiously – she was in fact writing the last pages of *Orlando* and the clock by the bed was at five minutes to one. She was sitting on the bed bent over her writing board and distant sounds from outside of crying and a sermon being intoned could be heard. Virginia was unaware of them. She was writing the final words and added three dots. The book was finished. The sounds from outside were continuing. Virginia became aware of them and she went to the door and looked out. A burial was taking place in the church yard at the bottom of the garden. Four women were weeping and there were two men and a child. Virginia saw shoes slipping on the muddy ground and the coffin tipping over on the canvas supports as it was lowered. She went back into the garden room and closed the door.

There was a sign saying 'Ears Pierced' and a drawing of an old-fashioned woman wearing ear rings. Vita and Virginia were sitting side by side in an uncurtained cubicle at the side of the shop and they both had almost identical shingled hair. 'They buried her *upside down*,' said Virginia in thrilling tones.

'Does it matter?'

'Oh, to the relatives. They are deeply concerned. The whole village is agog.' She paused and said suddenly, 'Did you know you died on Sunday? I have finished my book!'

'I couldn't be feeling more alive.'

'Didn't you feel a sort of tug as if your neck was being broken…at five minutes to one? That was when you stopped talking. With three little dots!'

Vita burst out laughing and put up her hand and ruffled Virginia's hair. 'And is it really about me?'

'My hair must feel like a partridge's rump.' She smiled. 'All about you!'

The jeweller came in with a shop assistant and a pair of piercing scissors. 'Who wishes to be pierced first?'

'Oh, I think I'll be first,' Vita said. The assistant came forward and put alcohol on a piece of cotton wool and rubbed the right ear. The jeweller advanced with the piercing scissors, and as he pressed them through Vita's earlobe she made a little face and Virginia gave a shriek.

The chauffeur-driven Daimler parked outside Monks House as Virginia was looking out of the window. Vita was sitting in the grey upholstered rear seat wearing a coat with a fur collar and earrings in her pierced ears. Virginia hurried out of the house. The chauffeur opened the rear door and Virginia, flushed with excited anticipation, climbed in to sit beside Vita. She also had earrings and a fur-collared coat and she was concealing something behind her back. As she sat down she brought her hand into view and put the first bound copy of *Orlando* onto Vita's lap. She gasped, looked at Virginia and kissed her cheek quickly and stroked the cover before opening it. There was a photograph of Angelica facing one of the pages. The chauffeur started the engine and Vita spoke with emotion. 'I think it is the most wonderful present I have ever received in all my life.' She turned back to the dedication page and she saw it was dedicated to V. Sackville-West. 'Dedicated to me! Oh, my darling, you have put me in such a turmoil of excitement and confusion…how am I going to cope with everyone?'

'I think I am going to be jealous of your friends tonight.'

Vita took Virginia's hands and pressed them. The chauffeur looked in his mirror and there was a glint in his eyes. Vita leant forward and slid the glass panel across before she answered Virginia in the privacy of the back seat. 'I'm going to be perfectly good tonight, I shall gambol like a dolphin.'

Half joking, half warning, Virginia said, 'Well, be careful, dolphin, in your gambolling, or you'll find my soft crevices are lined with hooks!'

The chauffeur drew up before mansion flats in a narrow, dingy street. They got out and Vita issued commands for when the car might return. They went into the building and the hall porter accompanied them to the upper floor. There were wrought-iron gates to the lift and the porter pulled them back and they went out and Vita pressed the brass bell beside the door of number 25. After a few moments the door opened. A stout woman in male dress, her hair cropped, held out her hands in welcome. 'Julian! We thought you were lost!'

Virginia watched Vita as she put her hands into those of the stout woman, and then she introduced them. They put their coats into the bedroom and Virginia was amazed to see Vita was wearing trousers under her long coat.

They went into the drawing room. Seated were a dozen women in male evening dress or velvet smoking jackets. Only one was young and pretty, the others were middle-aged with large bosoms compressed by stiff shirt fronts. Three held brandy glasses and some stood for introductions. One kissed Vita's hand. The stout woman said, 'Most of you know Julian, I think. May I introduce Mrs Woolf… Virginia Woolf… John, a great admirer of your work.'

The room was furnished with some Bauhaus pieces, a tubular chair, paintings after (or by) Kandinsky, a lot of books including Freud, Joyce, Lawrence and *The Well of Loneliness* by Radclyffe Hall. As Virginia smiled and shook hands she realised that the woman who had been introduced as John actually was Radclyffe Hall and Vita rushed to the bookcase and took down 'John's' œuvre.

After they had eaten the buffet supper and had coffee the room was full of smoke. One woman had a cigar between her fingers but the rest of them, Virginia included, smoked cigarettes. Radclyffe Hall handed round a cutting from the *Sunday Express* and the stout woman read aloud, ' "Literature as well as morality is in peril." Oh dear!'

Radclyffe Hall continued, ' "I would rather give a healthy boy or a healthy girl a phial of prussic acid than this novel." '

An attractive young woman, with Vita sitting at her feet, watched her.

' "Poison kills the body but moral poison kills the soul," ' John went on.

The young woman looked into Vita's eyes. 'Of course, everybody now wants to read it.'

John came over to Virginia and spoke. 'God created inverts, didn't he, Mrs Woolf? God created the Third Sex. I question the concept of Christianity held by the editor of the *Sunday Express.*'

Vita addressed the young woman. 'I wish I hadn't been away when the scandal broke!'

'You can sign Leonard Woolf's protest letter.'

Virginia gave a savage look at Vita, a mood of jealous revenge. ' "Julian's" proclivities are far too well known,' she said.

'All men's names, Leo...does one call them women? One had a pink face, rather like a piglet. I was almost repulsed...but I was fascinated in a kind of curious morbid way. And all obsessed by the banning of this *boring* novel, *The Well of Loneliness.*'

Virginia slammed down a copy of *The Well of Loneliness* onto the table in the Hogarth Press. 'Can you imagine! The wretched woman attacked me because Leonard didn't praise her novel as a work of art in his review!' She seated herself with Leonard, Saxon Sydney-Turner (who smiled and nodded and listened) and Morgan Forster who were already sitting round the table with tea in mismatched cups. Morgan had a letter in his hand. 'I'm afraid

that's the problem. She won't accept our protest letter supporting because…'
reading from the letter, "it deals merely with the legal aspects…etcetera,
etcetera…no opinion of either the merits or the decency of the book."

Virginia gave a snort. 'I suppose honesty is a merit. But where does
one place dullness?'

'Somewhere around Stoke Poges, I imagine,' said Saxon Sydney-Turner.

'And bad writing? Where does one place that?' She quoted, ' "and that
night they were not divided." Such brilliant prose! It is a pity it is not a
better book to fight for the freedom of the press.'

'Bookshops are being raided all over London,' Leonard said. 'The
publisher is being taken to court in order to have the copies legally destroyed.'

'One shouldn't say this…' everyone looked at Morgan, 'particularly in
view of one's own…but frankly, you know, lesbianism disgusts me. My
mother and aunts don't even know it exists.' Leonard hid a smile.

Virginia said, 'It disgusts me too, at times, but *love…*'

Leonard cut in quickly, 'But I assume, Morgan, you're still offering
yourself as a witness for the defence.'

'Of course! We are all writers.'

'I'm afraid we didn't give support to James Joyce over *Ulysses.*'

'And you'll have to offer yourself as a witness, Virginia,' Morgan cut
in. 'A respected novelist and a respectable married woman.'

A look of terror came over Virginia's features. 'I couldn't possibly. I'd
be petrified.'

Leonard said soothingly, 'No, I don't think you should.' He turned to
Morgan. 'Virginia is too honest. She'll forget what she's there for and tell
the truth. She's capable of telling the world that *The Well of Loneliness* is
second-rate.'

Morgan smiled a little. 'Most of our friends are trying to evade the witness
box for more obvious reasons.' He paused. 'I believe you have a moral duty.'

Virginia took a deep breath. 'Yes. I do.'

In Bow Street Magistrates Court Virginia sat in the corridor smoking
nervously. There was a sudden burst of activity as the doors of the courtroom
opened and Radclyffe Hall came out with her lawyer, Harold Rubinstein,
followed by members of the press and public. John wore a dark blue Spanish
riding hat, leather motor coat with an astrakhan collar and cuffs. A man
passing Virginia said to his companion, 'An affront to our wives.' The crowd

pressed forward, crowing. Leonard and Morgan, looking gloomy, detached themselves from the mob and came over to Virginia who rose to her feet.

'The book is banned! You won't be called. The case is over.'

'I know I should be weeping.' She sank back in relief.

Virginia was lying on the bed in the garden room with a damp cloth on her forehead. Louie knocked on the door and entered with a glass of milk. 'Mr Woolf said to make sure you drink it.'

'I will. I've wasted this afternoon. I should have been writing.'

Louie placed the glass on the bedside table. 'Let me help you sit up.' She put the pillow behind Virginia's back and Virginia took the handkerchief from her forehead and took a sip of the milk. 'It's getting exciting. I think we're winning!' Louie said.

'Winning what, Louie?'

'The election, mum.' She was impatient. 'The socialists are winning it. I've been listening in... Mr Woolf said it would be all right!'

Leonard and Virginia sat in Leonard's study listening to the radio. The announcer said, 'Labour 287. Conservatives 261. Liberals 59. Others 8. Mr Ramsey MacDonald will form his second Labour Government...'

Leonard switched off. 'Thank God!'

'That's what Louie says. It was rather extraordinary this afternoon. I realised we were on the same side!'

'Not really surprising, surely?'

'It was.' Virginia sat bolt upright to give emphasis. 'I was shocked.'

'Why?'

'Imagine being ruled by Louie. Total muddle. Utter chaos.'

'For heaven's sake, Virginia!' said Leonard. 'I trust you and Louie will both be spared disaster by MacDonald's good sense. At least he's aware that international policy has to be based on the League of Nations or Europe's in for another ghastly war. So I shouldn't be flippant about it.'

Virginia looked slightly ashamed. Leonard stood up. 'We need everyone on our side if we're going to avoid disaster. We'll have to work at it. The time is ripe for a progressive new political magazine...'

'The time is right for a new political magazine,' Leonard said in the Omega office the following morning. With him in the smoke-filled sparsely furnished room were Maynard Keynes and two other men.

Leonard was advocating the setting up of a new socialist magazine. They were listening as Leonard passionately propounded his ideas. 'I'm suggesting we call it simply *Political Quarterly*. Straight-forward name, straight-forward policy. If ever there was a need for a clearing house of ideas, a platform for constructive thought, it is now.'

'Presumably,' said Maynard, 'you intend to provide ideas for the "men at the top".'

'I'm hardly advocating a political *Peg's Paper*. We need the finest editor in the country. The contributors will be experts, writing for an elite. For members of Parliament and civil servants in the arena of practical politics.' Leonard thought for a minute before continuing. 'And in the academic arena *by* experts *for* experts, in sociology and law and history...'

'I have to say it, Leonard!' Maynard took a deep breath. 'It will cost money.' Everyone smiled.

'Bernard Shaw will give us money, and I hope many others.' Leonard looked at Maynard.

In the lecture hall Maynard was on the platform being introduced to a large audience. Saxon Sydney-Turner and Leonard were there, and Lydia, looking exotic and proud. A large man in an academic gown was in the centre of the stage. '...which we read in *Political Quarterly*. He is here tonight to expand and expound on the theory, and as the author of *A Treatise on Money*, and a member of the Prime Minister's Economic Advisory Council I know of no one better equipped to do so. Ladies and Gentlemen, Mr Maynard Keynes.'

Maynard rose to enthusiastic applause and took his position behind the lectern. He arranged his notes but when he spoke, he did not look at them, but straight out at the audience, with fervour and conviction. 'In this country – now – we have well over a million unemployed. We face the biggest slump in our history.' He paused. 'As does that bastion of capitalism, the United States of America. What are we to do? What is our solution?'

Lydia leaned forward, her hands clasped, her eyes intent on Maynard. He said, 'There is only one solution. We must spend money. Yes! Spend it! We must spend our way out of the crisis. Public work.' Leonard was agreeing, excited by what he heard. 'We must start employing the men on the dole. They will build bridges and roads and houses for us to beat this slump...'

'When I was a girl, my dream – my impossible dream – was to learn at a great university.' Virginia was at St Hughes lecturing the women undergraduates on Freedom for Women. 'You are lucky enough to be here in Oxford. Those are facts. Sometimes I think fiction contains more truth than fact, so the story I am about to tell uses the licence and liberties of the novelist!'

Among the audience were young women and academic staff and Vita sat beside an intense middle-aged lecturer, who wore a fluffy angora jumper under her gown. 'I...and the 'I' is not exactly me...' Virginia continued, 'was crossing a patch of grass in Oxford when a man rose up to intercept me. This was a beadle and I was not a scholar or a fellow of Oxford and – horror of horrors, lowest of the low – I was a *woman* and the grass was preserved for the hallowed feet of selected males.'

Vita and the lecturer turned to each other and smiled and Virginia watched them. She went on, 'Worse was to follow at the famous Oxford library. My way was barred by a kind of guardian angel – but with a black gown fluttering instead of white wings – who regretted that ladies are only admitted if accompanied by a fellow of the College – who are all men!' The audience laughed. The laughter continued as Vita murmured into the ear of the lecturer.

In a dressing gown and with her hair down, Virginia addressed Vita who sat, still dressed, on one of the single beds. 'She is twittering and gushing and second-rate. She gushed and twittered every time you whispered.'

'She is a friend!'

'Like your other second-rate friends. I can't have it said... "Do you know Vita's great friends? There is Dottie and Hilde and Virginia..."'

'You are apart...'

'The fact that you care about them, bother with them, think about them, *alienates* me from you. You are like schoolgirls, Vita.'

Vita was quiet, subdued, and she nodded. 'I know. I never seem to be able to stop what I have begun.'

'So many new beginnings...'

'You're going to make well over a thousand again this year,' said Leonard, looking up from the accounts on his office desk. 'The American sales are up.'

Small stacks of *The Waves*, *A Room of One's Own* and *Orlando* were waiting to be wrapped. Virginia, in the main room, was packing *All Passion*

Spent by Vita Sackville-West. 'Vita's still doing rather nicely with *The Edwardians*,' Leonard went on. 'I think the new novel should do the same.'

'All passion spent,' said Virginia in a whisper. She folded the paper, tightened the string and lit the wick of a stick of red sealing wax. 'And it is, Leo. It is.'

Leonard, abstracted, glanced up from his accounting. 'What's that? What is what?'

'Oh, nothing.' A blob of wax fell on the knot. She pushed the parcel aside and reached for *A Room of One's Own* by Virginia Woolf.

Julian was lighting fireworks on a winter night in the garden of Charleston. He wore a big brimmed hat and a muffler wound round his neck and he crouched beside a rocket set (with others) in the long grass beside the pond. He applied a light and his face was illuminated, and there was a cheer as the rocket soared and burst into pink stars. Clive and Vanessa were there, with Leonard and Virginia, Duncan, Maynard, Lydia, Quentin – who was twenty-three – and Angelica, of course, who would be sixteen the next day.

'Are you tired?' asked Leonard.

Virginia giggled. 'I am incendiary. If you try to take me home I shall ascend in pink stars!'

'We'll leave soon after supper. You mustn't overdo it.' A splendid rocket soared up and exploded.

At the top of her voice Virginia shouted, 'There I go!'

'There goes Ginia!' Angelica shouted, too.

They all laughed and Julian moved to the next rocket and lit it. Clive said, 'I'd never have described Virginia as *pink*.'

The rocket exploded, illuminating everyone. 'Sixteen... Happy Birthday, Angelica!'

Later, blowing out the candles on her birthday cake and with everyone singing 'Happy Birthday To You' Quentin said, 'Make a wish.'

'But I'm not sixteen until tomorrow.'

'You'll be sixteen at two in the morning.' Julian gave a smile. 'You're allowed to make a wish now.'

Angelica shut her eyes and screwed them up as she made her wish and opened them and saw Bunny laughing. 'I can guess!'

'No, you can't. It's my secret.'

'Someone to fall in love with?'

She blushed and said no, it was nothing to do with that. Lydia looked angry. 'It's wrong to tease, Bunny.'

'Anyway, she loves us,' Virginia said, 'don't you Pixerina?'

'Oh, do get a move on with the cake!' Quentin held a knife towards Angelica and she gave a relieved giggle. Everyone in turn passed their plate for a slice.

The meal was over and Duncan had his chair tipped back with his feet against the table. Angelica was kneeling on the window-sill re-arranging the holly and the ivy. 'I'm so glad everyone is here!'

A pause and then Vanessa said tautly, 'Except that everyone is not here. Roger isn't here. Neither is Lytton.'

'I think Angelica was referring to the living,' Clive gently reminded her. Vanessa's eyes swam with tears and Angelica bit her lip.

'I miss very much Lytton. He was a very tolerant, serious man. And he laughed at himself sometimes,' Lydia said.

'The end of "Old Bloomsbury", do you think?'

'Don't make us sound so passé, Maynard,' Bunny said.

'You weren't part of "Old Bloomsbury", Bunny. It ended with the war. And sometimes I think Roger Fry was the most important person in it.'

Leonard was gentle. 'You're not writing us off, I hope.'

When I said "Old Bloomsbury" I was implying a later Bloomsbury. We are all still working!'

'He write so hard I am very bore!' said Lydia.

'What are you working on?' Quentin asked Maynard.

'Riveting title. *The General Theory of Employment, Interest and Money*.'

Clive said laconically, 'Your masterwork?'

'Enough of all this "were" and "was". We're at our middle-aged peak. What about Duncan and Nessa doing panels for the new Cunard liner? What could be more contemporary than that?' Maynard went on to say that, as all Cunard ships had names ending in 'ia', such as *Berengaria* and *Mauretania*, the intention was to call the new Cunarder *Victoria*. The chairman had told him that he was writing to the King to ask if Her Majesty would be graciously pleased to name the new liner after England's greatest Queen. Of course, it all depended on Queen Mary's social calendar which was always arranged months, even years in advance.

'And you're writing your new novel... you are, aren't you, Virginia?' Bunny said. 'You always are…!'

'Don't talk about it. My head's in a cage,' said Virginia. Leonard put a calming hand on Virginia's and Vanessa looked at her sharply.

'Well, I think the Bloomsbury banner is in the hands of the beautiful birthday girl. How's that for a present?' asked Bunny.

Angelica looked pleased but embarrassed. 'Bunny! I'm still at school.'

'But you're going to be a famous actress.'

'Don't encourage her for heaven's sake.' Vanessa put her arms round Angelica while Leonard said, 'You're right. Second generation Bloomsbury. Quentin's a painter and Julian's a bit of a poet…'

'I'm afraid I want something more than a contemplative life,' Julian said.

'He always was a headstrong child!' Vanessa and Julian smiled at one another with understanding.

'I need action!'

'That sounds like youthful rhetoric.'

Julian replied hotly, 'On the contrary. Unlike 'Bloomsbury', I believe in doing rather than talking. Something has to be done about the things that are happening in the world, and I need…'

'What you needed, Julian, was a traditional Christian upbringing,' said Maynard. Leonard, Virginia, Duncan and Vanessa looked at Maynard open mouthed.

'*Christian?*' Vanessa said.

'You know perfectly well I don't mean in the religious sense. I'm talking moral framework, a sense of tradition, a sense of continuity.'

Bunny leant towards Julian, anxious to shift the balance. 'What kind of action do you feel you need?' he asked.

Julian rose to his feet and his voice was raised to Maynard. 'Not feel. I *know*. Continuity? If things continue the way they are, the whole of Europe will be dominated by Fascists.'

'And I suppose like the rest of your generation you assume communism is the answer.'

Lydia spoke warningly. 'Darling…'

'Is that "Old Bloomsbury" speaking? Because if so thank God it's dead. Pontificating over glasses of wine in middle-class Sussex isn't going to do a great deal for Spanish peasants. Pontificating about Adolf Hitler and his Brown Shirts won't stop them destroying the future of Germany. Something has to be done. Physically done by people who care about other people.'

Julian made a sweeping gesture. 'You're a bunch of old fogies living in the past.' As he stormed out he touched Vanessa's shoulder as he passed – a sign that she wasn't included.

'The New Bloomsbury speaks,' said Bunny.

Vanessa turned to Maynard, 'How could you?'

Bunny crossed the room, lifted Angelica off the window sill and whisked her under the mistletoe. 'Sealed with a kiss!' He swung Angelica round before he kissed her and she struggled with delight.

In Picasso's studio in Paris – a vast room in a 17th-century palace – Quentin, Duncan, Vanessa and, of course, Picasso stood in front of *Guernica*, his symbolic protest at the bombing of the Basque town during the Spanish Civil War. It depicted horror and violence with terror-stricken women, a flaming house, a dead child and a rearing horse. The painting was in black, white and grey and it filled the studio wall. 'Art is not compensation for human life, but if the Civil War brings nothing but death and destruction to the people of Spain, it will at least have inspired a great painting,' Duncan said.

'But the war is inspiring people outside Spain. Quentin's raising money for the children as you know, Mr Picasso…' Vanessa put her hand on Quentin's arm. 'And my darling Julian, my other son, is in Spain driving an ambulance…'

Three days after returning to Charleston, Vanessa was laying the table for lunch when the doorbell rang. It was the telegram boy. The message was from the British Consulate in Valencia and it said, simply, baldly, 'Regret tell you Julian Bell died during ambush by insurgent Forces. Signed G. Farrington, Secretary, British Consulate.'

Vanessa let out a howl of grief that was almost animal-like and Virginia came running to see what was the matter. Vanessa gestured to the telegram that had fluttered to the floor. Virginia glanced at it then took Vanessa in her arms. They clung together, sobbing. At last, taking a deep breath, Virginia said, 'First Thoby. Now Julian. At least Julian died for a cause.' Vanessa nodded, her tears continuing to flow. After a moment she managed to recover her composure and said, 'Since he grew up he couldn't bear the idiotic and infernal muddle of the world.'

On a wet November day Bunny and Angelica hurried into a teashop in Lewes High Street and took a table by the window. Bunny ordered tea for two and a plate of cakes. When the waitress had departed Bunny leaned across and took Angelica's hand. He smiled reassuringly and said, 'You have always looked so much like your mother...'

The waitress returned with the tea and Bunny said, 'Have a cream cake. You know you love cream cakes!'

Angelica sighed. 'Oh Bunny... you still treat me as if I were a little girl.'

'I don't think of you as a little girl.' She helped herself to a cream cake.

There was a minute's pause. 'My mother does. I'm nineteen!'

'Oh, probably all mothers...'

'No Bunny,' Angelica said, 'all mothers don't.' She unburdened herself, perhaps for the first time. 'She and Julian didn't even tell me he was going to Spain until he had almost gone. And now I can't even talk to her about it. Everything I say sounds so feeble when I know what she's been going through.' She paused. 'Did you know that Clive is not my father? Duncan is.' Bunny nodded. 'She only told me that after Julian died. You'd think I'd be the one who ought to know first. They don't even hug each other in front of me.' Bunny looked down at the table. 'They're always telling me how good I am at painting and how good I am at dancing, but they never tell me anything they think could upset me. Pretence, pretence, pretence. I'm even supposed not to know about Duncan's men friends.'

'They mean it well, Angelica.'

'Well, I feel I was brought up in a glass case. Not a very comfortable glass case. All my friends' houses are *warm*. Art isn't the only thing in the world!' Bunny laughed fondly.

'You have to talk to her about your feelings,' Bunny said. 'You have to be open about your love for each other. She needs to know how you felt when you were her age.' Vanessa was on a ladder repainting part of a mural on the dining room wall and Bunny sat on a chair pushed away from the table. Duncan stood, paint on his usual ill-fitting clothes.

Vanessa was helpless. 'I know I get on her nerves terribly at times.' She stopped painting and the brush dripped, forlorn. 'She probably thinks I'm gloomy and forbidding, but it's being unhappy...the young can't understand unhappiness...but she can be quite crushing sometimes and that makes me...'

'For God's sake stop making excuses,' Duncan said. 'If you'd grown up in my family... Your children have had care and freedom...'

'That isn't the way she...' The front door banged and they all froze. Running footsteps in the hall and then the door was flung open by Angelica.

'I saw your car,' she said softly. 'Why didn't you tell me you were going to be here.' She put her hands on Bunny's shoulders, kissed his forehead and perched on his lap, her cheek against his. Vanessa was shocked and met Bunny's eyes above Angelica's head.

Bunny and Duncan angrily faced one another in the bedroom. 'Morals, Duncan? Seduction? I'm not sure I'm hearing right. Isn't it a little late to be the Victorian father? *We* had some nights in this room, remember?'

'I have no intention of allowing Angelica to be hurt.'

'I'm not going to hurt her.' Bunny paused. 'I'm falling in love with her.'

'Who does she resemble most then? Me? Or Vanessa?'

'Are you jealous? Or is it some curious complex you have about sex?' Bunny stared out of the window and then turned round and stared at Duncan. 'She's of a sexual age, you know. If she has feelings for me you aren't going to stop them. What will you do? Tease her about me? Forbid her to see me? You'll cut her off from you for life.'

'I'd just like to think that her first love affair will be with someone rather less experienced and rather more her own age. Not someone old enough to be her father.'

'You *are* jealous,' Bunny said. 'Of me? Or Angelica? I have to tell you, Duncan, I intend to go on seeing Angelica as long as she wants to see me.' He turned and left the room.

The dogs were running around the gravestones and Adrian was sitting on a headstone as he was talking to Leonard. 'There is no point in alarming Virginia by discussing it over lunch.'

'I cannot say I share Chamberlain's euphoric confidence in Hitler's promises of peace in our time,' said Leonard.

'But in the course of my short stay in Berlin,' Adrian said, 'I saw the Nazis doing some pretty horrifying things.'

Leonard nodded. 'I've seen terrible, brutal photographs.'

'If… I am inclined to say *when* war breaks out, we will face the probability of invasion. From what I witnessed, I would commit suicide rather than let myself be at the mercy of the Germans.'

'As a sixty-year-old Jew already publishing an anti-Nazi pamphlet, how can I disagree?'

Adrian stood and looked at Leonard. 'You know as a doctor I have access to… Well… if you want an exit visa, I've got some pills.'

Leonard nodded and he called the dogs and began to walk on slowly towards the river. 'It is inconceivable that anyone in England in 1914 would have dreamt of committing suicide if the Kaiser's armies had invaded. And here we are now, in the heart of Sussex, seriously discussing it.'

'The Kaiser was a gentleman compared to Hitler.'

The air-raid siren started. Virginia and Leonard were playing bowls and Virginia straightened up from her shot. As the siren wailed to an end she said, 'Shall we wait for the all clear or, Drake-like, finish the game?'

'Oh, I think we go on.' As he spoke there was distant ack-ack fire, followed by the sound of a German plane approaching. 'No! I think we don't.' He took Virginia's arm and they ran to a covering of trees and threw themselves down into the long grass. As they lay there the shadow of a plane crossed the garden and then receded.

'I wonder what it would be like to be killed by a bomb,' Virginia said reflectively.

'That's one experience you won't be able to write about!'

'I try to imagine it.' Virginia said and Leonard smiled. 'I think I've got the sensation…but afterwards…' She rolled on her side to look at him. 'You never think about your death, do you? Sceptical Jewish fatalism!'

'I dare say two thousand years in the ghettoes of Europe have taught us that life is a good training for death!'

'And I'm "half in love with easeful death".'

'But don't think I don't resent it… I'd accept immortality tomorrow.' The distant sound of the plane faded completely.

'It's going to drop its bomb somewhere else. You know…' she spoke with a buoyant sense of discovery and sat bolt upright, '…I don't think I want to die just yet! I have never had a better writing season!'

In the garden room one early morning in March, Virginia was parcelling up her novel, *Between the Acts*. Leonard watched a little anxiously as she babbled on as she folded and refolded the brown paper.

'Well, I did it! And it pleases me! I enjoyed writing almost every page. But will they like it, will they *like* it, Leo…'

'No hurry to post it. It could wait until Monday.' He spoke calmingly.

'No. No. It has to go. Today. Now. Oh, why is it so painful. Cutting the umbilical cord.' She gave an over-excited laugh. 'I haven't cut this cord and I've already conceived another novel. Put your finger on this knot!' As he did so she kissed his cheek and gave another nervous laugh.

He was becoming more concerned but she was too busy tying the string to see. She took a pen and began to write the address and Leonard carried the parcel out into the garden. The dogs followed. Louie came out of a back door of the house with a bowl of potato peelings and eggs shells which she emptied onto the compost heap. As she turned to go inside Leonard's voice stopped her, and she waited. 'I want to have a quiet word with you, Louie… if you have a moment.' He looked back towards the garden room.

'Nothing's the matter, is it, Mr Woolf?'

He came closer. 'I hope not. Just a precaution. As you know, Mrs Woolf has been working very hard to finish her new book. I'm going into town to post it.' He indicated the parcel and Louie nodded. 'I don't want her to be alone too much. I've got a few errands to do while I'm there. She may need some extra looking after.'

'Don't worry, sir. I'll see she's all right.' She turned towards the door.

'Perhaps when she comes into the house later on you could find her something to do.' He looked at his watch and began to walk on.

She looked after him, puzzled. 'Do, Mr Woolf…?' He did not hear and Louie went into the house and got on with her chores. She was making Leonard's bed and she glanced towards the window and saw the rapidly disappearing figure of Virginia on a bicycle riding out of sight. She was wearing a green velvet suit. Louie went to the window and called, 'Mrs Woolf…' Virginia had gone, riding towards Charleston. On reaching it, she wheeled her bicycle through the gate and up to the front door. She opened it and entered the house just as Vanessa was coming out of a room carrying a canvas. She was wearing a loose smock and glasses, and her hair was in an untidy bun. She was startled to see Virginia – pleased, but anxious. 'Ginia! Why are you here so early? Does Leonard know you've come?'

'Don't fuss, Nessa. I'm perfectly well. He's gone to post the manuscript.'

'Come and have some coffee,' Vanessa said soothingly.

'I'm not staying.' Virginia took a letter out of her pocket and followed Vanessa into the dining room. Vanessa propped the canvas against the Omega table leg and poured some coffee. Virginia saw the signature – Matisse. She stood, tense and highly nervous. 'I came out to post a letter to stop them. I'm not going to let them publish it.'

'Leonard told me he likes it.'

'He was lying to please me. All the critics would attack it.' Virginia changed her tone. 'I think it's bad.'

'Well, if you've written the letter, there's no problem.' Grace, the maid, came in with some toast.

'Good morning, Mrs Woolf. I didn't hear you come in.' Virginia seemed not to hear her. She looked round in a distraught fashion and went to the window and Vanessa made a sign for Grace to leave.

'Where's Angelica?'

'Do sit down, you're making me nervous.'

Virginia sat down at the table. 'I don't want her to go up to London while the air-raids are on.'

Vanessa handed her a cup of coffee. She paused. 'Well, there's nothing I can do about it.' She paused again. 'She's living with Bunny.'

Virginia let the information sink in, shocked but not outraged. Her mood momentarily changed and she began her habitual probing. 'Do you mind very much.'

'Very much. But I have to believe he's making her happy.'

'But does he intend to marry her? I mean, eventually, are they going to have children?'

Vanessa said wearily, 'I told him if she gets pregnant to tell me immediately. Abortions are easier early on.'

Virginia drank her coffee, concerned now with learning every detail. 'Of course, he was always flirting with her. The disgusting way men do with little girls. What do you feel about it, Vanessa?'

'I honestly don't know what I feel any more.'

They went into the garden into the early spring sunshine. They walked around a little, then Virginia reclined in a deck chair and Vanessa went into the house to fetch some paper and charcoal. She sat on a wooden seat sketching Virginia, and without looking up she said, 'He took Duncan from me and now he's taken Angelica.'

Virginia leant back, reflectively. 'Could you imagine one of us telling father we were going to live with an older man – and not even twenty-one oneself!'

Looking up from her drawing, Vanessa said, 'A man who'd been her father's lover!' They both laughed – Vanessa ruefully.

'Your children grew up knowing that moral freedom was their right.'

'Julian's moral choice,' said Vanessa, 'was to go to Spain – and be killed.'

'Because of Bloomsbury! We did that for them. What an irony. We created the atmosphere for them to behave as they did.' They both fell silent, contemplating the full implications. As Vanessa bent her head forward to sketch again, Virginia heard the birds speaking Greek. She looked around her, frantically. Almost manic, she leapt to her feet.

'What's wrong...' Vanessa looked up fearfully at Virginia.

'I hate being drawn. You know I can't bear it.' Mimicking venomously, 'It's not like you at all, Virginia. Did you ever really look like that, Virginia.'

Very slowly Vanessa turned the sketch pad round. She stood at the gate as Virginia mounted her bicycle and, a gaunt, tense figure, pedalled away.

The radio was playing classical music in Leonard's study. A large book was in Louie's hands and she was banging the covers. Dust flew up and Virginia stood watching and listless, a duster in her hands. 'Mr Woolf thought you'd like to dust the books, Mrs Woolf.' Virginia turned her eyes blankly to Louie. 'Then you puts it back and does the same to the next shelf. Starts on the top shelf, see, and works your way down.'

As Virginia took the books under Louie's supervision and banged the covers and dusted the spines, she looked at her own books in various languages and Leonard's books and Clive Bell's books and books by John Maynard Keynes and Lytton Strachey, E.M.Forster's *A Passage to India* and David Garnett's *Lady into Fox* and *Old Possum's Book of Practical Cats* by T.S. Eliot. As Louie was leaving the room Virginia took out *Eminent Victorians* and stood holding it, not attempting to dust it. She gazed down at the little photograph of Lytton on the cover flap. 'He wanted to marry me once, Louie,' said Virginia dreamily. 'What a mistake that would have been. I wouldn't have written a word!' Louie went out and the book dropped from Virginia's hand onto the floor. She stood where Louie had left her and the distant sound of the vacuum downstairs reached her.

Suddenly, very loudly, the birds began to speak Greek again. Virginia went to the open window and slammed it shut. The sound diminished and the birds flew from branch to branch in the brilliant sunshine. She panicked and drew the curtains and stood leaning, terrified and exhausted, against the wall. The sound was now replaced by the vacuum cleaner again and she looked at the mantelpiece with the wireless still playing classical music, and Leonard's desk. Then she went to the desk and in a frenzy took a writing pad and pen and began to write.

Leonard got out of the Singer car with a couple of new books and a garden fork, and the spaniel scrambled out after him. He went into the house and propped the fork against the wall, put the books in the other hand and called out to Virginia. Louie came out of the kitchen, drying her hands on her apron. 'I got Mrs Woolf dusting the books in your study, sir. If you hurry upstairs you'll be in time for the one o'clock news.'

Virginia walked out of the garden into the churchyard. She carried a stick, wore a slouch hat and an old garden coat with deep outside pockets. At the water meadows she stopped, picked up a large stone and put it in her pocket.

Leonard went through the open door of his study. He stopped abruptly. Virginia was not there. Lytton's book was lying on the floor, the curtains were drawn and the duster was on the desk. On the radio the BBC was beginning the war news.

He looked around the room and his eyes rested on two folded letters by the radio. The one was marked VANESSA and the other LEONARD. He put out his hand to take them His hands were shaking as he tore open the envelope addressed to himself and read: "Dearest, You have been in every way all that anyone could be. All I want to say is I owe all the happiness of my life to you. I can't go on spoiling your life any longer. I don't think two people could have been any happier than we have been."

Reaching the riverbank, Virginia stooped and put another stone into her pocket. Slowly she walked along, looking for a way into the river. Finding a suitable spot she rammed her stick into the mud and stepped into the water up to her waist.

Letting the letter flutter to the floor Leonard dashed out of the house towards the garden room which was empty. There was evidence of her previous presence – a ball of string used for tying up the manuscript parcel, pens, paper, open books – but not Virginia. With growing panic Leonard began to run towards the river. Standing on the bank, gasping for breath, Leonard saw Virginia's hat floating slowly downstream.